MW00719977

RESTORING THE DREAM

Robert L. Ramsay

Thank you for reading my book.

BookLocker.com, Inc.
2017

First Edition

Dedicated to Johnny Townsend
and members of the Oval Table—
Kathy, Doreen, Karen, Eileen and David

UNIVERSITY OF MANITOBA
April 1988

Marc woke from his dream, one of those semi-nightmares that had him running for the school bus on rubbery legs. He couldn't understand why he kept having those miserable dreams. He had hated high school. He would never have run for the bus. He was always praying to the Blessed Virgin that it wouldn't show up. He hoped the engine would catch fire, or that Bill Harwood, the driver with the hooded bedroom eyes he liked to admire in the big mirror over the windshield, would have a heart attack; nothing fatal, just enough to give Marc one day off school, preferably a day when physical education was scheduled.

Marc shook his head to clear the panic, flipped onto his belly, saw the bedside clock reading five forty-six. He reached for Howard. He wasn't there, but his pillow was warm.

He heard water running, the clink of a glass against the sink, the snap of a pill bottle. At least Howard wasn't throwing up. He was a pretty placid guy who took life easy until a big examination or class presentation came along, then he couldn't relax until he'd heaved the contents of his stomach.

The bathroom light winked out. The door opened slowly.

"I'm awake. You don't have to tip-toe," Marc said.

"Sorry, I didn't mean to waken you."

"Got a headache?"

"Can't sleep." Howard stood still as a statue in the dim light bleeding through the closed venetian blinds of the dorm room they shared at the University of Manitoba. Marc marvelled once again at his good fortune in meeting Howard at the beginning of the year, their final year of graduate studies. *What have I done to rate such a hunky partner,* he wondered. Howard stood six feet tall, had a furry, muscular chest and a tight belly. His lightly furred arms and thick

5

thighs showed off muscles maintained by mucking out stalls during weekends spent on his family's ranch at Rock Lake. If someone had asked Marc to create his own dream man he couldn't have done any better, though maybe he would have opted for a stronger stomach, one more likely to hold onto its contents in sticky situations.

When Howard Hildebrandt had come lumbering through the door with his humungous suitcases in September, mumbling something about a mix-up at the student housing office which meant he couldn't have a room to himself, Marc had assumed he was a football player, a big, dumb and full of cum linebacker. Being the dumbest of the dumb when it came to throwing, catching or whacking a ball himself, Marc had been reticent around Howard. He was surprised and totally relieved when he extracted from one of his three suitcases, not a pigskin, or shoulder pads, but a scuffed up boom box and a truckload of classical cassettes: Beethoven, Bach and Mozart, lots and lots of Mozart. While classical music wasn't Marc's thing, it was easier to deal with than some jock spouting stats about passing, rushing and receiving. Marc was even more relieved the day he learned that Howard shared his minority affectional orientation.

That discovery had come about awkwardly one afternoon three weeks into the fall term. Marc had dashed back to the dorm to grab Margaret Atwood's novel, *Life Before Man,* which he needed for his Fundamentals of Teaching Canadian Literature class. When he burst into the room Howard was sitting on his bed, his jeans and boxers around his ankles, his hand gripping a part of his anatomy Marc had not until that moment seen, because Howard always undressed in the dark or modestly turned his back. At that stage of Marc's life he didn't have a large dossier of erect members to compare with Howard's, but it looked more than adequately long and thick, the tip slick with spit and dark plum red, about the same colour as Howard's face when their eyes met.

"Sorry man." Marc slammed the door and scurried back down the hallway, but not before noticing that several bodybuilding mags were spread out on his roommate's bed.

He had to go back to the room and get the novel because it was his day to make a presentation on it, but what, if anything, should he say when he went back? He was a daily devotee of newspaper advice columns, Ann Landers and Dear Abby, but neither of them had prepared him for this specific situation. Should he pretend he hadn't seen what he had seen?

Five minutes later when Marc opened the door Howard was seated at his end of the study table, his head buried in a thick engineering textbook. "I'm sorry Howard. I should have knocked. I never thought—"

"Yes, you should have, but forget it."

"I noticed you were looking at muscle mags. You into guys?"

"Look, I gotta study."

"Sure. Sure." Marc had retrieved the novel and dashed back to class.

If it had been left to Howard, nothing would have happened between them, but Marc wanted to talk about those magazines and what they meant. It was kind of awkward at first, but after Howard blushed and ran into the bathroom to throw up his macaroni and cheese supper, they'd talked. Then they'd hugged, and kissed, and began sleeping in the same bed.

Now the final term was winding down, a few weeks and they'd both be marching onto the stage to receive their degrees. "You're doing a good impression of Michelangelo's *David* by standing there in the gloom, my dear man. Aren't you coming back to bed?" Marc patted the pillow beside him.

"Nope. Can't."

"Come on, big guy. Crawl back into bed and tell me what's bothering you. Is it those electrical laws you were struggling with tonight? Are you afraid you won't pull off another A in today's test?"

Howard shook his head, then crawled back into bed where he scrunched himself against the wall as though he was bedding down in the barn on his father's ranch, sharing stall space with some skittish mare.

"Hey man, I haven't got the plague. Lie on your side with your back to me. That's the way. Let me hold you. Maybe you'll go back to sleep." Marc turned on his side, put his left arm over his buddy and snugged him in close, threaded his fingers through the hair on his chest, kissed the back of his neck. "I love you, Big Man."

Marc was dozing off when Howard flipped onto his back.

"Marc?"

"What is it?"

"Engineering isn't keeping me awake."

"What's eating away at you then?"

"I don't know how to tell you this, but—" Howard's voice broke and he turned his face into his pillow. Marc had never seen his roommate cry before, not even after his grandfather was killed when he wrapped his seventy-year-old bones around the power take off while operating the manure spreader.

"What is it, Big Man?" Marc caressed his broad back, reached for his shoulder to snug him back into the curve of his belly. "What's wrong, my love? You know you can tell me anything."

Howard sniffed. "I've done an awful thing."

"You have done an awful thing? I can't believe it. Not a good Christian boy like you."

"Stop calling me that. I hate it when you call me that. I may be a Christian but I'm not good."

"I'm sorry. What awful thing have you done that's making you tremble like this?"

"I've…I've accepted a job."

"You have? That's wonderful. Congratulations, my friend."

"No, you don't understand. I've accepted a job with Bronnel Engineering, here in Winnipeg."

"You've done what?" Marc reared up on his elbow.

"I've accepted—"

"I heard you the first time." Marc punched his pillow behind his back and sat up in bed. "Let me get this straight. You've taken a job right here in town after we both agreed that we'd move to Vancouver when we graduated, and you've done this after I've already accepted a teaching position on the coast?"

Howard's sobs shook the bed.

"Quiet down. You'll wake the whole dorm. Now tell me what this is all about. This is definitely not what you and I planned. You agreed with me that we'd both look for jobs on the coast, rent ourselves an apartment, save our money like crazy, buy a house with an ocean view, be together, you and me forever, the world's greatest love story. Now you're telling me you've accepted a job right here, in Winnipeg?"

"I know it's wrong of me, but I just can't go on like this."

"*Like this*? What is that supposed to mean?"

"You and me. In bed like this. You and me doing wicked things. It seems easy for you to love a guy, but I can't. I've tried, but the guilt is so strong inside me I can't stand it. It hurts to give you up, and I know this is going to hurt you, but I'm going crazy. I can't go on."

"You double crossing snake. You big double crossing, Christian devil. How long have you known about this?"

"Two weeks."

"And you let me go on sleeping with you, making love to you?" Marc flung back the covers, grabbed his pillow, and lunged across the room. He sat down on his own bed and wrapped his arms around the pillow, clutching it to his stomach as though to protect himself from this stranger in the bed across the room.

Howard was sitting up, his face twisted and red as tears poured down his cheeks, dripped off his chin onto his chest hair, flashing diamonds in the weak morning light seeping through the shades.

"I can't believe this is happening," Marc said, punching his pillow tighter against his belly.

"Go ahead. Punch *me* if it makes you feel better," Howard blubbed, reaching a hand towards Marc. "I know I deserve it, so come on over and punch me out if that'll make you feel better."

"The only thing'll make me feel better is to hear you say you're putting me on, but you're not going to say that, are you. You're going to cower in that lonely bed of yours and let that weird religion of yours control your life—and destroy mine, destroy our life."

"I wanted it to work. I wanted us to be a couple." Howard ran both hands over his eyes and down his cheeks.

"Well then, what's stopping you?"

9

"I keep praying the guilt will go away, but it won't. Every time you make love to me I can't enjoy it. I hear Apostle Thimble in our little country church shouting that God will hurl me into hellfire."

"Old Father Dann in my church back home would say the same thing—not that I step foot inside that hellish building anymore—but I know he'd be wrong. I know the love we feel for each other is something good, something to rejoice about, not feel guilty about."

"I wish I could feel that way." Howard wiped his face down again.

"I don't get how anyone can be so controlled by what some old priest or apostle says. Really Howard, everything was working out so well for us. How could you do this?"

At reading break they'd flown out to the coast, walked around Stanley Park, browsed the shops along Robson, seen a play, and Marc had arranged an interview with Surrey's superintendent of schools. Their final day they had looked at apartments to see what was available. Two weeks later Marc had received a registered letter in the mail, a contract to teach science and math in a French immersion elementary school beginning in September, subject to him graduating successfully.

"So what do we do now?" Marc asked.

Howard shook his head.

"Do you love me?"

"Yes, I love you." Howard began sobbing again. "I love you, but…but I can't get rid of this voice inside my head that says our love is wrong, totally wrong and sinful."

"Because of what your apostle teaches?"

Howard nodded.

"And you believe everything Apostle Thimble says?"

"Why would he lie?"

"Maybe you need to talk to some other apostle, priest, minister, whomever. This is 1988, not the dark ages. Some churches say it's okay for men to love each other."

"Maybe they're lying."

"Maybe your Apostle Thimble is lying, ever thought of that?"

"He wouldn't lie."

"Maybe not deliberately, but is he gay? Does he know what it's like to be born loving men? Has he ever studied the issue like we have, like his life depended upon it? I'm no high and mighty theologian, in fact I haven't been to church since my brother Claude's miserable funeral, but maybe your Apostle Thimble is wrong. He's not God. Do you agree with everything the pope says?"

"Course not."

"So why would you believe everything your Apostle Thimble says? Doesn't he burp and fart and take a dump like everyone else on this planet?"

"It's not the same."

"What isn't the same? The burping, the farting, the—"

"Don't talk like that. Everyone knows the Catholics believe in a bunch of weird things like bleeding statues and climbing stairs on their knees, but the tabernacle isn't like that. We're protestants."

"Sure you are, but you have to admit that some of those things written by that prophet of yours, Brother Tickoff or whatever his name is, are pretty weird too."

"Brother Tingley."

"Okay, Brother Tingley it is. I haven't said anything before, but when you've come back after a weekend at the ranch and told me some of the things you've heard at church, I've wanted to laugh my head off. Like does anyone really believe that your Brother Tingley went to heaven, that he had those little coffee klatches with Jesus, that he brought a leaf back from heaven with him?"

"It wasn't coffee. It was grape juice, and I know the leaf is real. I've seen it myself."

"Okay. Okay, my big, loveable man, but I wager if anyone did a scientific analysis of that leaf they'd discover it was just a big old maple or oak leaf from an ordinary tree like those outside this window."

"It is not."

"Fine, have it your way. Besides, I don't want to make fun of you and your beliefs, even if they are weird, but what are we to do now?"

Howard threw back the sheet, swung his legs over the edge of the bed and reached to hug Marc. "I do love you, Marc. I really do love you. You've got to understand that."

"So you say, but you can't have it both ways." Marc pushed Howard back onto his own bed. "Why reach for me now? If I hug you back won't that just make you feel guilty?"

"But I do love you."

"You sure have a queer way of showing it, accepting a job thousands of miles away from where I'll be this September."

Their final two weeks of term passed with awkward sluggishness. It felt to Marc like they were two strangers, cooped up against their will in the same hotel room by some emergency situation: a blizzard, an earthquake, or some other disaster. He tried to talk to Howard, pleaded with him to get some counselling, but he just mumbled that he had to study and buried his head deeper into his engineering textbooks.

On the last day when Marc came back to the room after defending his master's thesis, Howard's side of the room lay bare, like he and his Picasso prints, boom box and cassettes of *The Magic Flute* had been raptured, or whatever his queer religious group figured happened to you at the end of the age. Howard had sometimes talked about that when he came back from his weekend at the ranch, but Marc had never paid much attention. He figured it wasn't important, but apparently it was important enough to shatter their dream of a life together.

Chapter 1

"Excuse me, Jason." Marc grabbed his cell off the bedside table. "I need to get this call. My Auntie Belle had a stroke this morning and Maman said she'd call this evening to give me a report. You don't mind, do you?"

"Hey, no prob man. I'm not really into daddies anyway. I'll split." The blond wiped his spit-slick dick off on the sheets Marc had laundered the previous day.

"*Salut Maman. Ça va?*" They always began their conversations with a few words in French, the language Claudette, his French Canadian maman, had insisted the family speak around the supper table.

He watched the blond stand up and pull his boxers over his perfectly formed peach-fuzzed cheeks. He reached for him, squeezed his left cheek. "Please don't go," he mouthed as he listened to Maman a thousand miles the other side of the Rockies.

"*Fatiguée. Je suis fatiguée.* I feel so tired I almost wish it was me lying in that hospital bed."

"How is Auntie Belle?" The blond sat down to pull on his socks. Marc ran his fingers up the groove of his flawless back, stroked his golden hair, prayed he wouldn't leave.

"Belle is not good," Maman said. "She's in a coma. The doctor tried to dissolve the clot but it was too late. Whatever he gave her made things worse. Poor Belle."

"Oh Maman, I'm so sorry. Is there any hope for recovery?" He got up and followed the blond down the short hallway of his apartment, patted him on the butt, opened the door and inclined his cheek for a good-bye kiss that didn't materialize, then closed the door. Another one gone, not that someone so young counted when it came to a possible partner.

"Do you have company?" Maman asked. "I thought I heard your door."

"Just a guy from the gym. He came over for a drink. He's leaving."

"Is it serious? Someone new?"

"Maman, is anyone serious these days?"

"*Mon pauvre gar.*"

"Yes, I'm your poor little forty-eight year-old boy who will soon be fifty and nailed firmly to the shelf of chronic singleness. But never mind me. Tell me about Auntie Belle. You haven't said whether the doctor holds out any hope."

"He hasn't come right out and said, but I think it's probably too late to do anything more. My poor sister. I talked to her only yesterday. She must have had the stroke during the night, after she went to bed. If only I'd called her earlier this morning. Maybe it wouldn't have been too late."

"Don't blame yourself, Maman."

"It's too much for an old lady like me to bear alone."

"I'm coming home for spring break," Marc reminded her. "Just a few more days now. Can you still pick me up at the airport in Winnipeg?"

"*Mais oui.* I'll be there, but not alone. Your cousin Arlene wants to shop for a new dress and hat. Sondra is getting married in

May, but I suspect the real reason for the new wardrobe is to help her snag a new man."

"I'm not sure I want to tangle with Arlene so early in my visit."

"She offered to drive me into the city, so I could hardly refuse."

"Is she still with the Jehovah's Witnesses?"

"No. She abandoned them months ago. I think they shunned her after the divorce from Steve. I know she's my sister's own daughter, and I do love her, but I don't know how Steve put up with her for as long as he did."

"What's her latest craze?"

"Something she calls *the good old TBA*. Temple or tabernacle something. I'm sure she'll tell us all about it."

"Oh yes, that's Arlene. She'll preach at us all the way home."

"I think it's so sad that Carl left you, Marc. I liked him. Do you ever hear from him?"

"Not a word."

"He hasn't even called to explain why he left?"

"No, but it was pretty clear. When I refused to pay off his charge cards for the third time, he got mad and left. I came home from work and all his stuff was gone, plus the computer and stereo, things I'd paid more than half for. Two years down the drain."

"I'm so sorry for you. Too bad he couldn't have found more work."

"Carl had no trouble finding work. He was a good carpenter, but he knew how to play the system. He'd work long enough to qualify for employment insurance, then find a way to get himself laid off and collect as long as he could."

"My poor boy. You must be lonely. Living alone isn't any fun. I miss your father every day. I hope you'll find someone soon. Weren't you seeing a businessman of some sort?"

"You mean Barry, the guy who collected comic books. He decided my thighs weren't big enough. Can you believe it?"

"What's wrong with your thighs?"

"Nothing at all. I work them at the gym, but he expected me at five-ten, one seventy pounds, to be Superman with massive legs.

Besides, turned out he didn't want anything permanent. I think the thighs were just an excuse. He got scared when he found out I was looking for more than sex."

"I hope you're taking precautions, Marc. There's a lot of disease out there."

"I'm careful Maman."

"Being careful isn't enough. You shouldn't be seeing anyone in that way until you find someone decent and he's been tested."

"I try not to run around with indecent guys, Maman."

"I'm sure you do try, but there's so much sickness today, and murder and rape too. The news is full of horrible things. I wish you weren't living so far away."

"So far I haven't been raped Maman. I'm careful. I just can't seem to find anyone who wants something permanent." Marc tried not to chafe at Maman's advice. It was understandable that she worried about him after losing her eldest son Claude in such a miserable way.

"*C'est bizarre* that you haven't found anyone in all these years. Maybe you need to come back to Greenfield. There's a new pork plant coming into town which means more workers, and housing, and new schools. You could probably get a teaching job here, and maybe the men aren't so affected here. You might find yourself a nice farmer or a cowboy, someone who doesn't care about the size of your thighs."

"I've thought of that myself, but let's not talk now. It must be almost ten your time and you've had a stressful day. I want you to get to bed right now. You get some rest and I'll see you Sunday."

Marc placed the phone back on the bedside table and hurried into the bathroom. He hadn't gotten very far with the blond with the peach fuzz cheeks, but like he had assured his mother, he believed in taking precautions. He doused his crotch with rubbing alcohol, even dribbled a few drops into his slit. It stung like a razor cut for a moment, but hopefully it was shredding any bacteria the blond might have left behind. Lastly, he gargled with Listerine.

His mother was right. He was lonely. He wished he could attract a real man who wanted a real life, someone who wasn't a drunk, three hundred pounds overweight, or unemployed. He knew he wasn't as physically attractive as his brother Claude had been. Until his death he had been the knock-out dead handsome one in the family. With his stocky muscles, curly black hair and heavy uni-brow, he'd been a copy of his lusty voyageur ancestors.

Maman always told Marc he was a throwback to an O'Brien on his dad's side of the family, small boned with hair the colour of polished mahogany, a narrow freckled face with good teeth. After the Listerine, he stood at the mirror a moment and smiled. People said his whole face lit up when he smiled, but since Carl had left over six months ago, his pearlies hadn't helped him connect with Mr. Normal.

Marc grabbed some leftover pizza out of the fridge and ate his supper on the balcony. He never tired of watching the river traffic on the Fraser from his eleventh floor condo in New Westminster. When he first moved to the coast he had lived in a tiny bachelor apartment in Vancouver's West End. With its trendy shops, that had been a great place to be on weekends, but rather miserable for commuting to work in Surrey. He'd thought it would just be temporary. He'd expected that Howard would miss him, have a change of mind, and their lives would mesh once again.

That first year Marc had tried calling Howard in Winnipeg, but some snooty secretary at Bronnel Engineering had said he wasn't in. He'd written letters, none of them answered. He'd called several more times, left messages, but there had been no word from Howard. Now, twenty-four years and a string of aborted relationships later, he was alone again, picking up guys from the gym in the faint hope they could relieve his chronic case of skin hunger.

Chapter 2

Howard straightened up as much as he could while keeping one hand on the handlebars of the eighteen speed roadster. He fished a paper tissue from his pocket. He wiped the sweat out of his eyes, then blew his nose.

"Stop!" roared Rafe. "Pull over. Dismount." The six counselees pulled over to the curb. "Buck, what did you do?"

Howard hated the nickname. He wanted to punch Rafe in the face. He wanted to yell at him, *My name is Howard Hildebrandt. Plain and simple Howard, you big bozo of an ex-Marine.* But he kept his mouth shut. The nicknames Rafe had assigned Howard and the five other counselees at the Tingley Inversion Therapy Center were supposed to help transform them into red-blooded heterosexuals, men who sweated testosterone and drooled over female anatomy. Buck. Boxer. Baker. Brutus. Bullhead. Brick. The thick-necked slave driver must never have gotten past B in the alphabet in grade school.

"Buck, answer me. What did you do?"

"I didn't do anything, Sir."

"Think straight man. What did you pull from your pocket?"

"A paper tissue, Sir."

"Right. And what did you do with it?"

"Wiped the sweat out of my eyes, Sir." Southern California mornings, never mind the days, were too hot for Howard. He yearned for dear old Winnipeg. This early in March there'd still be patches of snow on the ground. He wanted to hear its crunch under his boots. He wanted to feel a northwest wind in his face. He wanted to smell the approach of a late-in-the season prairie blizzard.

"Are you paying attention to me, Buck?" Rafe laid a vice-like hand on his shoulder.

"Yes, Sir."

"What did you do with the paper tissue?"

"I wiped the sweat out of my eyes, Sir."

"And what else?"

"Blew my nose, Sir."

"Would a straight man do those things?"

"Not sure, Sir."

"How about the rest of you quivering blobs of biomass? Would a straight man use a paper tissue to wipe sweat out of his eyes?"

"No, Sir!" all six replied.

"What would he use?"

"Back of his hand, Sir."

"Would a straight man use a paper tissue to clear snot out of his nose while on a bike ride?"

"No, Sir."

"I didn't hear you, you useless bags of bones." Rafe, being a member of the Tabernacle of Believers' Assembly like all the counselees, couldn't swear, but he sure made up for it with his own quirky brand of gutter talk. "Say it like you mean it, you miserable morons. Would a straight man clean snot with a paper tissue?"

"No, Sir."

"What would he do?"

"Snot rocket, Sir."

"Right. Do I need to teach you bulging belugas how to rocket your snot?"

"No, Sir."

"How do you do it?"

"Cover and snort, Sir."

"Right! So no more paper tissues. Mount your bikes. Fast forward. Hold it. Dismount. Boxer, how do straight men mount bikes?"

Howard was thankful to have the spotlight taken off himself, but he felt sympathy for his roommate, little Boxer. He was a runt of a southern boy who couldn't get anything right. Howard knew Rafe would nail the poor guy for mounting his bike like a girl, left foot on the pedal, a running push off, then swinging his right leg elegantly over the rear wheel and dropping his tiny butt onto the saddle.

After Rafe had chewed out little Boxer, they got on their bikes—like real men this time—and set off on the last leg of the morning's ride. Howard knew the exercise was good for him. It was paring away the jellyroll that had accumulated around his middle during twenty-four years of sitting at his desk at Bronnel Engineering in Winnipeg. Since coming to California in January his weight had dropped from two-thirty to two twenty-two. By the time he headed home in December he should be down to two hundred, or even a bit less.

The seven men crested the last hill and glided along Temple Avenue where it passed the campus of Cal Poly. Rafe often brought them that way and frequently hollered for everyone to slow down when he saw one of the female joggers bending over, stretching, or jogging past, her tits bouncing. Howard supposed he and the other guys would be slowing of their own accord to ogle the females by the time they graduated from the sexual inversion change program, but so far he hadn't felt any change. As they cycled Howard kept his eyes on Baker's muscular butt, a much more alluring carrot than any pair of bouncing breasts.

Rafe yelled for them to swing onto University Drive, then up Mansion Lane for a quick U-turn in front of the Kellogg estate. At last they were on the final stretch, racing downhill, around the corner, and through the stone gateposts guarding the Tingley Inversion Therapy Center, T-I-T-C, or Titsy as the counselees called it.

Rafe herded everyone into the pool house that served as shower and change room. This time both Boxer and Howard caught hell together.

"Boxer! Buck! What are you barf bags doing?"

"Taking a shower, Sir."

"What are you doing with your sweaty togs?"

"Taking them off, Sir."

"I can see you're taking them off. What did you do with them when you got them off?"

"Sorry, Sir," Howard said, grimacing in disgust at his inability to remember to act like a real man twenty-four-seven.

"Sorry for what?"

"For folding my shorts and shirt, Sir."

"Boxer?"

"Sorry, Sir."

"Sorry for what Boxer?"

"For folding my shorts and shirt, Sir."

"What do straight guys do with their sweaty togs?"

"Shuck, drop and kick."

"That's right, shuck 'em off, drop 'em on the floor, kick 'em under the bench. Everyone get dressed again. Now then, strip like real men. Shuck! Drop! Kick!"

After showering, the six men dressed in loose fitting grey sweats. As they paraded into the main house for breakfast they looked like refugees on the six o'clock news, boat people perhaps, clothed in castoffs from the Salvation Army donation bin. They hadn't been told why they had to wear such shapeless clothing, but Howard assumed it was so they wouldn't tempt each other by wearing tight-fitting shirts and pants.

So far he hadn't felt any change in his affectional orientation. Even though he didn't find Boxer attractive—his head no wider than his skinny neck—there were moments, like when the little fellow was sleeping with the sheets thrown back, that Howard felt a tenderness stirring. But he didn't play with those ideas. *Jesus, take these thoughts. You deal with them. Give me something else to think about,* he prayed, and so far Jesus had kept him clean.

Chapter 3

Marc spotted his mother standing near the baggage carousel as he came down the escalator from the arrivals level in Winnipeg's James Richardson International Airport. She was a tiny lady but easy to pick out of the crowd, for she was one of the few fashionably dressed women. She was wearing one of her Jacqueline Kennedy outfits, a light blue skirt and matching jacket over a white blouse, a little blue hat perched well back on her head. It was after Claude's death and consignment to hellfire by Father Dann, the parish priest, that his mother became fixated upon the former American first lady.

"That Jackie knew true sorrow," she would say. "She had so many miscarriages, suffered the death of her baby Patrick, and finally, her husband shot to death right beside her, his brains in her hands. Can you imagine it? Oh *mon Dieu*! If she can get on with her life, then I can too."

As Marc bent to hug her he sensed that she had shrunk since his last visit. He kissed her lightly on both cheeks, being careful not to peck holes in her perfectly applied makeup. "Maman, you look fabulous. *Ça va?*"

"*J'ai la langue à terre*," she said, shaking her head.

Marc laughed and gave his mother another hug. "I love that expression, Maman. *My tongue's dragging on the ground.*"

Claudette led the way to the parking lot where Cousin Arlene was nesting in the back seat of his mother's black Volvo, the floor and seat strewn with shopping bags from *Sears* and *The Bay*. Apparently her shopping trip had been a success.

"How you, Arlene?" Marc asked as he slipped into the driver's seat after opening and closing the passenger door for his mother.

"I am extremely well, cousin Marc. The Lord is very good to me. And you?"

"I'm fine too, Arlene. Maman tells me Sondra is getting married in May."

"She is. I hope you'll be able to come to the wedding. It'll be in Greenfield's tabernacle. Did you know I'm going to the tabernacle now?"

"Yes, Maman told me. Say Maman, how is Auntie Belle doing? Any change for the better?"

"No change. Like a wax dummy lying in that bed. The nurses have to do everything for her, everything."

"Have you thought about letting her go?"

"I think about it night and day. I know it's what I should do but it's not easy to tell the doctor to let a sister die, my last sister. When she's gone I'll be alone, completely alone, so I do nothing, and keep praying for a miracle."

"Aunt Claudette, you mustn't pray for that," Arlene said, popping a piece of Dentine into her mouth and offering the package to Claudette and Marc. "Death is nothing to fear, just the entrance to a better life. I've been learning so much since I joined the tabernacle. Our prophet, Brother Tingley, who started the tabernacle, was actually taken to heaven."

"How do you know that's true?" Claudette asked.

"He wrote many books about his visits with God, Jesus and the Holy Spirit," Arlene explained. "He used to visit frequently, having lunch with them. One time he brought back a leaf from the tree of life."

"*Vraiment* Arlene, you are not serious. *J'ai vu neiger.* "

"What does that mean?"

"It means she wasn't born yesterday," Marc said. "She's seen a bit of life."

"Well, you may think you have lived, Aunt Claudette, but you haven't really lived until you've read some of Brother Tingley's books. And you both need to worship in the mother tabernacle, visit the Bible research centre, see the leaf with your own two eyes."

"Is that in Beeverville, Saskatchewan?" Marc asked.

"Yes. Do you know it?"

"I had a roommate in university who talked about Beeverville."

"He must have been a Tabber."

"A Tabber?"

"That's what we call members of the Tabernacle of Believers' Assembly, the good old TBA. You should let me take you to Beeverville while you're here. It's just a day's drive. You could see the leaf for yourself."

Over the years Marc had forgotten about Howard's strange religion. In fact, in the turmoil of his loveless life, there had been days, sometimes whole months, when he'd forgotten about Howard, forgotten how lonely he was those first few months in Vancouver after graduation. He'd blocked out those endless nights with the rain pelting against the window as he lay awake in his tiny West End apartment, clutching his pillow to his chest, pretending it was Howard, running his fingers across the cold cotton, willing himself to feel the tangle of dark fur on Howard's chest that should have been snugged next to him.

"You haven't answered me," Arlene said, reaching forward to touch Marc's shoulder.

"Sorry Arlene. My mind was somewhere else. What was your question?"

"Will you come to Beeverville with me?"

"Mother and I'll be going to the hospital every day."

"We should never let worldly things, even something as important as Auntie Belle, get in the way of our eternal salvation. I don't need to tell you that the world's in a mess, that King Jesus will soon come zip-lining down from the sky to rescue all those who are righteous. I mean, just look at what's happening to marriage in this country, letting people of the same sex marry. Can you believe it?"

"I think it's wonderful," Marc said. "I'd give anything to have a husband."

"Oh right, you're one of them," Arlene said. "I'd forgotten. I thought you'd be all over that by now."

"Now that you and Steve are divorced, are you all over wanting to be with a man?" Marc asked.

"Well no, but I think it's disgusting for two men to pretend they're married. It's like they're little kids playing house, and for what purpose? A few hours of lust-filled pleasure before God hurls them into hellfire?"

"You talk like God's a terrorist, like he's going around with a flame thrower, getting his jollies by roasting people."

"I'm sure I don't need to remind you what happened to those filthy Sodomites." Arlene smacked her lips with satisfaction.

"And don't forget the woman caught in adultery who was flung down in front of Jesus," Claudette said. "Remember how Jesus poured gasoline over her and then struck a match."

"Very funny Aunt Claudette, but this isn't something to joke about. He told the woman to quit sinning. These homo folk need to remember that."

"*Je suis fatiguée*," Claudette said, reclining the back of her seat. "Let's be quiet and I'll have a little nap."

After dropping Arlene and her packages off at her house, Marc drove with Maman to the hospital. As they walked into the room he realized that he'd never before seen Auntie Belle lying down. On his last visit to her home she'd been putting in a bed of asparagus along the back fence. He had volunteered to help dig the trench, and had felt a might embarrassed because he could barely keep ahead of her. Now her customarily rosy cheeks were as white as the sheet she was lying beneath, her mouth that had always been smiling or laughing as she recounted some tale was slack, drooping to the left.

It was Auntie Belle who had inspired him to be a teacher. His family's tradition was to gather at her house on Sunday afternoons. Everyone sat around her kitchen table eating oatmeal cookies still warm from the oven, while she delighted them with tales of the goings on in her classroom: the pranks, the outlandish excuses for homework not done, the tussles with difficult parents.

Auntie Belle was the first person Marc had told of his attraction to men. He'd been eighteen years old, in twelfth grade, and the hazing at school, especially in the gym's change room, had become too much to bear alone. His own classmates in the 12A class never made an issue of his preference for drama club over football and basketball, but the boys in his class were paired for physical education with the jocks in 12D, loud talking yokels with necks as thick as their heads, though they certainly didn't need the extra support for brains.

The crisis that sent him sprinting to Auntie Belle transpired one day after physical education class. Marc had just stepped out of the shower.

"You lookin' at my dick, LaChance?" Paykum, the school's star quarterback, had bawled, wagging his cock at Marc.

"Course he's lookin' at it," Ludlow, the wide receiver, had said. "The whole fuckin' school knows LaChance likes dick."

"You wanna suck it?" Paykum had stalked over to where Marc was sitting on the bench running the towel between his toes.

"I'd rather kiss a skunk's ass than touch that warty thing," Marc had said. In hindsight it probably hadn't been the wisest thing to say to someone who put so much store in his physical attributes.

"Come on Ludlow. Let's teach this faggot a lesson." The next few moments had been a blur of swaying green and white floor tiles, meaty thighs and hairy bellies viewed upside down, a white ceramic toilet bowl, splashing sounds, loud laughter, a kick in the butt, and then Marc had been crawling into the shower on bloodied knees. He knew he couldn't go on with life without unloading on someone, and Auntie Belle had seemed the likeliest sympathetic ear.

"Is this a news flash you're giving me?" Auntie Belle had exclaimed when he burst through her door with the news.

"You know the truth about me, Auntie Belle?"

"From the day you were born I could see that you were special, different from your brother Claude, different from other boys, and of course I saw young men like you in my classroom every year. You're all so creative and such a pleasure to teach. Come here. Let me give you a hug. *Je t'aime, mon petit gar.* I've always loved you like you're my own little boy. Now let's get those scrapes on your elbows and knees cleaned up."

She had helped him break the news to his family, and after Maman had had a good cry, and Papa had smashed his pipe by hurling it at the mantelpiece, she convinced them it was nothing Marc had chosen. "*C'est normale comme la tête sur ses épaules,*" she had said. In time his parents had come to accept that.

Now Marc kissed Auntie Belle on both cheeks, then pulled up another chair so that he and his mother could sit down, one on either side of the hospital bed. He took his auntie's blue-veined hand in both of his. It was like holding a tiny leaf that might crumble into dust if he so much as blew upon it. It was the hand that had written weekly letters to him in Vancouver, encouraging him when love affairs had withered away or exploded in a torrent of angry words and flung keys. Now she was the one who needed assurance that all would be well, but there was nothing he or his mother or anyone else could do. He brushed a tear from his eye.

Just then a pleasant-faced lady with dark hair pulled back in a ponytail came hurrying into the room. She was wearing a light blue top festooned with little red hearts and fuchsias. She was carrying a stethoscope. "Hello, Madame LaChance. How are you this evening?"

"Very tired. I just got back from Winnipeg. This is my son Marc, from Vancouver. He's come to visit."

"Hi Marc. I'm Amy. I'm just going to give a listen to Belle's heart, take her temperature, check the catheter and then turn her. We don't want her to get bedsores. You can wait in the lounge at the end of the hallway. I won't be long."

"She's *très gentille,*" Claudette said as they left the room. "Amy Hildebrandt is her name. She drives into Greenfield from Rock Lake every day."

"Hildebrandt? I used to know a Hildebrandt from Rock Lake. You must remember Howard, my roommate in university?"

"Isn't he the fellow you invited for the weekend and he ate half a dozen cinnamon rolls for breakfast? How your father laughed at that boy. Maybe Amy's related to him."

"I'll have to ask her." Marc sat in one of the leather recliners in the lounge, then turned it slightly so he could keep watch down the hallway. He didn't want to miss Amy when she came out of the room, but when she did, she hurried into the next room, and Marc could see that his mother was exhausted. He could ask Amy about Howard tomorrow.

"Come on, Maman. Let's go say good night to Auntie Belle. Then we'll go straight home. You've had a long day."

Chapter 4

It was letter-writing day at TITC. Upon registration, the counselees had been advised to leave all communication devices at home: cell phones, Kindles, laptops—anything that could be used to contact outsiders. The brochure had explained this was so they would immerse themselves fully in the straight lifestyle, and avoid any outside influences that might encourage them to abandon the program. After three months they had finally been issued pens, paper and envelopes so they could write to friends or family.

Howard began his first letter.

Tingley Inversion Therapy Center
Pomona, California
April 4, 2011

Dear Mom and Dad,
I hope you are both well and that everything is fine on the ranch. Forgive me for not writing sooner.

This is the first chance I've had. Let me tell you about a typical day.

We get up at five every morning. I was used to that on the farm, but my rich little roommate, Boxer— his family has something to do with Coca Cola in Atlanta—is a southern gentleman who never had to do any work. Sometimes I have to throw off his sheets to wake him up. Oh, you don't need to worry that I might see something tempting—we have to wear pyjamas at night and there's a screen behind which we take turns dressing and undressing.

Rafe, our physical trainer, is an ex-Marine, a huge guy whose neck really is as thick as his head. He leads us on early morning bike rides. Pomona is kind of pretty. The hills are covered with pine and palm trees. There are little valleys with farms.

We ride for an hour every morning. Rafe always rides behind, bawling out directions. He stops us if we do anything girlish. I've never wanted to be a girl but he's bawled me out several times. The other morning I wiped the sweat off my forehead with a paper tissue. He says a straight man wouldn't do that. Dad, I remember you carrying a big red handkerchief on the farm. You wiped your brow with it on hot days. I can't see anything wrong with that, but Rafe does. He has a short temper and yells at us a lot.

After the bike ride we shower and change our clothes. We have breakfast on the terrace beside the swimming pool. Rosanna, a Mexican lady, is our cook. Everything is spicy. I didn't care for it at first, but I'm starting to enjoy it. We usually have beans and rice for breakfast with fruit. The estate has several orange and lemon trees. I wish you could leave the snow and cold behind and come and pick oranges from the tree like we do.

Howard paused. Boxer was sitting across the table from him, his pen flying back and forth across the page. "Who are you writing to, Boxer?"

"Rickie, my boyfriend. He's an ophthalmologist in Atlanta."

"An eye specialist?"

"Yes. I miss him like I'd miss my own skin if someone peeled it off me."

"I still don't understand why you're here."

"Why are any of us here? My parents insisted I attend. 'Just give it a chance,' was what they said, so here I am, trying to become a good little hetero so their only son can bless them with grandkids before they take leave of this planet."

"What does Rickie think of you being here?"

"He thinks I'm nuts, but of course there is the money factor."

"Oh yes, I remember you telling me you'll be written out of your parents' will if you don't give this a try."

"Exactly, and Rickie loves clothes. You should see his closets, three walk-through closets stuffed with *my finery* as he refers to his clothing. So here I am at TITC, but it's not working, is it?"

"I don't know about that."

"Be honest, Buck, no amount of bike riding, snot rocketing and kicking our clothes under the bed is going to make us straight. It's just turning us into filthy, dumb-ass jerks like Rafe."

"But there's the counselling. Isn't that doing you any good?"

"Sister Bergus doesn't know whether her asshole is drilled or punched. Now I gotta finish this letter to my honey bunch before lights out."

Howard went on with the letter to his folks.

After breakfast there's an hour of Bible reading. The readings are assigned. We can sit wherever we like—by the pool or under the palms, or in the pine woods up the hillside. I like going up the hillside. From the top I can see distant fields—I don't know what the crops are. They look like wheat and remind me of Manitoba.

Boxer always sits beside the pool. He's afraid of the lizards. They're tiny things, not even as big as the palm of my hand. Rafe says they're called geckos. If I sit very still they come out from under the bushes. I try to pet them, but they're very shy.

After Bible reading we gather in the living room. It's huge, about the size of the tabernacle in Winnipeg. It has three large chandeliers hanging from the ceiling. The man who built the house made money racing horses. He must have won a lot of races to have built such a big house.

Apostle Motchkess, the program director, leads us in discussing the Bible passage. I like him because he doesn't yell at us like Rafe. He listens to what we say. The readings are supposed to help heal us. This month we're reading the Song of Solomon. After reading one verse Apostle Motchkess asks us to talk about what it means. Yesterday he asked me to talk about this passage:

I have compared thee, O my love, to a company of horses in Pharaoh's chariots. Thy cheeks are comely with rows of jewels, thy neck with chains of gold. We will make thee borders of gold with studs of silver.

I told him the horses reminded me of our horses on the ranch at Rock Lake. They look so beautiful on a summer morning when the mist is rising off the grass and you can only see their backs and heads. Apostle Motchkess liked what I said, but he wanted me to compare the horses to women. I didn't know what to say. I figured it had to do with wearing jewels, though we never put jewels on our horses, did we. He said women in Bible times wore jewels.

Lunch is usually quesadillas and a salad. Then we spend the afternoon reading other books and having our counselling sessions. Sister Linda Bergus is the counsellor. My time is from two to three every day. There's a long couch in her office, but I don't have to lie on it. I sit in a chair across from her and she asks me questions. She wants to know how I got on with everyone in our family when I was a kid. I don't see how talking about that's going to change me, but I try to think she knows what she's doing.

Some of the things she says are stupid. She has never met you, Dad, but she thinks you abused me in some way. She keeps asking if you beat me. I told her if she met you she'd know you couldn't beat anyone. I remember how you were always so gentle with the cows, even when they didn't like being milked.

She was pleased when I finally remembered one spanking. Do you remember the night I called sis a bugger? I heard Billy Jensen use the word at school. I thought it sounded funny. Do you remember how I asked sis to pass me the butter. She didn't do it right away, so I said, "Pass me the butter, you little bugger." I thought I was being smart because it almost rhymed. I deserved the licking you gave me.

Howard looked at his watch. It was a quarter to ten. He guessed he'd better write to Maxine.

Dear Maxine

I am well. I hope you are too, and that you haven't had too much snow. It's like summer here.

Yesterday evening we had our first dance. I know that must shock you, since good Tabbers know that dancing is wicked. Apostle Motchkess thinks learning to dance will help us feel comfortable around women. I do my best but I feel so awkward. It feels like

I'm wearing big rubber boots. Sister Higgins, who's teaching us, keeps shouting, "Light on your feet, men, light on your feet". So far I haven't broken any lady's toes which is a miracle. My roommate, little Boxer, is the best dancer. He took ballroom dancing when he was a teenager.

The girls are from the Pomona Tabernacle. They smile and laugh a lot like they're having fun, but I think it's all an act. None of us counselees—that's what they call us—enjoyed the evening. After the last dance, Boxer grabbed me and started dancing even though there was no music. I thought that was fun, but Apostle Motchkess was not amused. He warned Boxer to stop ruining my progress.

Another thing that will shock you is that one evening a week we have to watch movies. I know movies are a sin, especially porn movies, but Apostle Motchkess says they're good for us. They'll teach us how to have sex with a woman.

I probably shouldn't have told you about the movies. Please don't tell anyone else. I wouldn't want word about that to get back to Mom and Dad.

The lights just flashed off and on, which means I've got five minutes to get ready for bed. I'll write again later.

Love,
Howard

He could have told her a lot more, such as how they were treated like children. There were no doors on their rooms, presumably so there'd be no funny business going on. Instead there were two door frames for each room, offset like in an airport restroom. No one walking by could see into the room unless they peeked around the first doorframe. Jim Raynard, the gray-haired night watchman, shuffled down the halls like he was too tired to lift his feet. Several times

Howard had awakened to see Jim standing in the doorway. In the gloom he couldn't tell who he was staring at, him or Boxer.

Chapter 5

After a quickly prepared supper of Habitant tinned pea soup—the only brand Marc's mother would buy—and garlic bread, Marc cleared the table, washed the dishes and put things away while his mother had a hot bath. When she came padding into the living room in her pink bunny slippers and housecoat she said, "I suppose we should check Belle's house. I've been going over every day, just to make sure everything's okay."

"You can take a break while I'm here. Where's the key?" As a little boy Marc had loved going to Auntie Belle's house, though at first it had been *Grandmère's* house. When *Grandmère* had died Auntie Belle had stayed on, continuing her mother's tradition of offering French Canadian hospitality—*tortière*, pancakes drowning in real maple syrup, *pouding chômeur*—to anyone who came through the door.

As Marc turned onto Greystone Avenue with its old elms arching over the street like cathedral buttresses, he noticed that everything was the same as the last time he'd visited, except the grey fieldstone Anglican church on the corner. It had morphed into Greenfield Independent Christian Centre.

Auntie Belle's house was one of many honey-coloured brick houses sitting well back from the street. They resembled a row of self-satisfied matrons ready for a Sunday afternoon concert, competing with each other to look their best in an excess of stained glass piano windows, gleaming white gingerbread, and herringbone brick accents.

When he fitted the key into the front door and pushed it open he was greeted by the same delicious scent that had enticed him as a child: a mixture of herbs and spices, perhaps sage, poultry seasoning, ginger and cinnamon.

"*Salut,* Auntie Belle, he called from the front hallway. "You home?" He'd seen the little lady with the crumpled features in the hospital; still, he expected Auntie Belle to stick her head around the kitchen door and call, "Come in, my boy. Don't worry about your shoes," and there she'd be, stuffing a chicken, or mixing up a batch of molasses cookies.

He swallowed the lump in his throat and started touring the house with a check of the lock on the back door. Her gardening boots were set neatly on the throw rug, like she'd just come in from doing some little chore. He peeked inside the fridge but his mother must have cleaned it out. There was no sweating jug of lemonade, no jiggling bowl of cherry-red Jello or frosted chocolate birthday cake seeded with dimes, quarters and buttons. Getting the button in your slice had meant you were going to be an old maid or an old bachelor. Marc remembered getting those big ugly buttons rather frequently, so perhaps it was engraved in his genetic structure that he'd never find a congenial partner.

He tiptoed across the polished hardwood floors, brushing his fingers against things that had meant so much to him as a boy. The pocket doors between the living and dining rooms had made a perfect place to play elevator, though the game always involved a bit of a fight because cousin Arlene, as the eldest, thought she should get first turn as elevator operator, the privileged one who got to slide the doors open and closed.

"Going down. Second floor toys. Everybody off."

"Going up. Fourth floor notions." They had all laughed because *notions* was such a funny sounding word and no one knew what it meant.

In the front parlour he struck a note on the upright grand, remembering how at Christmas Auntie Belle would play. Everyone would gather around and sing carols, and not just adult songs, but the children's favourites too like *Jingle Bells* and *All I want for Christmas is my two front teeth.* Arlene and some of the other cousins had taken piano lessons but Marc never had the patience. Even so Auntie Belle had let him bang on the piano whenever he liked. Well, for a few dreadful, skull-fracturing moments anyways.

Upstairs the bedrooms seemed to be holding their collective breath, waiting for someone to snuggle beneath Auntie Belle's patchwork quilts. Grandmère's room, now Auntie Belle's, was at the front of the house, the four bedposts topped by polished brown balls which the cousins and Marc had believed were cannon balls left over from the war, though they weren't sure which war since the only shots fired around Greenfield were to bring down ducks or deer. Between the two windows that looked out on Greystone Avenue, was Auntie Belle's sewing table. On top, a pattern for a dress was pinned to a light yellow fabric sprinkled with red poppies.

Marc sighed as he went back downstairs. What would Auntie Belle think if she could see his tiny one bedroom condo in New West? It would easily fit into her high-ceilinged dining room, and leave space to spare.

It had been Marc's dream to own a house like this in Vancouver. One fall after he moved out west, the dream had started to come true, though not with Howard. Brian was another teacher. They dated for several months: cycling the Delta dikes, running up and down the Grouse Grind, kayaking Buntzen Lake. They traded growing up stories long into the night and read to each other from *The Male Couple, How Relationships Develop.*

Their relationship had reached the stage where they visited Sunday afternoon open houses with a view to buying a place of their own when the romance came to a fiery end. It was a dark, west coast evening. Brian was stopped in rush-hour traffic on the approach to the

Patullo Bridge when a dump truck's brakes failed. It roared down the hill, horn blaring, stampeded up the viaduct and turned Brian's little blue Volkswagen Golf into flaming road kill.

Marc had been twenty-seven then, young enough to recover from the grief and hope for someone new. However, except for a couple of years here and there, the long term relationship he coveted had never jelled. At forty-eight years of age he was now at that place in life where he no longer cared to stare too closely at himself in mirrors. He knew he'd see more strands of gray threading his copper hair and new lines etching the delicate skin at the corners of his eyes. Both were scribbling the message that he'd soon be consigned to hunting for a partner in that dustbin of gay dating, *Older-for-Younger*.

He didn't want to be fifty. He didn't want to live his whole life without having a man of his own, even one who might drop and kick his underwear under the bed, one who would leave stray curlies all over the bathroom sink and floor.

The next morning Marc and his mother took up their vigil at Auntie Belle's bedside. "Her left eye's still halfway open," Marc said. She seems to be looking at me." Marc took her hand. "Auntie Belle, this is Marc. Squeeze my hand if you can hear me."

"I tried that," his mother said. "I've been talking to her every day, asking her to squeeze my hand, but there's nothing, *rien*."

Just then the doctor, a surprisingly young man with curly dark hair and features fine enough to win him a role as a philandering husband on a television soap, came striding into the room.

"Madame LaChance, how are you this morning?"

"I'm fine Dr. McCrae. This is my son Marc. We need to talk with you. We need to know—"

Marc shook the doctor's hand, then put his arm around his mother's thin shoulders. "Dr. McCrae, we need to know whether Auntie Belle is likely to make a recovery."

"As I explained the other day, your sister, your aunt, has suffered a cerebral infarction." He looked at them with eyes of such an intense blue and so full of sparkling light that Marc had to physically steel himself so that he wouldn't lean forward and plant a kiss on his cheek. "That means a clot formed in one of the blood vessels supplying blood and oxygen to the brain. We tried to dissolve it but instead she suffered substantial brain haemorrhage, or bleeding."

"Can that not be stopped?" his mother asked.

"The damage is already done and there's no way we can reverse that. I'm sorry, but considering your sister's advanced age, it would be dishonest of me to hold out any hope of recovery. If we continue to give her fluids and nourishment intravenously, we can keep her alive for a few days, maybe even weeks, but that won't change the outcome."

"She will die?"

"Yes. I'm sorry."

"And if you withhold everything?"

"Three or four days perhaps."

Marc felt his mother trembling. He was struggling to hold back the tears too, partly from the expected bad news, but mostly because of his reaction to Dr. McCrae. Looking into the young doctor's eyes he felt his face flush as a wave of desire swept over him. What kind of a monster was he, he wondered, as sweat exploded under his arms? How could he be having these feelings when behind him the dearest person in his life, save for his parents and brother Claude, was lying still as a wooden dummy, her life ticking away with each heartbeat? Yet there it was, an almost overwhelming desire to have Dr. McCrae's arms around him, to press his flesh against the young doctor's, to run his fingers through his curly blond hair, to have him hold and rock him into a world where no one died, where no relationship turned sour.

"What do you think, Marc?"

Marc shook his head to clear his mind. "Maman, we have to let her go as quickly as possible." He felt his mother's shoulders stiffen. He gave her an extra hug.

She looked up at the doctor. "Yes, Dr. McCrae, I must do the right thing. It's what I would want her to do for me. Please let her go quickly."

"I believe you're making the right decision," Dr. McCrae said. "I'll instruct the nurses accordingly." He reached for his mother's hand, then Marc's.

"Thank you for being honest with us," Marc said, holding onto the doctor's hand a little longer than he should have. When he finally let go Dr. McCrae squeezed his shoulder and patted his mother's arm. Then he turned and walked briskly from the room. Marc supposed he was used to having patients and their relatives fall in love with him. It was probably one of the little annoyances of his position as arbiter of life and death.

A few minutes later Amy came into the room. "Dr. McCrae told me of your decision so I'm going to carry out a few procedures here. You may leave if you'd rather. It will take me just a few minutes."

"Maman, do you want to leave?"

"*Mais oui*. I'll get a coffee."

"I think I'll stay," Marc said, pulling one of the chairs back so he could sit down out of Amy's way. He watched as she pinched off the drip from one of the clear bags of fluid that hung from the frame attached to Auntie Belle's bed.

"I'll leave this one drip in."

"What for?"

"I can administer morphine through this one. We want to keep your aunt comfortable. She's had a lovely, long life hasn't she? I've never seen anyone with so many get well cards, so much love. Often the older ones have very few left who care."

She gently turned Auntie Belle, tucking pillows in behind her so she could lie on her side. "There we go, Dear. Are you more comfortable now? Let me straighten your pillow. I'll lift your head...and there you go. You just rest easy now, Dear. I'll be in to check on you every hour or so."

"Thank you for taking such good care of Auntie Belle," Marc said. "My mother tells me your last name is Hildebrandt. Are you related to Howard?"

"Howard's my brother-in-law."

"Howard and I were roommates at university."

"I'm married to his brother Doug."

"Is Howard still in Winnipeg?"

"He's on leave this year, in Africa. He's volunteering with some mission program, drilling wells and building water systems for villages. We haven't heard from him for several months now. Apparently he's in a very primitive area that doesn't have cell phone coverage."

"His family go with him?"

"He doesn't have a family, at least not yet, though I believe he has an understanding with a lady in Winnipeg. They'll be getting married when he returns."

Marc and his mother sat beside Auntie Belle's bedside for three more days. Marc had lots of time to think about Howard, and to learn more about him from Amy, without being too obvious, he hoped. She told him Howard still worked for Bronnel Engineering, that he hadn't gone bald but his thick black hair was turning a handsome salt and pepper. He rented a one bedroom apartment in downtown Winnipeg which he was subletting to someone from work while he was in Africa.

Late on the third day Auntie Belle was breathing noticeably shallower and her heartbeat was weaker. Cousin Arlene came up to the hospital for a visit. She hugged Marc and his mother and handed over a spray of tinted carnations. Marc went down to the lounge to get another chair and when he got back to the room his mother and Arlene were gazing down at Auntie Belle.

"*Belle est décédée,*" his mother whispered, grabbing his arm. "*Ma pauvre soeur est décédée.* I had three sisters, and now I have none. I'm all alone in the world."

"I'm here, Maman."

"Yes, Marc, and I'm so fortunate to have you, and you too, Arlene. Poor Belle had no children. All alone in the world."

"She's in a better place now," Arlene said. "Imagine what it must be like, trapped in this broken body of hers one minute, the next flying through space to heaven where she'll have high tea with God and the angels. I think we should all be happy for her."

The official mourners were few in number: Marc's mother in a black dress and hat, two strands of pearls around her neck—Marc was relieved she hadn't copied Jackie Kennedy's full veil as that would have been a bit too melodramatic for Greenfield. There was Arlene and her ex-husband Steve, their daughter Sondra and her fiancé, and a few elderly friends hobbling in the procession with walkers and canes. The rest of the chairs in the small room were filled with strangers whom Marc later learned were Auntie Belle's former teaching colleagues and students.

Much as his mother had admired President Kennedy's full requiem mass, she was determined to keep Auntie Belle's service free from religious rigmarole. At one time she had been a devout churchgoer, but Claude's funeral had inoculated her against all religious ceremony. Claude, always a hot head like his lusty voyageur ancestors, had thrown himself off the Twentieth Street bridge when a teenage love affair had gone wrong. If he'd jumped during the summer he'd only have gotten a slimy, algae infused baptism, but the frozen Greenfield River hadn't offered any second chances at life in the middle of January.

Father Dann, their parish priest, had consigned Claude's soul to hellfire. It wasn't surprising that now Claudette wanted no clergy at Auntie Belle's farewell. One of the men from the Greenfield Seniors Centre was master of ceremonies. Marc read the life history and during an open mike, friends, former students and ladies from the *Quilts for Kids* chapter Belle had started, lined up to remember her.

Marc wanted his mother to sit down at the reception, but she refused. "Haven't I told you how Jackie gave an audience to visiting statesmen when they came to the president's funeral?"

"But she was less than half your age when she did that, and I doubt there are any statesmen here today."

"If Jackie could walk behind her husband's casket surely I can stand for a few moments." Marc worried that his mother was taking her Jacqueline Kennedy mode a bit too seriously. In a few years she might be in some nursing home, wearing a little pink suit and hat, standing at her window, waving a white-gloved hand to passersby.

"My condolences on the death of your sister, Mrs. LaChance," said a stout man who walked with a limp, one boot sole built thicker than the other. "I'm Tim Grant and your sister inspired me to be a teacher. She taught me in Grade 5, and years later I actually taught in the same school as her. She was always so much fun, and thanks to the faith she had in me, I'm a principal now. I'll be opening a new school in South Greenfield in September."

"This is my son Marc. He's a teacher too."

"Where do you teach?"

"In a French immersion school in Surrey."

"Why don't you come and teach for me next year? My school won't be French immersion, but I'll need someone to teach French to the upper grades." He reached into his jacket pocket and pulled out a business card. "I'll want to finalize staffing before the end of June. Give me a call if you're interested."

Marc nodded, stuck the card into his pocket and turned to shake hands with the next person.

Chapter 6

Howard couldn't decide which was worse, workouts with Rafe ranting at him to man up, or counselling sessions with Sister Bergus who was always trying to break him down. She was determined he was covering up childhood sexual abuse.

"Who behaved inappropriately around you when you were a child?" Sister Bergus asked after settling her wide-as-a-haystack butt into the swivel chair behind her desk.

"No one, Ma'am."

"Think carefully, Buck. There must have been some incident. Perhaps you've tried to forget it because it was someone close to you: your father, or one of your brothers." She gave her Dubble Bubble pink nails a frown as she waited for him to reply.

"No one abused me, Ma'am."

"What about the teacher at that little country school in Rock Lake? Did he touch you inappropriately? Or maybe the apostle at the tabernacle?"

"No Ma'am."

"What about the organist? What did he do to you? Was it so terrible that you have sublimated it, forced it out of your consciousness?"

"Ma'am, there was no organ in the Rock Lake Tabernacle. We had a piano."

"What about the pianist then? Did he touch you—"

"Yes, Mary Dyson touched me all the time. She used to hug me and give me peppermints. She hugged all the kids. Besides playing the piano she was our Sunday School teacher."

Howard got so weary of this game. Sometimes he was tempted to lie.

All right, he wanted to say. *I'll tell you about it. It was the AI man who touched me inappropriately.*

AI stands for Artificial Insemination, Sister Bergus. Dad would call the AI man anytime one of our Holsteins went into heat. Do you know what it means to be in heat?

You know a cow's in heat when she starts jumping up on the other cattle. When she does that she's showing that she's got eggs that need to be fertilized. Only problem was, Sister Bergus, that we didn't have a bull. You need a bull to fertilize the eggs. Do you understand how that works, Sister Bergus or do I need to explain how a cow and a bull make a calf? Should I draw a diagram for you on that legal-sized pad of yellow foolscap you scribble on?

So this is how it happened. When bringing the cows home from the pasture I might see a cow jumping.

"Dad, Daisy Belle's jumping," I'd say, or "Dad, Buela Mae is jumping tonight." I know they're strange names, but you see Sister Bergus, Mother had family in Alabama and she liked to name the cows after her cousins. It was a bit of a joke.

You don't think it's funny. Fine. Just forget it.

Dad would phone the AI man and ask him to come out the next day to take care of things. If it was a school day I'd play sick. I'd stick my finger down my throat and throw up my oatmeal and toast. Then I'd watch out my upstairs bedroom window for the little white Volkswagen Beetle to drive onto the farmyard.

*I watched the AI man get out of the car. He opened the hood—
the trunk was in the front of those cars. He lifted out a bucket, a roll of
paper towels, a bottle of antiseptic, and from the cooler in the back
seat, he took the tiny vial of frozen semen—bull semen, Sister Bergus.
Do you understand?*

*As soon as he disappeared into the barn I sneaked out of the
house. It was easy to do. Dad was fixing fences or cutting hay. Mother
was hanging out the wash or working in the garden.*

*I sneaked into the barn and stood quietly watching the AI man.
First he washed the cow's—What's that, Sister Bergus? You don't
want to know every detail?*

*Okay, I'll skip that part. After satisfying Buela Mae he'd turn
his attention to me. First, he would soften me up with a jawbreaker.
They were my favourite candy. While I was sucking on it he would
undo his zipper and—Oh Sister Bergus, it was awful! You have no idea
what he made me do.*

Howard said none of these things. He just shook his head and
stared at the ugly growth on Sister Bergus' forehead. It was the size of
a pencil eraser with three black hairs growing out of it. Sister Bergus
appeared to be mid-forties and, despite her weight, a decently
attractive woman. He wondered why she didn't make an appointment
to have the growth removed. An X-acto knife would do the job, one
quick slice and the ugly knob would be gone.

Her short hair was dyed copper. To Howard it looked like
someone had used her skull to wind the armature wire from an electric
motor. His girlfriend in Winnipeg Maxine sported the same industrial
colour, but Howard kept his mouth shut. His mother had taught him
never to comment on a woman's hair.

And he wasn't going to tell Sister Bergus about being abused
as a child, because there had never been any abuse, though he
wouldn't have put up a struggle if the AI man, a slim, curly-haired
fellow who wore skin-tight jeans, had tried something funny.

When Sister Bergus failed to unearth any scandals from his
childhood, she quizzed him about his adult relationships. "Maybe you
weren't a child when this awful thing happened. The brain is a
powerful instrument. It can block out unpleasant events."

Howard shook his head.

"Have you ever been with a man?"

"Nothing unpleasant has ever happened to me."

"You've had no disappointments in life?"

"I meant nothing of an unpleasant sexual nature ever happened to me. Like everyone else, I've had my disappointments."

"Have you ever had a relationship with another man?"

"No one made me gay, Sister Bergus. I just grew up this way. I thought it was weird and uncouth, the way my brothers talked about girls. I just wasn't interested in the same things."

"You didn't answer my question, Buck. Have you ever been intimate with a man?"

Howard shook his head and studied the wood grain pattern of Sister Bergus' desk. He hated when she badgered him like this, but she could say whatever she liked, he'd never tell her about his last year in grad school, the year he roomed with Marc LaChance. He wasn't going to let her turn that into something dirty, something perverted and life destroying.

"I feel you're holding something back from me, Buck. Howard, please be honest with me." She always used his real name when she thought he was about to disclose something important. "I can only help if you're brutally honest with me. Now tell me, have you ever had intimate relations with another man, with anyone?"

Howard shook his head again. He couldn't get Marc out of his mind, and thinking about him made him tense up. Tears blurred his vision.

"For someone who has never been abused, you show a lot of emotion," Sister Bergus said, handing him a paper tissue. "Why don't you tell me about it? You'll feel much better after you talk about it, after we unpack it and take the hurt out of it."

Howard shook his head and mopped the tears off his cheeks. *Marc. Oh Marc, how could I have been so cruel? What kind of a religion do I belong to that makes me think I'm doing God's will when I reject someone's love? How could I have been so callous, so deceitful, as to grab that job with Bronnel Engineering behind Marc's back?*

"Well?" Sister Bergus stared at him through the thick lenses of her narrow-framed glasses.

Howard shook his head again. There was no way he could tell her how Marc and he used to sleep together, how Marc used to hold him, run his fingers through the hair on his chest. It would be a betrayal of Marc's memory to tell her how good it had felt to snuggle together every night. Even though Howard knew their actions had been sinful, he wasn't going to let Sister Bergus turn it into something unspeakably foul.

"Well, don't you have anything to tell me?" Sister Bergus tried again.

"I did have a few sleepovers with my friend Lenny Maxted," Howard said.

Sister Bergus grabbed her pen and adjusted the thick pad of yellow paper to a comfortable angle. "Who is Lenny Maxted?"

"He was a school chum."

"And you slept with him?"

"Yes."

"In the same bed?"

"Sort of."

"And what happened?"

"What do you mean, *What happened?*"

"Did Lenny touch you inappropriately?"

"We were seven years old."

"Exactly the age when little boys may begin exploring their bodies, doing inappropriate things."

"We slept together. That's all."

"Go on."

"Mom and Dad were nervous about letting me go."

"So there was some concern on their part. Had Lenny or someone in his family been known to abuse others?"

"Lenny's family never went to church. Mom and Dad said I could spend the weekend at Lenny's if I promised to tell them about Jesus Christ."

"And were you able to point them to God?"

"I promised, but that night Lenny wanted to watch the Chiller Thriller movie on television. I knew I should tell him movies were sinful but I didn't. I watched it with him."

"Were his parents in the room with you?" Sister Bergus was scribbling as fast as Howard could speak.

"They went to bed."

"So you were staying up very late while everyone else was in bed? What happened when the movie was over?"

"We planned to stay up all night."

"Was Lenny planning something?"

"You know what kids are like. They think it's fun to stay up all night."

"And did you?"

"No. After the movie we both lay down on the couch."

"Beside each other?"

"No. They had one of those L-shaped couches so we lay down, one of us on each section. We must have fallen asleep. When morning came someone had put—"

"Put what, Howard? You can tell me."

"Someone had put a blanket over me. And another over Lenny."

Sister Bergus dropped her pen. "That's not the type of experience I'm thinking of, Buck. You know, you're never going to heal from homosexuality if you keep on blocking whatever despicable act caused you to veer onto that pathway. You must be honest with me. Between now and tomorrow's appointment I want you to think very carefully about that weekend with Lenny. Try to remember what really happened. You can send Boxer in now."

Chapter 7

"I love what you've done to the living room," cousin Arlene said, plunking herself down on the sofa. It was almost the end of July, three weeks since Marc had moved into Auntie Belle's house. "The room looks so much bigger this way. I could never understand why Auntie Belle had the furniture arranged around the outside of the room. This is so much cosier, the sofa and chairs facing each other beside the fireplace."

"A place to curl up with a book on cold winter days," and snuggle next to my husband, Marc thought, though he didn't say it. No point getting Arlene riled up.

"Exactly, but I didn't come to check on your decorating skills. I wondered if you'd like to come to the art gallery's summer gala on Friday evening. There'll be guided tours of the William Kurelek exhibition, a string orchestra and food and drink, not that I touch the latter."

"I'm not really an arty type."

"I know that, but you've been so busy cleaning up this house you haven't had a chance to get out and do anything. This will give you an opportunity to meet some people. Besides, I don't have a date and I always feel queer going to these things on my own."

Marc couldn't think of anything more boring than being screeched at by violins while trying to talk sense to artistic types, but it might be an ideal spot to meet some of his own kind, so he agreed to go. Arlene hugged him like he'd just bailed her out of jail.

Marc was pleased to discover that Kurelek's paintings depicted recognizable scenes of everyday life on the prairies: snowy city streets with kids playing shinny, adults pushing a car out of a snowdrift, and yellow school buses tearing along lonely country roads. It helped that the tour guide was easy to look at. Jordan Cloutier appeared to be in his mid-forties, salt and pepper hair in a layered cut, blue jeans, yellow shirt open at the neck showing off a coarse tuft of hair. His face was angular, like it had been chiselled from a block of wood by teenagers in the school shop, a rash of pock pits on his cheeks, which made him look vulnerable and loveable.

Marc listened to Jordan's every word and even asked a question or two, hoping to be noticed. Jordan was wearing a platinum ring on the fourth finger of his right hand which he flapped around a good deal while pointing out interesting aspects of each painting. The ring might be a wedding band or a mere decoration. Marc hoped it was the latter.

When the tour was over Arlene rushed across the room to talk to someone while Marc lagged behind to shake Jordan's hand and thank him for such an interesting tour. He made a point of holding his hand long enough to send him a signal if he was inclined to recognize it, but not so long as to make him uncomfortable. Jordan smiled, thanked him for his kind words, and turned to a young lady with long blond hair who had also been on the tour.

Marc went looking for Arlene. He found her at the buffet on the front lawn. They grabbed paper plates and browsed their way through the delicate little sandwiches with their crusts sawed off, and tiny gingerbread men and women, each one decorated by a different artist. Marc's little man was wearing a bright green shirt with red polka dots and orange pantaloons. He had thought the green shirt might be mint frosting, but he had been deceived. It tasted of the same bland sweetness as the rest of the little man's clothes.

"What did you think of the Kureleks?" Arlene asked.

"Very pleasant, and Jordan did such a good job of leading the tour. As a volunteer, do you work closely with him?"

"I don't see that much of him. He travels a good bit, searching out new shows, visiting artists."

"That must be hard on his wife and family." He was praying she'd say he was a single man, but instead she pointed to the woman ladling out the punch at the far end of the buffet.

"That's his wife over there. She goes with him when he travels." Arlene lowered her voice. "I've heard he's quite the ladies' man, and that's why his wife travels with him, to keep him out of trouble, if you know what I mean."

Deceived again. Apparently the flapping wrist was not an indicator of affectional orientation, or if it was, he was hiding his true self behind the skirts of his punch-pouring wife.

Marc and Arlene were finishing their lunch when two ladies joined them: a mother and daughter. The daughter focused her attention on him, quizzing him like she was a television reporter and he a person of some import. Finally he excused himself and returned to the gallery. Maybe if he hung out away from the ladies he'd bump into someone his own gender, someone single and on the lookout for a husband.

He wandered through the galleries, pretending to look at the paintings and sculptures. He thought he'd found someone when he came upon a lone guy a few years younger than himself examining what looked like a road kill pizza on a man-sized canvass. The fellow's body screamed gym bunny, for he didn't have even a hint of a belly, and his legs and butt fit perfectly into his chinos. Marc was about to make a clever comment about *Honeymoon Orgasm*, the painting's title, when a woman came out of the ladies room and wrapped herself around the fellow as though she was anxious to get on with her very own honeymoon orgasm.

Marc turned away, disappointed. Across the room he saw a rusty haired guy examining some vases displayed in a glass case. He was wearing blue jeans, a mauve shirt under a light grey sports jacket, a pale yellow-chequered scarf tucked into the neck. He had a bit of a belly, but nothing unmanageable. Marc wandered over and looked at the display.

The fellow turned to him and smiled. "Hi. Do you collect Wedgewood?"

"No, I don't collect anything," Marc said. "How about you?"

"I do indeed. In fact, these pieces are from my own collection. Every year I lend a few of them to the gallery for their open house."

"Are they valuable?"

"This is a Portland vase in black jasperware, a limited edition, so it's worth several thousand dollars. Interpretations of the scene vary but I like to think he's Dionysus, chief of the Olympians. Look at the detail in his thighs. "

At that moment an elderly fellow with a cane tapped his way over. He sidled up to the fellow Marc was talking to and slapped him on the shoulder. "Ready to head back to the hotel, Prince?"

"I was just showing this fellow the Portland vase. By the way, I'm Colin and this is my partner Jeff. He calls me Prince, for some unknown reason."

"Marc. Marc LaChance. I just moved to Greenfield," Marc said, shaking both men's hands.

"We're from Winnipeg. We just came out for today's open house. I'm assistant curator at the Winnipeg Art Gallery, and Jeff, well, he's retired, does a bit of painting. I was just pointing out the design on this vase," Colin said.

"Ah, yes, the thigh vase. Colin likes thighs, especially when they're wrapped around him, don't you Prince, and yours aren't too bad either," Jeff said, taking a step back and pointing his cane at Marc, as though judging a bull at the fair.

"Jeff can be rather rude," Colin said, "but I think he's saying that he'd like you to join us for dinner. We're staying at the Manitoba Inn, and after dinner, if you care to stick around and—"

"Play thigh ball," Jeff finished the sentence for him.

"Thigh ball?"

"My partner is known for getting straight to the point," Colin said, "but the invitation's for dinner, and anything else is up to you."

"You guys aren't monogamous then?"

"That soon gets boring," Jeff said, still eyeing Marc like he was a prize bull.

"Thanks for the invitation, but I'll take a rain check. Thigh ball isn't exactly what I had in mind for this evening."

"We're open to suggestions," Jeff said, winking and licking his thin lips.

"No thanks. I better be going. I came with my cousin and she's probably looking for me. You guys have a good evening."

As Marc and Arlene drove home, Marc wondered if he would have responded positively to the invitation if Jeff hadn't resembled a leering cadaver from some horror movie. Would he have taken the couple up on their offer?

When he'd moved to Greenfield he'd promised himself there'd be no more cruising for one-hour stands. From the little experience he'd had with long-term relationships, he knew what he wanted, and it wasn't an hour of bedtime here and there when some stranger felt the pangs of skin hunger. He knew from those last few months in New West when he'd been promiscuous, that no-strings-attached sheet-twisting could never compare with the joy of knowing he had someone special to come home to every night. But was he going to find a soul mate in Greenfield, or were the birthday-cake buttons set in stone?

By the time Marc bid good-bye to Arlene and let himself into Auntie Belle's big house, he was questioning whether he'd been wise to move to Greenfield where there was no visible gay community. When Tim Grant had handed over his card at Auntie Belle's funeral, Marc had shoved it into his pocket and forgotten about it until he was back in the classroom on the coast.

It had been a week later, a Friday evening when he'd remembered it. It had been a difficult week at work and he was feeling drained of energy. Teaching had a way of doing that to him. Like an actor on the stage, he had to be turned on while at work, pretending he really cared about multiplication facts and magnetism and all that other exciting grade school stuff. When not actually teaching he had to show an intense interest in his students' little lives—how Billy had taught his new puppy to sit up and beg, how Diana's dad had yelled at her mother the night before because she burned the roast.

That Friday evening Marc had been too tired to burn a roast or anything else. He'd walked down to Tugboat Willy's for dinner. He was sitting by himself at his favourite table in the farthest corner where the floor was raised a couple of steps, letting him keep tabs on the whole bar. He supposed it was the schoolteacher in him that impelled him to choose that table, though he managed to suppress the urge to tell others to keep the noise down, spit out their gum, or line up quietly at the cash desk when they got up to leave.

He liked to read when he dined alone, figuring folks would think him some high-powered businessman who had to work through lunch or dinner rather than a loser who wasn't able to snag a dinner date, never mind a full-time partner. That evening he'd taken David Sedaris' book, *Me Talk Pretty One Day*. Sedaris always made him feel better about living alone. What a hellish life it would be if he was hitched to Sedaris, a fellow who found things of interest in people's toilet bowls, and not only studied them at close range, but felt compelled to write and share his experiences with millions of readers.

That night Marc got through the salad and the fish and chip courses okay, but then had to wait for his dessert, a slice of triple layer chocolate cake—he didn't worry about his developing paunch when depressed—and when he turned the page he came to one of Sedaris' chapters clogged with scatological references. He slammed the book shut and looked around the bar. A couple of guys were sitting down at a table across the room. As soon as the waitress had retreated to get their drinks they started playing footsie under the table, and as Marc watched, a feeling of desperate loneliness came over him. He happened to be wearing the jacket he'd been wearing at Auntie Belle's funeral, and reaching into the pocket to snug away the book, he felt the business card.

He pulled it out and remembered Tim Grant's offer of employment. His personal life couldn't be any more bankrupt in Greenfield than in New West, and besides, his mother had hinted that he could have Auntie Belle's house, no charge, if he moved back to Manitoba.

He had called Tim Grant on Monday morning, verified his offer of a job, and given notice to Surrey. As he'd packed his few precious things into his RAV4 and headed east through the coast range, he'd hoped he was putting twenty-four years of disappointment behind him. Surely whatever lay ahead could be no worse, and perhaps his mother would be right about prairie men being easier to connect with. Perhaps he'd meet that hunky cowboy with whom he could play *Brokeback Mountain, the Revised Version*, the one with a happy-ever-after ending.

Now, barely three weeks into his new life, he was sitting at home alone, picking away at a micro-waved rice and vegetable dish that had left the whole house smelling like an outdoor biffy. He was sitting at his desk in the upstairs study, surfing the web, searching once again for local gay organizations. So far there was no place where he could meet his own kind, not even an HIV/AIDS group where he might volunteer. Greenfield seemed to be a town of the fifties, where *gay* still meant happy-go-lucky.

He checked out the local college, to see if there were fall courses that might attract his own kind. *Agricultural Methods of the Eighteenth Century* and *Maximizing Efficiencies in your Cow Calf Operation* didn't seem to hold out a lot of promise. He shut down the computer and went to bed.

He awakened at two in the morning, momentarily disoriented by the faint glow of street light coming through a window that shouldn't be at the foot of his bed, and by the dead quiet: no gulls, no traffic sounds. Once he'd sorted out that he was in Greenfield, and not in New West, he made a trip to and from the bathroom, then lay awake reviewing his past almost-loves.

There had been Michael, a guy at the Y, short, stocky, with thick slabs of muscle on his furry thighs. He'd had a six-pack belly, and shoulders like soccer balls, the complete opposite of his own slim frame. They'd become after-workout lovers before Michael changed his workout days and quit answering Marc's telephone calls. When he'd finally tracked him down he'd muttered something about Marc being too intense.

Next had been Rejean, an Air Canada flight attendant, sporting the same testosterone-soaked voyageur genes as Marc's brother Claude. After making love, Marc had enjoyed playing with his shaggy head, tracing his thick black eyebrows, drawing a line down his profile, grabbing handfuls of his coarse black hair. Marc couldn't recall what had gone wrong with that almost-relationship, but they'd drifted apart. When Marc next heard of Rejean it was to read his obituary in the *Vancouver Sun*. In lieu of flowers, loved ones were invited to contribute to an HIV organization.

There was John who lived to drive his Mazda RX-7 so fast that he had to cut into the opposite lane to negotiate mountain curves. He had been looking for a long-term relationship. Perhaps in time Marc would have come to love his less than handsome features, even his nose which was porker like, letting him look right through his nostrils into his head. At the time Marc just couldn't see himself sitting across from that nose at the breakfast table every morning. How shallow a reason was that for giving up on a good man?

September brought the beginning of school with the excitement of new routines, lessons to prepare and staff members to get to know. He hoped there might be another gay guy on staff.

Marc was assigned a fourth grade homeroom class as well as forty minutes of French as a second language in both grades five and six. It was a small staff, just one class of each grade from Kindergarten to sixth, plus itinerant music and physical education specialists. Tim Grant confided that he'd been hampered in staffing by the seniority list. There were a couple of old biddies looking after Kindergarten and first grade, two middle-aged women in second and third grades, Marc in fourth, another biddy in fifth, and Bill Fuches in sixth.

Within moments of meeting Bill, Marc felt an aversion to him. He had a pasty, round face, and cemented down his few strands of greying hair in a comb over. He favoured sixties style brown corduroy jackets with leather patches on the elbows, one of them usually flapping in the breeze. When asked to help out with something extra he groaned as though it was a great imposition upon his precious time. When he talked to Marc, he got far too close, invading his personal space and enveloping him in his stale, tobacco tainted breath.

While the old biddies and middle-aged women were pleasant enough to work with, the brightest spot was Ian Hiddley, the physical education teacher. About thirty-five years of age, he bounced into the school three days a week, full of energy and hot to look at whether in baggy sweats or shorts. Of course he had a wife, three kids, and a house in the suburbs. Marc was always glad to offer him assistance with the after school sports program, not because he harboured any hope of prying Ian's affections from his loved ones, but because he was one of those people whose enthusiasm for life made Marc feel more alive.

Marc's life settled into a routine: school during the week, preparing lessons and doing a few chores around the house and yard on weekends. Occasionally Arlene dropped by to enthuse about her latest religious experience, or to invite him to the opening of some new art exhibition or a musical event. He didn't always go, but when he did venture out, meeting single, gay men proved as elusive as at that first gala.

Was this going to be the sum of excitement for the rest of his life?

Chapter 8

Apostle Motchkess was taking the six counselees on their monthly field trip, this time to White Glove Auto. As he drove them over to West First Street in Pomona he explained that they would learn how to change the oil in their cars. That didn't sound very thrilling to Howard. He'd helped his dad with jobs a lot more complicated than that around the ranch.

White Glove Auto was as grubby as its neighbourhood, railway tracks on one side of the street, an electrical substation on the other. Beside the service station was a vacant lot full of waist-high weeds dry enough to burst into flame at the first whiff of cigarette smoke. The sign tacked above the service bays showed a grinning fellow in a blue uniform. He was looking up from the open hood of a big-finned 60's Caddie, a can of motor oil in his white-gloved hand. His grin may have brought customers in at one time, but now his face was pock-marked. His white gloves were speckled with rust where chips of paint had peeled off the metal sign.

Apostle Motchkess led them into the shop where he introduced the owner, a stocky thirty-something guy named Rocko. His face displayed several pits and pock marks of its own, but his large brown eyes beneath thick eyebrows exuded masculinity as he levelled his gaze at each of them and flashed a mouthful of perfect teeth. He was wearing dark blue coveralls, stained with grease and oil. His sleeves were rolled up, showing off a muscular pair of forearms. Before shaking everyone's hand he pulled an oil-stained rag from his back pocket and wiped the sweat from his brow. Apparently Rocko hadn't heard that real men wiped sweat with the back of their hands. Howard winked at Boxer.

"What are you going to show us?" Apostle Motchkess asked.

"I'm guessin' it'll be best if I jest go on with my work," Rocko said, shuffling his steel-toed work boots. "Changin' the oil in this here one, and got a half dozen more waitin' out there." His speech was drawled, like Boxer's, only sloppier sounding.

"Y'all can watch me finish this here one. Then I'll get y'all to help with the rest of 'em. Coveralls inside the office there. Better cover up them fancy threads some of you is wearin'."

Even Boxer started acting macho once he'd pulled the coveralls over his black pleated pants. He left the zipper half-way down, exposing his hairless chest, set his hands on his hips, spaced his feet widely apart, and stood on tip-toe to peer into the engine compartment of the SUV Rocko was working on. His little freckled face was framed by the crook of Rocko's furry arm.

"Count the clicks as I fill 'er up," Rocko said, sticking a nozzle into the oil filler cap and squeezing the lever.

"One...Two...Three...Four."

"Y'all know how to check if four quarts is enough?"

"You pull out the dipstick," Baker said.

Rocko nodded. "Y'all know where to find the dipstick?"

Boxer turned and took a step toward the workbench that was spread with tools. "Y'all won't find it over there," Rocko said. "Y'all find it under the hood."

Boxer turned around and gazed up at the raised hood.

"Not *on* the hood. *Under* the hood. Watch now, here's where y'all find it." Rocko pointed to a loop of metal near the back of the engine. "Y'all know how to use it?"

Baker yanked it out, waved it around, spattering them with droplets of oil.

"You take it out all right, but wavin' it round won't do nobody no good. Y'all know how to read the thang?"

Boxer grabbed it out of Baker's hand. "Here it is, Sir. I can read it. Let's see. F-U-L-L. It says Full."

"You're telling us it's full, are you?"

"Wait." Boxer held the stick closer. "Down here it says A-D-D, Add, and there's another word down here at the end. L-O-W. Which is it, Full or Low?"

"Any you guys know how to measure oil proper like?"

"Here. Give it to me, you dipstick," Baker said, almost taking Boxer's nose off as he whipped the dipstick out of his hand. He dragged it across the leg of his coveralls, then shoved it back into its sleeve, jamming it down. He waited a second, then yanked it out. "It's on Add." He looked triumphantly at Boxer and Rocko.

"Right," Rocko said. "I know this vehicle takes five and a bit quarts, but I never put that in to begin with. I put in four, take a reading, then add a bit more. It's easier to add more than take out what you've already put in. Remember that. There's a good lesson in that for y'all."

He winked, then clocked in another one and a half quarts. He motioned for Boxer to check the level. Boxer gripped the clip, tugged, stood on tiptoes, finally pulled the stick all the way out. Rocko yanked the rag out of his back pocket and handed it to Boxer. He looked at Rocko with a puzzled look, then wiped his brow.

"No, the rag's for the stick," Rocko said. "When I was addin' that last bit of oil some may've splashed up on this here stick." He took it from Boxer. "You wipe it off like this, then stick it back in gently. Pull it out, and then you read the thang. Now let me see y'all do it."

"What else should we check when we change the oil?" Rocko asked when they'd all satisfied him they knew how to use a dipstick.

"All the bodily fluids," Baker said.

"That's right. What are them fluids?"

"The rad," said Baker.

"And the window washer fluid," volunteered someone else, "And the tranny. Don't forget the tranny," added Baker.

"And what's special about the tranny?"

"You gotta have the engine running when you check it," Howard said.

"I thought a tranny was like a man who wants to become a woman," Boxer said, "but that can't be what you're talking about."

"The transmission, you dipstick," said Baker, punching Boxer affectionately on the shoulder. "The transmission fluid has to be checked."

The morning was spent doing oil and lube jobs. One car needed new plugs so everyone got to remove and install one. While this was going on Howard noticed that Boxer was completely smitten by Rocko. He was hanging as close to him as he could, *accidentally* brushing arms with him as they bent over the engine.

By the time the job was completed, everyone was sweating and had their coveralls zipped down as far as they dared. Howard couldn't tell whether Rocko was wearing any shorts or underwear beneath his greasy costume, but he was sure it wouldn't be long before Boxer found out. He seemed one excited breath away from jumping inside Rocko's coveralls and snuggling up to his bearish belly.

After lunch Rocko directed everyone to the last bay where he was restoring a classic. He said it was a '59 Chevy, though with nothing but the frame and engine, it was impossible to tell which model it was.

"Y'all can help me hoist this engine out of here," he said. "I've loosened all the motor mounts so it should come out easy. We'll use this hydraulic crane to lift it. Then I'll get you to remove the carburettor, the valve covers, all that junk, and clean 'er up."

Howard recalled Marc saying he wanted to restore an old car once they got established in Vancouver. He used to talk about helping his brother Claude work on some old Pontiac. As Howard helped winch up the engine and push it over to the bench he wondered if Marc had ever got the chance to do that kind of work. Then, since only he and Baker knew anything about engines, they started ripping it apart, handing the components to the others to be cleaned. Howard tried to keep his eyes off Baker, but it was difficult to do since it took both of them to remove valve covers and spark plugs that hadn't felt a screw driver or wrench in decades. Several times he felt himself becoming aroused, but he did as Apostle Motchkess had taught them. He silently prayed, "Deliver me from evil, Lord. Give me something else to think about," and most of the time it worked.

Meanwhile, Boxer, wearing rubber gloves, was spraying the valve lifters with degreaser, scrubbing them and laying them out on paper towels as though they were fine china.

On the short drive back to TITC Apostle Motchkess gave a pop quiz on automotive terminology. He threw out automotive terms and asked for definitions: "Two eighty-three…Four barrel…Four on the floor…Super-charged…Dodge hemi." Judging by the answers, most of the guys were going to have to spend a lot more time with Rocko at White Glove Auto if they wanted to become straight.

Chapter 9

As soon as Marc had made Auntie Belle's house his own, and the school year had gotten underway, he resumed his workouts at the gym. The price of an annual membership at the Greenfield Y was half the price he'd paid on the coast. He followed a lite maintenance schedule, exerting himself just enough to keep his pecs and biceps in decent condition. At forty-eight years of age he realized he'd never be a muscle hunk, but he wanted to keep trim, just in case he met Mr. Right.

The gym's downside was that the sight of so many fit men underlined Marc's loneliness. The flash of a sun-ripened shoulder, a glance at a well-muscled butt, and the sight of fine, sun-bleached hairs on the back of a sturdy hand wrapped around a dumbbell were enough to inflame a blaze of overwhelming desire. He would hurry home and search the web again for any hint of a gay community in Greenfield, but there was nothing. He even called the hospital to ask if there was an AIDS support group, thinking he could become a buddy to someone, meet people that way, but again he struck out. A couple of weekends he drove into Winnipeg to hang out at Club 200. There he could be with his own kind, but it was too far away to foster any ongoing friendships.

As September's leaves fell and the cold winds started blowing down from the north he grew more impatient. Why had he left the coast? Sure, he was enjoying Auntie Belle's house. It was such a treat to be able to walk inside with a sack of groceries instead of unlocking a zillion security doors and waiting for an elevator to carry him home. As for his mother, she didn't really need him. Physically and mentally she was doing fine, if he discounted the strange fixation upon Jackie Kennedy. She certainly didn't need his help, though he enjoyed her company on weekends.

Finally he signed onto an online meet-up site. As he scrolled through the profiles he saw that most of the guys in Greenfield classified themselves as *bi*. That was probably their code for *married*. They were looking for NSA, no strings attached, and could not host a meetup. His brief liaisons on the coast had taught him there'd be no satisfaction in hooking up with those guys.

He managed to stay on the straight, narrow, and lonely until a Thursday night in late October. He got to the gym later than usual due to an annoying staff meeting. A lot of time had been wasted stroking Bill Fuches' delicate ego as he complained that his sixth graders were wasting too much time on physical education and music.

"How do you expect me to teach math and reading when they're out of the classroom half the day playing sports and singing stupid ditties?" While that compliment to Ian Hiddley and the music teacher had sunk in he'd turned his attention to Marc. "Of course, I guess it really doesn't matter how they do in my subjects so long as they learn to speak Froggie, as if that's going to be any help to them in this town."

"What makes you think all your students will be staying in Greenfield after they graduate?" Marc had shot back, though he managed to put the brakes on and not say, *They're not all going to be big losers like you.* The poisonous atmosphere had hung about for the rest of the meeting.

By the time Marc got to the gym he was feeling bruised, both professionally and emotionally. He began plodding through his workout, stretches on the mat, followed by crunches, then the Roman chair, a feeble attempt to recapture a six-pack, though he wasn't sure it had ever been there. As he progressed through his workout he kept waiting for the endorphins to kick in, but they were proving elusive, and then a new guy bounced in. Fortyish, a smidgen shorter than Marc, he stepped onto the scale which was snugged into the corner beside the Roman chair.

"Lies. It's all lies!" he said, turning to Marc, showing off a mouthful of perfectly aligned teeth. "Never trust a scale, especially after a night at the pub with the guys."

"You look pretty fit to me," Marc said.

"Always room for improvement," he said, sticking out a hand. "My name's Trevor. Just moved to Greenfield. This is an excellent gym, eh?"

"I'm Marc." They shook hands. "It's as good as any I guess. Where'd you move from?"

"The big T-O, Toronto. Had enough of the big city so I've come to take over the family farm."

"I'm new too. Been here about four months, from Vancouver."

"You farming too?"

"No. Teaching."

"That's awesome, man. Hope to see you around. Maybe we can catch a beer sometime. Now I better get a move on. The cattle give me quite a talking to if I'm late. Wife and kids don't like it either. They get hungry for their feed too."

They shook hands again. Marc did a few more crunches, but the momentary lift he'd felt during his chat with Trevor had evaporated. The guy *would* have to be married. All the decent guys were married. He would live out the rest of his life alone, just like Auntie Belle. He plodded through the rest of his workout, using lighter weights than usual.

When he exited the gym he intended to go straight home, but at the traffic light his Toyota RAV4 turned left instead of right, and within minutes it was taking him through the big stone gates at Riverside Park. The park was his mother's favourite place to walk. Most Sunday afternoons they came to stroll around the gardens, and sit on a bench by the duck pond to read. His mother read mysteries while Marc had become addicted to gay autobiographies, which for some unknown reason the local library had in abundance.

When glancing up from his book Marc had seen things that were probably of no account to straight park users—single men driving around and around the circle. Finally they'd park at the far end where the woods sloped down to the river. From his vantage point in the shade of a big old cottonwood, he watched them get out of their cars and dusty pickups, mosey along the pathway, throw glances over their shoulders to see if anyone was following, then slip into the woods, to be followed a moment later by someone else, if it was their lucky day.

That October day Marc parked the RAV4, reclined the seat and tried to remember when he'd last snuggled inside a pair of masculine arms. Discounting the quick gropes and furtive hand jobs of one hour couplings, it had been the previous Christmas when he and Sam, his love interest of two, or had it been three weeks, had flown to Maui. The trip had been spoiled by Sam's preference for the hotel's bar, where he knocked back a rainbow parade of those colourful drinks the Hawaiians were so good at concocting.

As they'd flown home to Canada Marc had known their brief fling was over. Sam's furry arms and chest had been comforting to cuddle into, but Marc could do without the alcoholic fumes emanating from every pore, the slurred speech, and the morning hangovers.

The park was quiet. He supposed most of the cruisers were married guys, sitting around the dinner table with their loving families at this time of day. That was what Marc wanted to be doing too. He thought of the life he had planned with Howard. He wondered how that would have worked out, and whether Howard was really that special, or was he fixated upon him just because he'd been his first boyfriend?

In many ways they had been opposites, Howard quiet and reflective, whereas Marc wasn't shy about speaking his own mind. Howard had loved art and classical music. Closing his eyes, Marc could still see him sitting at the study table in their dorm room, looking like a handsome airline pilot with the headphones clamped over his ears, listening to Bach and Mozart. Howard had pitied Marc's preference for country music.

"Nothing but moaning and groaning and crying," was how Howard had described it. "How can you listen to that depressing stuff? It just pulls you down," and then he had quoted some Bible verse about filling your mind with beautiful things.

Howard's overt piety might have been enough to eventually separate them, though Howard had never been pushy about his beliefs. He prayed before meals, even in the university's cafeteria, which Marc found endearing. Every morning he sat up in bed, grabbed his Bible and read for half an hour. He called it his morning devotions, and Marc had loved snuggling against him while he read. Howard would hold his Bible with one hand while tracing trails down Marc's chest and belly with the other. Marc had fully approved of that kind of religion.

Now he watched as a red Ford pickup approached for the third time from behind. He jacked his seat up a couple notches to get a good look at the guy who slowed to a crawl as he came abreast of the RAV4. The driver was fifty-five or sixty, a thin salt and pepper moustache above his lip. He was wearing a blue and white Winnipeg Blue Bombers jersey and baseball cap. He nodded as he drove past, then pulled into the curb in front of Marc and sat with the engine idling.

Finally he opened the door and got out. He walked in Marc's direction. In the light of the streetlamp he looked half-way decent, a hint of a belly, but nothing gross. Marc rolled down his passenger window, intending to call Hi, when another vehicle came up behind. The Ford guy adjusted his baseball cap against the oncoming headlights and in that movement Marc saw the flash of a wedding ring. He rolled up his window, started the engine and tore out of the park. There was no point connecting with a married guy who would only be available on his own terms.

A block down Fifteenth Street Marc's skin hunger reasserted itself. He let the RAV4 do a U-turn. As he drove through the park gates a second time the red pickup was exiting. Marc braked and rolled down his window. "Hi there. Kind of a slow night eh?"

Mr. Ford grinned, noticeably widening his attractive moustache. "Always find it slow this time of day," he drawled.

"Care to join me for a coffee?" Marc asked.

"Sure thing. Starbucks?"

"How about my place?"

"I'll follow you."

When they were upstairs in what had been Auntie Belle's bedroom Marc's conscience pricked him. He wished he'd taken control of the RAV4 and fought that U-turn, but it would be rude to kick the guy out now. Mr. Red Ford pickup said his name was Ralph. As he dropped his clothes on the chair in the corner, Marc noticed him slip off and pocket the ring. His chest and belly were as smooth as those of a baby mouse. His pubes had been trimmed, as seemed the fashion. Being a bit lite in the body hair department himself, Marc preferred darkly-furred partners, a foil to the reddish blond fuzz on his own chest and belly, but this guy would have to do.

As Marc stepped out of his clothes and tossed back the sheets he wondered if this would be the first time two men had coupled inside Auntie Belle's house. It was possible, but maybe a couple of randy carpenters or Italian brick layers had connected while it was being built around the turn of the century.

Ralph smelled a tad sweaty, and Marc again regretted bringing him home, but didn't know how to order him to put his clothes back on and leave. He'd get it over with as fast as he could, a quick grope and come, and then he'd get rid of Ralph and never again bring home a one-nighter.

He began with a tentative kiss. Lots of married guys didn't care to kiss, but Ralph was really into it. His mouth carried a hint of beer. What was that other smell? Brylcreem, coming from his hair? Did they still make that stuff? Howard had always kept a fat tube of it in the dorm's bathroom cabinet to grease down his thick black mane.

Like prepubescent school boys playing doctor behind the schoolhouse, the sex with Ralph was lite and furtive, groping hands, a quick lick or two, a hasty suck, a sudden climax followed by a glance at the bedside clock.

"You got a cloth I can mop up with?" Ralph was out of bed the moment the deed was done. Marc padded across the hallway for two facecloths and a towel. Without looking at each other they wiped away the evidence.

As Ralph walked to the front door he said, "I really enjoyed that. Can I see you again sometime?"

"Sure thing. Hit me up if you see me in the park. You take care now."

As he closed the door the grandfather clock on the mezzanine struck eight-thirty. The encounter from park gate to *Take care* had taken less than twenty-five minutes. He watched Ralph pause to put on his wedding ring before getting into his red pickup. What a pitiful guy if he truly felt he'd had a good time.

I didn't have a good time, Marc thought as he went back upstairs. *Howard, oh Howard, why did you run out on me?*

Marc gargled with Listerine, ripped the sheets off the bed, hauled them down to the washer, sprayed the mattress with Lysol disinfectant, and took a shower. After that he was too exhausted and depressed to cook anything, so he grabbed a handful of chocolate chip cookies and a glass of milk. Two hours later he was getting into his remade bed when he remembered that he'd forgotten to disinfect himself. He dashed into the bathroom, grabbed the bottle of rubbing alcohol and doused his crotch.

Chapter 10

Howard hated Sundays when Apostle Motchkess shepherded the six counselees up the hill to the Pomona Tabernacle. He wouldn't allow a bike ride or any kind of exercise, claiming it was a sin to break a sweat on Sunday. Howard had been surprised and shocked to find California Tabbers so conservative. He had thought the Golden State's relaxed lifestyle would have penetrated the tabernacle, but no. A Sunday walk along a lakeshore might be okay, but swimming, and even wading, were fun, and therefore a sin. Some Tabbers even boasted how they threw the electrical breakers on Sunday morning so they wouldn't be tempted to bake a cake or watch television.

Their Bible teacher, Apostle Limross, was a forty-something guy who wore fitted, short-sleeved shirts in pastel colours. He owned a citrus orchard. He was darkly tanned, his cheeks glowing like there was a 100 watt light bulb inside his head.

"That Apostle Limross is as ripe as a Georgia peach, a big, juicy Georgia peach," Boxer had said after their first Sunday at tabernacle.

Howard had agreed. Apostle Limross definitely was the sort you'd want to make eye contact with if you passed him on the street. However, judging by the tone of his Bible studies, neither Boxer, Howard, nor any other man stood a chance of sinking their teeth into him.

That particular week the lesson was based on Psalms 11. Apostle Limross focused on verse 6. *Upon the wicked he shall rain snares, fire and brimstone, and an horrible tempest: this shall be the portion of their cup.*

After reading the verse he paused, his head bowed, then recited a litany of the world's ills. There was unrest in the Middle East, an earthquake in New Zealand, and a typhoon hammering Japan. According to Apostle Limross these were God's doings, his judgments on a wicked world. He loved everyone so much that he was using natural disasters to try to scare them into his camp.

"Isn't it kind of hard to wake up and repent if you're dead?" Baker asked.

Apostle Limross pretended not to hear him. "There is wickedness right in our own backyard," he thundered. "Do you know that in the bars and clubs right here in Pomona both women and men dance naked on top of the tables?"

"Which is the sin, *dancing*, or dancing on *top* of the tables?" Boxer whispered to Howard.

"Oh my brothers and sisters," Apostle Limross went on, "we are living in the days of Sodom. What other conclusion can we come to when men are lobbying our God-ordained government to marry each other?"

"If God is so mad at gays, why doesn't he drop a twister onto the Golden Gate bridge?" Howard asked Apostle Limross. "Wouldn't that be more likely to grab the attention of gay folks than one that destroys a mobile home park full of poor trailer trash in Kansas?"

"Perhaps those poor folk in Kansas are righteous enough to enter the heavenly kingdom. They don't need a second chance like those who practice filth in San Francisco."

That Sunday the preaching dragged on until a quarter past one. As Howard stood to leave, Apostle Motchkess put a hand on his shoulder and called out to the others. "Not so fast fellas. I've arranged a special service for you men today."

"But what about lunch?" Howard could already taste Rosanna's chicken enchiladas and sugary cinnamon-dusted crullers heaped with fresh strawberries.

"It's getting close to your graduation," Apostle Motchkess explained. "Some of you have expressed concern that you haven't sensed any change in the bent of your thoughts towards men. I've arranged for the apostles to have special prayer for you. Please follow me into the Fireside Room."

"Oh no, they're going to exorcise us," Boxer squealed, putting a hand on Howard's arm. "Please don't let them exorcise me. I've heard about those things, people foaming at the mouth and writhing on the floor."

"No one's exorcising anyone," Apostle Motchkess said, standing back to let them into the Fireside Room. "That sacrament is for non-Tabbers. You men know God, so you don't need any demons purged. As you've learned in your counselling sessions, your thoughts need only a little tweaking and then you'll bloom into full heterosexuality. "

Howard questioned his use of the word tweaking. Apostle Motchkess made it sound like some surgeon was going to slice open their skulls, reach in with a needle-nosed pliers and flip one or two dip switches. Even before their scalps had time to heal, they'd all be bursting out the tabernacle door, chasing women up and down Pomona's hills.

Inside the Fireside Room, twelve chairs were arranged in a circle. "Sit on alternate chairs," Apostle Motchkess instructed. "Ah, here are the rest of the apostles now. We'll sit between you counselees."

Apostle Motchkess inserted himself between Howard and Boxer. An unfamiliar apostle sat on Howard's other side. "Now then, let's all hold hands," Apostle Motchkess said. His hand was bony, cold and damp. It reminded Howard of a kitten he'd picked up on the ranch one spring morning, stiff and cold in death. The other apostle's hand was small too, but soft, like a Holstein's teat.

"You want us to hold hands?" Baker sat up straight. "Are we going to play kissy kissy too?"

"There is nothing erotic or evil about holding hands with fellow brothers," Apostle Motchkess said, ignoring Baker's derisive snort. "Holding hands creates a circle of Christian brotherhood. As we pray we will gain strength from each other, strength to resist the devil. So, let's get started. Holding hands, we bow our heads, close our eyes, and I'll begin. God, we are gathered here in your presence, twelve men, twelve heterosexual men, though among us are six who have yet to discover their latent heterosexual desires."

He quoted scripture, a passage that had nothing to do with love or sexuality. The other apostles chorused loud *Amens* at every pause. Howard cracked his eyes open. Baker was sitting directly across from him, bolt upright. When he saw Howard looking his way he winked and smiled wickedly.

When Apostle Motchkess had exhausted his store of platitudes about sin and deliverance, the next apostle picked up the litany. Howard groaned, wished he could put a hand over his stomach to ease its grumbling. All he could think about were Rosanna's enchiladas. She had a special way of cooking the chicken. She boiled it, then sprinkled it with spices and browned it under the broiler.

"Oh God," bawled the next apostle, "we are gathered here to rejoice in our heterosexuality. With these six men who are seeking healing, we bow in humble expectation. We celebrate and thank you for the healing that has already taken place in their lives…"

To get his mind off the ache in his stomach, Howard tried to think of ways he had changed. Before coming to TITC he'd felt awkward in social situations, especially around men who talked nothing but sports. The intense physical training classes with the annoying Rafe had been good for him. Besides the bike riding and gym workouts, Rafe had coached them in baseball. Howard's brothers had always scoffed at him for throwing the ball and holding the bat like a girl. Now he rarely struck out when the counselees played an evening game of scrub, and he wasn't afraid to get under the ball and catch it.

Rafe had taught them how to cheer while watching sports too, something Howard had never been comfortable with when his brothers were turning their lungs inside out while watching Hockey Night in Canada or the Grey Cup football match. Thanks to Rafe's cheering drills, he could now yell with the best of them—

Punt, you fool.

Pass it, you moron.

Grab him, you useless goon.

Touchdown!

Pass the fool puck!

Shoot when you've got the chance, you dummy!

Smash him into the boards!

It was a relief to finally know what all those words meant, and be comfortable using them, but what good would they do him after his wedding, when he was alone with Maxine? Those words weren't exactly bedroom vocabulary. When was the big change going to happen that would make him feel comfortable with her?

It was late October already. He'd been in the program almost ten months. When was he going to start going ape over women? If men loving men was such an abomination, why was it taking him so long to change? What was God waiting for?

Howard's hands were losing feeling as the apostle droned on and on. It was like his tactic was to bore the good Lord, try his patience with empty words until he healed the bunch of them just to be rid of them. If the fool didn't quit his prayer soon and let the others get on with theirs, Howard's hands were going to turn gangrenous and fall off.

Howard thought of his dorm days. He and Marc would sometimes awaken during the night and search for each other's hands. Marc's hands had been strong due to his workouts in the gym. It had been comforting to hold his hand, whether on a cold prairie night, or before an important examination. Why was that debauchery, while sitting here in the tabernacle holding hands with relative strangers was considered righteous, something God would honour?

Now Howard's hands were really numbing up, and two apostles hadn't yet prayed. He wanted to flex his fingers—the dead kitten had a particularly tight chokehold on his hand. Did he dare extricate his fingers to restore their circulation?

"Oh man, save me!"

Howard felt the circle of men jerk in surprise at the exclamation. He opened his eyes. Baker was standing up, both arms reaching towards the ceiling. "Save me! Save me!" he cried. "Oh man, I feel it. I feel the power."

Every eye was on Baker as he dropped his arms to his side and his chin to his chest, then stuck out his tongue, letting a gob of drool fall to the carpet. The apostles looked as startled as the counselees. Howard wondered if they were as surprised as him that it was Baker, the scoffer, who was feeling the power, and not one of the meeker men. But he looked genuinely, clearly under the power of some sort of spirit.

They watched as Baker slowly lifted his chin, his tongue wagging from side to side like a wary serpent sniffing the air. As he once again looked toward the ceiling he crossed his eyes. His head swivelled side to side as though following the flight of some bird. Suddenly he flung both arms into the air and extended his fingers. He stood on tip-toe and hollered. "I can see it."

"Amen. He can see the healing power," Apostle Motchkess said. Encouraged, the other apostles added their *Amens*.

"I can almost touch it. The power is within reach."

Howard watched, completely mystified, as Baker writhed like a snake-charmer's serpent. Baker was the cynic in the group, always making light of TITC's program of treatments. When the counselees were alone he entertained them by impersonating Sister Bergus and Rafe. Why was the spirit using Baker and not someone who was serious about changing?

"Amen. Amen. Praise God," chorused the apostles.

Settling back onto his heels Baker looked around the circle, his crossed eyes staring at everyone and no one. "Oh, my dear comrades, I have a message for you."

"Listen to the message," Apostle Motchkess motioned for everyone to be quiet, not that any one was saying anything at the sight of such a spectacle.

"My brothers, I can almost touch it. Oh, can't you smell it? Can't you taste it? There!" Baker licked his lips, sniffed, and pointed to a far corner of the ceiling. "There it is."

"What do you see, Baker?" asked Apostle Motchkess.

Baker pointed to another corner of the room. "Look over there beside the light. Oh my comrades in this battle for our lives, can't you see it?"

Everyone was staring at the stone chimney rising up from the fireplace. "What do you see Baker? Tell us what you see."

"I see golden brown with little green lights. Can't you see the lights, the little green lights? Can't you smell them? They're coming closer, closer." Baker stepped back, knocking over his chair. He raised both arms again, extended his fingers, stood on tip-toe. "Here it is. I've got it. I've got it."

"What have you got? Is it the healing power?" Apostle Motchkess was sweating with anticipation.

Baker dropped his arms, his chin, and uncrossed his eyes. He looked directly at Apostle Motchkess. "What have I got? I've got a vision of Rosanna's golden brown enchiladas sprinkled with green onions, and topped with sour cream. If you apostles don't stop this nonsense and let us out of here I'm going to be so hungry I'll start biting you in a place you'll remember long after I'm history."

Howard and the rest of the counselees broke into relieved laughter.

"Silence!" Apostle Motchkess took a step towards Baker. "You are one of the most thoughtless young men I have ever known. These apostles have selflessly delayed their Sunday lunch to help you fellows, and this is the thanks they get?"

He turned to the apostles. "You men might as well go home to your wives and families. Clearly we are not going to welcome God's spirit into this room after such a rude performance. We'll try this again next Sunday." As they left the room he closed the door.

"Aren't we going home too?" asked Howard.

"We came to pray and that's what we're going to do," Apostle Motchkess said. "We're going to pray that the Lord will remove our doubt."

"Pray the gay away. Pray the gay away. It's what the ignorant say," Baker chimed in a sing-song voice.

"Stop it! Don't mock the Lord."

"I'm not mocking him. I'm mocking you, you and your fool ideas."

"Baker, I have had enough of your insubordination. If you don't want to be healed you can just pack up and—"

"You want me to pack up and go home? Is that what you want me to do, because if that's what you want I'll—?"

"I think we're all tired and hungry." Apostle Motchkess pulled a white handkerchief from his pocket and wiped his brow.

Howard exchanged glances with the other counselees. Baker had told them back in January that his father, a Southern Baptist pastor at a mega church, had bankrolled TITC several hundred thousand to repair his son and save the family from embarrassment. It was unlikely Apostle Motchkess would carry out any threat to send him home unchanged.

"We'll head back to the Center, but don't discount heaven's power," he said. "Miracles have happened, but for them to occur, you need to clear all doubt from your minds."

"I have absolutely no doubt that Rosanna's enchiladas will be as delicious as always," Baker said. "Now let's get a move on."

Chapter 11

Marc was hit with the burning sensation on Saturday morning when he got up to empty his bladder. He ripped off the boxers he wore as pyjamas and held them up to the light. There it was, an ugly yellowish-green stain on the black material.

"Damn you Ralph, what kind of a disease have you given me?" he wailed. Since his first cruise through Riverside Park, he had connected several times with Ralph and never come down with anything. He thought back to the last time. Arlene had called just as Ralph was leaving and he'd run to answer the phone. It was her fault he hadn't doused himself with alcohol immediately. Now he was going to pay for his negligence, and what was worse, since moving to Greenfield he hadn't yet found a family doctor. He'd looked on the web a couple of times for names of physicians taking new patients, but hadn't found anyone. Now he'd have to line up with all the other medical orphans at a walk-in clinic.

As he showered, he pleaded with God to make the discharge disappear, or to morph it into something other than what he knew it was. *Please, let it be a reaction to something I ate, or drank, or to the water in the Jacuzzi at the gym*, but he knew such a prayer wouldn't be answered. How could he have neglected to ask Ralph if he was clean, not that his word would have guaranteed anything? Married guys cruising the park weren't usually poster boys for truth telling.

Marc waited until evening, then put on clean underwear and wrapped his dick in a paper towel to catch the oozing pus. Greenfield's only walk-in clinic was in a strip mall on Eighteenth Street, a ten minute drive from home. He parked on a side street, hurried around the corner and nipped through the door, hoping no one would see him going in, not that it would matter. Even if he ran into a neighbour or someone from work it's not like he had *HORRIBLE SEXUALLY TRANSMITTED DISEASE* tattooed on his forehead.

A half dozen patients slumped on the chairs in the waiting room, thankfully no one he knew. After signing in, he filled out a two-page questionnaire about his medical history, and returned it to the receptionist. He picked up a National Geographic and sat down to wait. It was an ancient copy, featuring Australia's Surf Life Saving clubs. He started flipping through the pages of Speedo-clad lifeguards, then slammed it shut and tossed it on the table. No more naked men. He truly would give up men so he'd never again have to deal with swollen glands in his groin and a fresh ooze of pus every time he tightened his sphincter.

Finally the nurse, who looked half-a-day past puberty, called his name. She escorted him into the examination room where she took his blood pressure and temperature—the latter was a couple degrees elevated—and then asked the reason for his visit.

"Urinary tract infection," he said, hoping she wouldn't ask for details.

"What are your symptoms?"

"Burning sensation when urinating. Pus."

"What colour is the pus?"

"Sort of yellowish, greenish white."

"How long have you had these symptoms?"

"Started this morning."

"Are you sexually active?"

"I wouldn't call my sex life active."

"Have you had unprotected sex in the last few days?"

"Yes. Two, three days ago."

Her face betrayed nothing. No doubt she'd heard it all before. She dropped the chart into the slot on the outside of the door. "Dr. Beale will be with you in a few moments."

Marc breathed a sigh of relief. Another five, ten minutes and the embarrassment would be over. He'd be on his way to the drugstore to get the antibiotics and he'd never touch another man so long as he lived. He'd fill his life with other interests: his teaching job, longer workouts at the gym. Maybe he could build up his thighs a little. He'd start looking for a classic old beater he could tinker with, eventually restore it to running condition. He'd buy some cross-country skis. He'd heard the city groomed trails on the frozen river in the winter. Surely all those things would be enough to keep him out of the bushes—

He sat bolt upright in the chair. What name did the nurse say when she told him to wait for the doctor? Wasn't it Dr. Beale? Marc felt his blood pressure skyrocket. He taught a Roderick and Matthew Beale. Was their dad a doctor? He had noted a couple of physicians among the parents when he'd updated the student records.

What a fuck up I've made of myself if Mr. Beale walks into the room and asks me to drop my pants, Marc thought. He stood up. He could just walk out. The nurse and receptionist would just think he had some sort of mental problem, a phobia about doctors perhaps. He could drive to the next town, attend a clinic there. He had his hand on the doorknob when he heard the clipboard being slid out of its slot.

"Hi. I'm Doctor Beale." The young lady smiled and shook his hand. "I see your name's LaChance. You wouldn't happen to be Monsieur LaChance, the French teacher at Southside Elementary?"

Marc felt the blood rush to his face as he sat down. There was no point in lying. "Yes. That's me." He'd probably meet her again at parent-teacher night or the Christmas concert.

"I've been wanting to meet you. Roddy and Matty love your classes. They say you make learning French fun, and every day they come home with some new word or expression. What was it on

Friday? Oh yes, the tableware. They insisted that we all had to speak about the plates and forks and things in French."

"I'm glad they're enjoying it."

"What brings you to see me?"

Surely it was on the chart and she didn't need to ask him to name his misdemeanour. He felt the sweat trickling down his flanks. "Well, Dr. Beale—it's kind of embarrassing. Is there another doctor I could see, not that I don't think you're a good doctor—"

"I'm the only one here tonight, but you need not worry about confidentiality. Nothing in this room goes further than these four walls. I never speak of my patients at home."

"Still, perhaps I should—"

"I see by the chart you've got a urinary tract infection. It happens all the time. In fact I've seen several tonight. People should take precautions but they forget. We're only human. If you've got a discharge I'm sure you're pretty uncomfortable so you might as well let me take a look. Drop your pants and sit up here on the examining table while I get the supplies." She turned to a cupboard on the other side of the room.

Marc shifted his brain into neutral, stood up, undid his belt, dropped his jeans and boxers to the floor, sat on the table, then noticed the paper towel still wrapped around his oozing member. He had meant to remove it while still in the RAV4. He was gingerly peeling it away from the head of his dick when Dr. Beale turned around.

"Oh, that bad, eh?" she bent down to examine the pus on the towel before pointing to the waste basket at the end of the examination table. "That looks very nasty. Can you milk your penis a bit so that some more pus moves down towards the end?"

Marc felt like a complete fool as Dr. Beale unwrapped a wire probe. "You may want to close your eyes if you're squeamish, Marc," she said, but he didn't. He was determined to watch, to engrave on his grey cells the picture of the mother of two of his favourite students jabbing a wire up his dick. Maybe that would keep him from stepping out of line again.

"Can you spread the glans a bit so it's easier for me to get in there?" Marc watched the tip of the wire disappear inside his cock. As it came in contact with his raw urethra, Marc felt his brain do a back flip. He closed his eyes, afraid he might fall off the table.

"There, that's all I need," Dr. Beale said, inserting the wire into a tube of culture. "You can pull up your pants now. From the colour of the discharge I'd guess this is gonorrhoea. Is that a possibility?"

"Yes."

"I need the name of your partner so she can be treated too."

Marc's mouth went dry. When he tried to speak, only choking sounds came out. Gay relationships were celebrated by law in Canada, but how about Greenfield? Should he pretend he had a wife, give some fictitious name at his address?

"It's okay, Marc," Dr. Beale said. "This will be strictly confidential, but I need her name so that she doesn't re-infect you, or anyone else."

"I understand, but you see, well, well it wasn't a she. It was a guy."

"Then I'll need his name."

"You're going to think me an awful slut, Dr. Beale. I don't know his name. He says his name's Ralph, but that might not be correct."

Dr. Beale patted Marc on the shoulder. "A pickup, was he?"

"Yes."

"I won't lecture you, Marc, because we both know you're old enough and wise enough to know better, but do take precautions, and when you see this fellow again tell him to come in and get tested."

"I won't be seeing him again, or anyone for that matter. I'm going to swear off men for good," Marc said, playing with the zipper on his jacket.

Dr. Beale shook her head. "No need to do make empty promises, Marc. We all have emotional and sexual needs, and though I said I wouldn't lecture you, I will remind you that this is the twenty-first century. Two guys can get married. I'll tell you straight out that I'm pleased about that. It makes life a lot easier, and healthier, for everyone concerned. I'd suggest you find yourself a partner and be faithful to him. Then you won't have to make these inconvenient visits to see me.

"End of lecture. Now, here's the prescription. It's for ten days because we want to ensure we get this thing licked. You have a good night now." She patted him on the shoulder as he walked out the door.

Chapter 12

The day Howard had been dreading for months had finally arrived. Sister Bergus had mentioned *the life lesson* when she outlined the course of treatment at his first counselling session in January. Now it was December 13th. Howard's appointment with Sister Bergus, Rafe and his wife, was for two o'clock.

The counselees had jokingly speculated that Rafe owned a whorehouse in downtown LA. They weren't far wrong. He and his wife Rheanna were sex therapists to the movie stars. That seemed odd to Howard. As a Tabber, he'd been told movies were wicked. They were full of sex and violence. If that was true, why did movie stars need counselling about sex? You'd think they'd know everything about it, but judging by the silver Porsche Rafe drove, they needed a lot of coaching.

Howard had lain awake most of the night, trying to figure a way to escape this last step towards heterosexuality. Practicing on the plastic blow-up doll had been difficult enough. When he'd walked into the counselling office and seen the life-sized doll lying on the couch, he had thought Sister Bergus was having him on. But it was no joke.

After talking about foreplay, she had instructed him to go over to the couch. She told him to sit on the footstool. Then she had him run his hands over the doll's breasts and other parts he couldn't bear to name. He'd felt such a fool, such an imposter. He'd never needed instructions on where to touch Marc in those long-ago nights in the dorm room at university.

The doll's smelly latex had given him the heaves. After his session he'd run back to his room and taken a long shower, desperate to scrub the pungent odour off his hands. Twice during the night he'd awakened in a sweat, having replayed the experience in his dreams.

Today he would be asked to touch a real woman. He wasn't ready for that. TITC had changed him in some ways, like giving him more self-confidence about his own abilities, but he would never have enough confidence to touch Rafe's wife, with Rafe sitting there, coaching, just like he did with the bike rides and baseball. He'd seen Rheanna with Rafe at tabernacle. She looked like a movie star from times past: round, rosy cheeked, and blond.

The thought of touching her made him feel sick to his stomach. He wished he hadn't eaten lunch, but it had been too tempting to turn down: tortillas filled with tomatoes, thick slices of avocado, and slivers of spicy, blackened chicken.

Too jumpy to wait in his room, Howard took his Bible and went out to sit by the pool. "You seen Boxer?" he asked Brick, who was slumped on the next deck chair, his nose in that week's assigned reading, *The Joy of Sex*.

Brick pointed toward the hill behind the mansion. "He went that direction."

"Boxer, who's terrified of geckos and rattlers, walked up the hill?"

"Yup. Thinks Sister Bergus and Rafe won't find him up there."

"Poor guy. I told him to just grit his teeth and get through it."

"Is that what you're going to do?"

"I grew up on a ranch. When we had a nasty job to do, like shovelling manure out of the calf pens, or castrating the calves, Dad told us to shift our minds into neutral and our muscles in gear."

"You think that'll help get you through this life lesson nonsense?"

"What else can we do? We want to graduate and get out of here, don't we?"

"Yup. What're you reading?"

"Sister Bergus advised me to read Song of Solomon to prepare for the life lesson. I'm reading how Solomon's getting all excited at the sight of his lover's breasts."

"Is that helping?"

"No. In fact it's having the opposite effect. Excuse me."

Howard ran back to the room, hurled himself into the bathroom and bent over the toilet. By the time he'd rinsed his mouth and re-brushed his teeth it was one forty-five. He dropped to his knees beside his bed and began praying harder than he'd ever prayed before.

"Heavenly Father, deliver me from this evil. Get me out of this life lesson. I can't go through with it. Let there be a fire alarm, nothing major, just some little glitch to set off the fire alarm, or a small earthquake, anything, so long as I don't have to go into that counselling room. Please God, if you really exist as the prophet Brother Tingley reported, help me now."

"Excuse me." Baker stuck his head in the doorway. "You're next Buck. Your turn to play with pussy."

"How was it?"

Baker opened his mouth and stuck his finger down his throat.

"That bad?"

Baker nodded. Howard stood up, started out of the room, then went back and picked up his Bible. He'd feel safer with it in his hand. Surely they couldn't make him touch another man's wife if he was holding God's word.

Sister Bergus was standing outside her office. She beckoned Howard inside. Rafe and his wife were sitting on the sofa. "Welcome to the life lesson," Sister Bergus said. "You know Rafe, of course. This is his wife Rheanna. At our last session I told you that they are both licensed sex therapists. They have kindly agreed to donate their time to help with this lesson."

Rafe was dressed in his usual pleated khaki shorts and green muscle shirt. His wife was wearing a white bathrobe. Sister Bergus sat down in her swivel chair behind her desk and pointed for Howard to take the chair across from her, the one he sat in during the counselling session.

"We talked about and practiced foreplay at our last session. Do I need to review that with you?"

Howard opened his mouth to speak, but choked on the sticky glaze of mucous coating the roof of his mouth and throat. He shook his head.

"Good. We can get started then. Rafe and Rheanna will show you what to do."

"I don't think I can—"

"It's normal to be a wee bit nervous," Sister Bergus said, "but Rafe tells me you've been making great progress."

"He sure has," Rafe said. "Buck has come a long way since January. In fact, he has excelled at so many things: cycling, weight training, baseball."

"I still don't think I can do this."

"Now, now," Rafe said. It was odd to hear him speaking in a normal tone of voice instead of yelling at him to man up. He stood up and came over to where Howard was sitting. He laid a hand on his shoulder. "Trust me, Buck. I'll be with you every moment, just like I am when we're out cycling the hills or working out in the gym. Remember what I've taught you: straight men never say they can't do something. I'm sure you, being a professional engineer, can understand that. No problem is too difficult for an engineer. They can always find a way to solve a problem.

"Just like all the other activities, I'll coach you through this life lesson. Rheanna understands that you're nervous, don't you, Darling?"

"Of course I understand, Buck. It's only natural. Will this be your first time with a woman?"

He nodded, at the same time trying to relax his stomach muscles. They were in spasm, searching for remnants of his lunch to throw up.

"Let's begin then," Rafe said. "Rheanna will recline on the sofa. Buck, you come over here beside me. Sit down on the footstool."

"Please Sir, I can't. It's not right. It's sinful for me to touch someone else's wife."

"God understands what we're doing in this room," Sister Bergus said from behind her desk, her pen and yellow legal pad ready. "I'm sure He's rejoicing at this very moment, thrilled that you are turning into a heterosexual."

"I don't know what God's thinking, but I can't do this. I really can't."

"I don't want to hear the *can't* word again," Rafe said, returning to his US Marine voice. "Now come over here, soldier. Sit down."

Howard thought of his dad's advice to shift his mind into neutral, and stood up. He laid his Bible on the desk, then walked over and sat down on the footstool beside Rafe and Rheanna.

"It'll be alright, Buck. I'm here to help you," she said, smiling and patting his arm.

Rafe patted his shoulder. His voice reassumed its soothing tone. "As Sister Bergus explained to you yesterday, men like to get to the real thing, cut to the chase as they say, but a woman enjoys the lead-up to an orgasm. As Christian men, we have to consider our women and make sure they enjoy the sexual experience too. A woman likes to be wooed with foreplay. Ordinarily that would begin with oral stimulation, kissing the lips, but we do things safely here at the Center. We don't want any exchange of bodily fluids, so we'll skip the kissing and go on to stimulation of the breasts.

"Now that Rheanna is reclining, I'd like you to loosen the tie on her robe. Then gently pull the top aside, exposing just one breast."

"Sir, I can't do this."

"Let me help you. Let me take your hand. Don't resist. Just relax. We'll just lift the robe, like this, and move it back. There. Watch as I lightly touch her breast, give it a gentle squeeze, run my finger around the aureole—that's the dark part around the nipple. See how I'm gently circling? Put your finger next to mine."

"Please, Sir."

"Here, let *me* take your hand," Rheanna said. She took his hand in hers and cupped it over her breast. "Just lay your hand here. Take a moment to get used to the feel of my breast. Now you can squeeze, but gently, very gently. Doesn't that raise a feeling of tenderness in you?"

The only feeling Howard had was that he would puke if she asked him to do anything more. Besides, he didn't like the softness of her breast. It felt too malleable, a word he sometimes used as an engineer to describe a metal that wouldn't stand up to hard usage. Rheanna's breast felt nothing like the slab of hard muscle he used to knead on Marc's chest those long years ago in the dorm.

"Now I'm going to remove my hand so you can explore on your own." Rheanna threw off the other side of her robe. "You can feel this one too. Isn't it lovely?"

"You're doing very well, Buck," Rafe said. "Now, like I was showing you before, using just the tips of your fingers gently run them around Rheanna's aureole. That's the way. Very good, Buck, but use the flat part of your finger. You don't want to scratch with your nail. You're doing great. And now move to the nipple. Like this." He brushed the tip of Rheanna's right nipple. Her nipples were dark, almost black, and prominent. They reminded Howard of those on their collie bitch when she was nursing pups.

"That's the way. You're getting the hang of it," Rafe said. "What you're doing is called stimulating a lady's nipples. Both hands now, one on each nipple." Rheanna's legs twitched and Howard quickly withdrew his hands.

"No, don't stop," Rheanna said. "Keep on. You're going to be an excellent lover. I enjoy what you're doing. It's only natural that it gives me the shivers, prepares me for the ultimate sexual act by stimulating lubrication of my vagina. Would you like to feel what's happening down here?" Rheanna threw wide her robe.

"No! Please don't."

"Steady, Buck." Rafe put a hand on his shoulder. "Don't stop now. You're doing so well, but if you're not quite ready for the vagina yet, just go back to stimulating the nipples. Your future wife won't mind if you play with her nipples for a lengthy period of time. To vary the sensations, you can substitute your tongue for your fingers. Just bend down and give Rheanna's nipples the gentlest flick with the tip of your tongue."

That did it. No remembered advice from his dad could help now. Howard knew he was going to be sick and if he didn't get back to the room immediately he'd barf all over Rheanna. Ignoring Rafe's barked order to sit down and man up, he ran from the room.

For the second time that afternoon he bent over the toilet, his trembling hands clinging to the cold lip of porcelain. Heave after empty heave threatened to split his belly wide open.

"Here's a damp cloth. Wipe your face." Rafe was standing behind him, holding out a facecloth. "Don't be upset, Buck. Your reaction is quite common the first time, but don't let it defeat you. Come back and we'll skip the oral stimulation for now."

Howard followed Rafe back to the counselling room. He sat down on the footstool. He tried to hold his breath, sure that it stunk of stomach acid. Rheanna had covered herself up. Now she loosened her robe's tie, but didn't flip it open.

"Perhaps you'd prefer for me to keep my robe on," she said. "Some fellows prefer to explore without me exposing myself completely. Let me take your hand.

"That's it. Don't be nervous. Just relax and let me guide you. You did a very good job of stimulating my breasts. You are a very gentle man. Some woman will consider herself very fortunate to get such a tender-hearted husband. In fact, while you were taking a break Sister Bergus shared with us that you have a lady friend back in Winnipeg. Is that right?"

Howard nodded.

"What's her name?"

"Maxine," he squeaked, after swallowing twice.

"That's lovely. Now just imagine that I'm Maxine, your very own wife." She reached for his hand and moved it from breast to breast, then with her robe still loose, but not fully open, she moved his hand down her tummy. She paused at her navel. Howard could feel that it was an outie. He remembered that Marc's had been an innie. He'd always made a joke of blowing the lint out of it.

Rheanna guided his hand further down. Soon he could feel a bush of hair. He closed his eyes tightly, fearful that her robe might fall open.

"Doesn't that feel nice? Just relax. Keep running your fingers lightly through my bush. Ah yes, that feels sooooo good."

"You're doing great, Buck," Rafe said, touching his shoulder.

"You'd better speed it up just a little," Sister Bergus said. "It's almost time for the next appointment." Howard could hear her pen scratching across the yellow pad.

Rheanna pushed his hand further, then curled his fingers into a damp, warm place. "There. Doesn't that feel good? Don't you feel like you've finally come home to what God intended you to enjoy?"

Howard shook his head.

"Never mind, Dear. You did very well for your first time with a woman." She released his hand. "Of course you're nervous because this situation is very artificial. When you make love to Maxine for the first time, it will be totally different, so much better, because you love each other. You'll be able to relax and take your time." She patted his hand. "You may go now, unless Sister Bergus has anything extra."

"No. No, that's fine. Please send Boxer in."

"You did very well," Rafe said, squeezing his shoulder one last time.

Howard stood up, grabbed is Bible off the desk, whipped the door open, and strode down the hallway to his room. They could go in search of Boxer themselves. He could think of only one thing—getting into the shower and scrubbing the skin off his hands. He stripped off his clothes, adjusted the water as hot as he could tolerate and stepped in. He pumped a truckload of soap onto his palm. He lathered his whole body, rinsed, then lathered again—four, five times. He wished he could flip his brain out, scrub it, soak it in bleach, erase the memory of what he'd just done.

Chapter 13

Marc's life slipped by in a steady grind of preparing lessons and teaching. Sometimes he stayed after four to help Ian Hiddley with extra curricular sports. Three days a week he made time for the gym where he did a quick circuit of the weight machines, then spent twenty minutes on the bike or cross trainer.

The down side of the gym was that it continued to fuel his yearning for male flesh, and after recovering from his STD, he found himself wandering back to the park. He told himself he was just going to find Ralph, to warn him that he should get himself checked, but after he'd done that—and Ralph had sped out of the park like a frightened rabbit—he kept on cruising, bringing home other guys. He knew it was a stupid thing to do, dangerous even, but he ramped up his disinfection procedures, even carrying a bottle of ninety-nine percent isopropyl alcohol in the RAV4's glove box.

He was not looking forward to the Christmas break. His mother was expecting him to spend this first Christmas in Greenfield with her, but what would he do the rest of the two weeks? He was truly starting to regret leaving the wet, west coast. Lonely and frustrating as his personal life had been, at least he'd been able to get outdoors for some exercise without bundling up like a space walker against the cold weather. As the days grew shorter and the northwest wind piled drifts of snow around the house, he thought of Howard. If he could reconnect with him, just to be friends even, that would be a bright spot in his life.

Mid-month he googled Bronnel Engineering to get the phone number. The receptionist was as snooty as the one from years ago. She refused to divulge any information, but finally put him through to the owner, Jim Bronnel. He said that Howard was expected home in late December and would return to work early January. Marc should call back then.

Southside Elementary's Christmas concert was the last evening before the holiday. When all the children had stumbled through their recitations and carols, and Marc had bid *Au revoir* and *Bonnes vacances* to the last of his students, he pulled on his winter gear and trudged through the snowdrifts to the parking lot. He unplugged the block heater, let the engine warm up, then drove off slowly, the bottom of the tires squared by the cold.

The prospect of heading home to the big house where two weeks of solitude awaited him didn't appeal, so at the stop sign the RAV4 turned towards Riverside Park. Maybe there'd be someone looking for some skin to skin tonight, but after a couple of blocks Marc pulled a U-turn. No way was he going to spend the entire two weeks trolling the park, waiting for Mr. Right who would never come along.

It was only nine o'clock. He'd head out to the mall. It was open until midnight every day until Christmas Eve. Even though he didn't need to buy anything—he'd ordered a series of spa treatments for both his mother and cousin Arlene—he could grab a coffee and muffin and entertain himself watching the other shoppers hyperventilate during the final stage of Christmas panic. If it wasn't too busy he'd get some new bed sheets to replace his that were getting so badly stained from sweat and other bodily fluids that they would no longer come clean in the wash.

When he got to the mall, the parking lot was jammed, but he finally found a spot out back. He decided to avoid the crowds and just nip into Canadian Tire to see if they had a sale on GPS units. It took him awhile to find a clerk to unlock the cabinet containing the precious instruments, and after he'd made his selection, he had the clerk open the box and check everything out—if there was anything he hated more than shopping, it was returning faulty merchandise. When he got to the checkout he was three back in the line-up. There was a lady with a popcorn maker ahead of him, and ahead of her a guy bent over the card reader. There was something familiar about the back of his head, especially his finely formed ears. Was it some guy from the gym?

When the customer retrieved his card and straightened up, Marc's heart literally skipped a beat. Howard Hildebrandt? Could it be him? But no, Howard had thick black hair and a matching paintbrush moustache. This fellow's moustache was paint brush wide and thick like Howard's, but it was threaded with gray, same as the hair. Of course, a quarter of a century had gone by. Marc's hair wasn't the mahogany colour it had been in his university days either. He watched as the guy picked up his purchases and started for the exit. Maybe he was one of Howard's brothers.

Marc dropped the box with the GPS unit on the counter, excused his way past the customer ahead of him, and ran out the exit. The fellow was yanking up the fur-lined hood on his parka and hurrying across the parking lot.

"Howard?" Marc yelled. "Howard Hildebrandt, is that you?"

The fellow kept on walking. Maybe he couldn't hear Marc with that hood over his ears. Marc followed him to a green Toyota Tundra.

"Are you related to Howard Hildebrandt?" Marc asked when he turned to open the door.

The fellow scowled at Marc while keeping a hand on the door's armrest. "Nope," he said, then morphed his guarded look into a quizzical stare.

"Sorry," Marc said. "You look like someone I once knew."

"And who are you?"

"Marc LaChance. I had a roommate in university looked like you, minus a few years. His name was Howard Hildebrandt from Rock Lake."

"Well I'm not related to Howard," the fellow said.

"Sorry about the mistake." Marc turned to go.

"Hey, don't go," he said. "I'm not related to Howard. I *am* Howard. He jumped down from the Tundra and made a grab for Marc's tuque, ripped it off his head and ruffled his hair. "Marc LaChance. You really *are* Marc LaChance, though I'm sure your hair used to be thicker, and redder than this."

"And yours used to be black as the night."

"I guess we've both changed over the years," Howard said. "Imagine running into you in Greenfield. Is this really you?" He ruffled Marc's hair again.

"And is this really you?" Marc reached out and tweaked Howard's moustache. "I heard you were in Africa."

"Who told you that?"

"Your sister-in-law Amy. She nursed my aunt."

"Good old Amy, a regular Florence Nightingale. That why you're in Greenfield, visiting your aunt?"

"That's what brought me here, though she died last spring. I'm now living in her house."

"That's fabulous, Marc, but are we going to stand out here and freeze our butts off all night, or do you want to hop in while I fire up the engine?"

"You got time for a coffee?"

"I'm headed out to Rock Lake for Christmas. Just stopped to buy something for Mother, but I can spare a few minutes."

"Let's head over to Tim Horton's on Eighteenth."

"Sure thing."

Marc felt like crying and laughing at the same time as he skidded across the icy parking lot to his RAV4. What a miracle, running into Howard in Greenfield on a busy shopping night!

Howard was standing in front of the donut shop looking up at the sky when Marc got there. "Get a load of those northern lights," Howard said. "Listen! Can you hear them?"

Marc looked up at the flickering sheets of green and blue undulating across the northern sky. "I hadn't noticed them until you mentioned them."

"Science says they don't make a sound, but listen. Can't you hear that ripping sound, like someone shredding an old shirt?"

Marc couldn't hear anything, but thrilled to the sight as he stood beside Howard, dear Howard Hildebrandt, his man. "Come on in. I'll buy you a coffee."

"You've forgotten that I'm not a coffee drinker. I will have a hot chocolate though."

"Oh right. You go find a table and I'll bring the brews."

"This weather must be a bit of shock to your system when you've been in Africa," Marc said, setting the cups on the table. "When did you get back?"

"I've been home a week and will be back on the job with Bronnel come January."

"I'd like to hear all about your trip. Was it some mission project?"

"A lot of villages don't have proper water systems, but even more interesting are some of the projects I've worked on in Winnipeg and right here in Greenfield. Take that new bridge over the river and railway tracks. It posed a real challenge…"

As Howard talked Marc searched his face and mannerisms for the twenty-three year old man he had loved. The face was a bit more filled out with fans of tiny lines radiating from the corner of each eye, but it was still Howard's face. When searching for a word he still squinted until his eyes all but disappeared, like country singer John Berry singing one of his tear-jerker lost love songs.

"What's wrong?" Howard asked, halting his bridge story.

Marc shook his head. "Nothing's wrong. In fact, everything's good, everything's very good. I'm remembering those months we roomed together at university, you and me, you and me together. You look really good, very trim and fit." Howard nodded, swished his hot chocolate, tapped his fingers on the table.

"I'm talking too much," Howard said. "What are you doing back here in Greenfield?"

"Mother offered me Auntie Belle's house. It was an offer I couldn't refuse, so I came back. I'm teaching at a new school in the south end of town. Other than that, everything's about the same."

"You married?"

Marc spread out the fingers of his left hand. "No ring. No husband. Amy told me you may be getting married."

Howard hesitated, shifted in his chair, tapped his fingers on the table and swirled the dregs of his hot chocolate again. "That's right. Haven't set a date yet, but I won't be marrying a man. It's a woman— Maxine."

"I'm kind of surprised to hear that you're going to marry, a woman I mean."

"I'm surprised too," he said, setting down his cup and folding his arms across his chest. "I never expected to marry, but Maxine's a decent woman. I think we'll make a go of it."

"I'm afraid a woman wouldn't do it for me, and I don't mean just sexually," Marc said. "Much as I can appreciate a beautiful woman, deep inside I need a man to make me feel satisfied, complete. I thought you were the same. Are you not like that anymore?"

"I've put that behind me." Howard scraped his feet on the floor and picked up his gloves. "I guess I should be getting on the road again. It's an hour to Rock Lake and the folks will be waiting up for me."

"They're both still living?"

"Yes. Dad's ninety-one, still helping on the ranch."

"They must be excited about your wedding plans."

"It's what they've always wanted for me."

"Hopefully, we can keep in touch now that you're back."

Marc pulled out his phone. "What's your contact info?"

Howard pulled a business card from his wallet and handed it to Marc. "Best place to get hold of me is at work."

"If you're staying at Rock Lake for the whole week," Marc said, "maybe you can come into town or we can meet somewhere, do some cross country skiing just like old times?"

"I don't know what the family's plans will be. We might all head out to Beeverville for the annual CarolFest, but if we come into town I'll give you a call."

"I'd like that. Is it okay if I email you now and again?"

"Sure. If I don't answer right away it'll be because I'm out on a job somewhere."

They shook hands, got into their vehicles, and turned in opposite directions as they exited Tim Horton's.

Marc was too excited to sleep when he got home. Instead he dusted off the photograph album from his university days, got into bed and sat there reliving those magical months in the dorm when Howard and he had discovered their love for each other. Oh Howard, if only you hadn't rejected me, Marc thought. What might our lives have been like? What could they still be like? He got out of bed, padded across the hallway to the study and fired up his computer.

Hi Howard. It was so very good to see you tonight. I hope you'll have a happy Christmas and a good new year—and I hope we can keep in touch. Love, Marc.

Before pressing Send, he deleted *Love*. He'd better not spook the guy.

Chapter 14

Howard turned onto the highway and racked up the heat in the Tundra. The dashboard thermometer told him it was minus thirty-eight outside. It was hard to believe that three days ago he'd been sitting under California palms reading his Bible. He laughed as he remembered how he'd found the heat exhausting and wished for Manitoba's clean, cold air. Thirty-eight below zero was a bit more than he'd asked for.

As soon as the engine had warmed up, he pushed cruise and settled back to enjoy the drive, and to replay his encounter with Marc. Imagine running into him at Canadian Tire after almost a quarter century? After bailing on Marc that last month in university, he hadn't expected to see him again, and man, he still looked good, real good. His reddish hair was a bit faded. There were hints of grey in front of his ears—quite attractive really.

The weekend he'd taken Marc home from university to the ranch, his mother and father had labelled him Mr. Smiley. It was maybe a nervous tic, or habit, like a cue for others to agree with what he was saying—every few phrases his face lit up in a handsome smile, one that crinkled the freckles sprinkled across his nose.

Howard shivered when he remembered that night in the university dorm when he'd rejected Marc. What a messy business it had been, spurning Marc's love. And afterwards, he'd refused his phone calls, and stashed his letters in his underwear drawer without replying to them. Yet what choice had he? The guilt of living with a man would have eaten away at him. Eventually he'd have been forced to end the relationship. Better to have done it at the beginning than after they'd moved half-way across the continent.

He wondered what life would have been like if he'd been able to put behind him the tabernacle's horror of homosexuality. Would they still be living in Vancouver? Would they have bought that house with a sea view, a boat? Or would they have tired of each other? Rather than splitting, would they have done like he'd heard some gay couples did: become free range husbands?

Oh well, no point thinking about that now. He had been to TITC. He was going to marry Maxine. He looked across the snowy fields at the full moon rising, hoping to distract himself from the butterflies that flitted at the walls of his stomach every time he thought about marrying. Everyone at TITC—Rafe, the program director, the therapist—had told him it was normal to feel nervous about his upcoming marriage. Every groom was uptight, but once the ceremony was over, a whole new life would open before him. Even if he didn't feel great passion for Maxine at first, over the years he would grow to love and respect her.

Howard's thoughts went back to Marc. He sure had looked good, sure had brought back memories of the fun times they'd had: hiking, skiing, going to art shows and symphony concerts. Marc hadn't cared for classical music and art, but like a good sport, he'd gone along.

Howard was glad Marc hadn't pushed for information about Africa. He wasn't a good liar. Hopefully his family wouldn't ask too many questions either. His mom and dad were the only ones in the family who knew of his affectional orientation. They knew he'd been to TITC, and not to Africa. When the previous year he'd revealed to them the reason he was unmarried, his mother had exclaimed, "Oh Howard, what will people think? You haven't told anyone, have you?"

His father's reaction had been more primal. He'd covered his face with his wrinkled rancher's hands and wept, great heaving sobs. The sight of his poor old dad in such distress was what had finally impelled Howard to enrol in the program at TITC. He remembered hugging his father and saying, "Don't cry, Dad. I'm going to do something about it. Apostle Farida in the Winnipeg Tabernacle tells me there's a place in California where I can get help. I can start in January and when I come home twelve months later I'll be as normal as you are. Please Dad, don't cry."

"Well then no one ever need know," his mother had said. "It's no different than some little medical condition, a disfiguring wart or high blood pressure. It's something that can be cured."

Now, as Howard drove south through the frigid night, he pondered what to tell his folks. Knowing his mother, she would probably avoid the topic. If it wasn't spoken of, then it didn't exist. It would be enough for her to see that he had been getting three square meals a day and that he was looking fit. His father would be pleased to see how confidently he handled the ball if his brothers wanted a game of touch football in the snow. His folks were both probably looking forward to his marriage to Maxine, after which they'd be able to forget he'd ever had his *little medical condition*.

Maxine was the one who had told him about TITC. After her husband was killed in a car wreck on the auto-route north of Montreal, she moved back to Winnipeg. For a couple of months she lived with her parents, Apostle and Mrs. Farida. One Sunday after tabernacle they invited Howard home for lunch. He discovered that Maxine shared his love of classical music and the outdoors. They started going to concerts together, and hiked local trails, sometimes with a group from the tabernacle, other times just the two of them.

One autumn evening when he brought her home from hiking in La Barriere Park, she surprised him by kissing him on the cheek.

He had blushed. "What's that for?"

"Just a good night kiss, Howie. I do enjoy spending time with you."

"I enjoy our outings too, Maxine, but—"

"But what?"

"Maxine, there's something you need to know about me."

"What's that Howie?"

"You have to promise not to tell anyone else." She had nodded agreement. "I wouldn't tell you this if I didn't trust you completely, Maxine."

"I'm glad you feel that way about me." She patted his arm.

"We can never be more than friends."

"Should I not have kissed you? It was just a peck on your cheek, Howie, friend to friend, saying good night."

"I know, but you see." He paused. "I might as well just say it. I'm one of those guys your dad sometimes preaches about, a man who loves men."

"Well I love men too."

"You don't get what I'm saying, Maxine. When I was in college I had a roommate, Marc. He was the same as me. We used to sleep together."

"You mean you're a homosexual?"

"Yes." Howard had felt such relief when she had pronounced the word for him.

"Well, that's nothing to worry about. Don't you read the *Tabernacle Times*?"

"I don't have time to read outside of work."

"A month or so back there was an article about this place in California where homosexuals can be healed."

"I didn't know the tabernacle was into that type of healing."

"Oh yes. Apparently it's very successful. I'll ask Father about it. I remember him saving the article for his files in case he ever met someone with that problem. So don't worry," she'd said, patting his arm as she got out of the truck. "Isn't God wonderful. He has a solution for every problem, if we just trust him."

He'd listened to Maxine, to her father, to the tabernacle council, and to his own mother and father. He had used his one year sabbatical from work to seek healing at TITC. Now he was home and before he had a chance to talk to any of them he had run into Marc. Was it some sort of sign?

He didn't really believe in signs, unlike Maxine and her folks who were always imagining signals from God in everyday events. When Maxine first got into his Ford 150 pickup after Sunday lunch at her folks' house, she'd said it was an exact match for her late husband's truck, and therefore a sign from God.

"But it's not my truck," Howard had said. "See the name on the door. *Bronnel Engineering.*"

"But you're driving it. I always liked riding in Frank's truck. I felt so safe up there, above the rest of the traffic, and so I think this is God's way of telling me that you and me are going to be great friends."

Howard had never viewed life that way. He believed God might be interested in small details, but wasn't sitting in heaven waving wands and pushing buttons to make people do things they didn't choose to do.

But what about running into Marc at Canadian Tire in Greenfield? Had that been a chance happening, or had God arranged that to test him? Was the meeting, with the only man he had ever loved, divinely arranged to assure him that he was no longer attracted to men? Was it to show him that he felt nothing for Marc, that he had been right to reject him so long ago?

But he sure did look good, and Howard was pleased that he might get to see him now and again, become friends, maybe do some hiking and skiing like they'd done so long ago.

The reception by his parents was easier than he'd expected. His mother exclaimed over his muscular slimness and his California tan. His father hugged him with trembling arms. "You're looking good, Son."

"Your father and I missed your weekend visits," his mother said, "but we understand why you had to go away, and now that little problem you mentioned last year is all taken care of, is it?"

"I feel good about myself," Howard said.

"I'm so happy for you. And you and Maxine Farida will be getting married sometime soon?"

ROBERT L. RAMSAY

"I haven't seen Maxine yet. She and her parents are out to
Beeverville. She's singing in CarolFest this year. She had to go early
for rehearsals."

"But you're still planning to get married?"

"We talked about it before I went to California, but we haven't
discussed it while I was away," Howard said.

"But you will discuss it soon?" his mother asked.

"Yes, I suppose so."

"Of course you must propose properly. Now that you're home,
I'm sure she's anxious to go ahead with her plans. Oh Cal, can you
believe it? One of our sons will finally marry an apostle's daughter. I
always prayed for that."

"Good boy," his father said, hobbling back to the recliner
where he'd been sitting when Howard arrived.

"You'll be wanting to head out to Beeverville then, to see
Maxine," his mother said.

"No. I thought I'd spend Christmas with you folks."

"But we'll go with you. Your father, bless his poor, dear heart,
wants to go to CarolFest."

"I'd like to see the Mother Tabernacle one last time before I
die," his father said.

"Oh Dad. Don't talk about dying."

"It's true son. I don't think I'm long for this world."

The drive to Beeverville on the banks of the North
Saskatchewan River usually took six hours. This time it stretched to
almost eight. Howard had to stop frequently so his father could take a
bathroom break. Howard didn't really mind. He was anxious to see his
brothers and sister and their families, but the butterflies kept nipping at
the lining of his stomach every time he thought of Maxine. Would the
months of physical training and counselling sessions work? Would it
be enough to just *go forward in faith*, as Sister Bergus had advised him
at the last counselling session? Would trusting God to make his
marriage work, really work?

When they finally turned off the highway and the big stone
tabernacle came into view, his father started crying. "Look Bella.

There's the tabernacle. We're in Beeverville. After my bout with pneumonia, I never thought I'd see the good old Mother Tabernacle again. Praise God."

The rest of the family were already checked into the Super 8. Much to Howard's relief, everyone was too excited about the festival to quiz him about Africa. After getting his parents settled in their hotel room, Howard supposed he should look up Maxine, but his nephews and nieces mobbed him.

"Uncle Howard, will you come skating with us?"

"Uncle Howard, will you pull us on the toboggan?"

It had been a year since he'd seen them, so how could he resist their eager pleadings? Maxine would probably understand, and there'd be time to see her later.

It was dinner time when she caught up with him in the cafeteria line-up. He felt a hand on his arm as he was contemplating whether to indulge in a slice of triple-layer chocolate cake, a reward for all those sweaty miles he'd cycled in Pomona.

"Who is this handsome stranger with the California tan?"

"Oh, hi Maxine. You're done with rehearsal for now?"

"We had our last rehearsal this afternoon. I've been looking all over for you. Your folks said you'd gone skating."

"My nephews and nieces wanted me to pull them along the ice."

"Of course. They must be excited to have their uncle home again. And so am I." She gave him a one-armed hug and kissed him on the cheek. "I've really missed our times together: the hiking, being at tabernacle service, and Sunday dinner with my folks."

Howard blushed at Maxine's show of affection. In the Tabber's world, where unmarried folk were pitied and considered defective in some unsavoury way, the tiniest flutter of affection between two people was snatched up like lost treasure. The gossips would rapidly extrapolate a simple gesture into serious courting, marriage, children, and grandchildren. He'd just as soon keep their plans under wraps for as long as possible. The wedding would be stressful enough without involving all the old biddies at this early stage. Besides, Maxine might have changed her mind while he was away. That comforting thought sent the butterflies in his stomach back into hibernation.

Without being invited, Maxine and her parents joined Howard's family in the cafeteria's far corner. In the commotion of reminding children of their table manners, and gossip about who was, and who was not, at CarolFest, Howard didn't have to field any difficult questions about Africa. He and Maxine didn't get time alone together either, which was okay with Howard. After the months with the half dozen counselees in California, it felt odd to be among such a large crowd.

The next morning Maxine called to suggest they meet on the front steps of the Tingley Research Centre at nine o'clock. The three-storey stone building held Brother Tingley's writings, including accounts of his meetings with God in heaven. The most popular exhibit was the leaf he had brought back from the heavenly tree of life. It was displayed in a glass case in the centre of the room. The leaf was in the shape of a lily pad, though about three times the size of any lily pad on Earth, and as thick as a leather belt. Despite its thickness, it was translucent, a deep green with a golden sheen on the surface.

"Imagine what it will be like when we get to the heavenly country." Maxine reached for Howard's hand. "Won't it be exciting to see the tree this leaf came from?"

"I guess we'll eat fruit from the tree," Howard said, conscious of how tiny Maxine's hand felt in his compared to Marc's all those years ago in the dorm.

"And we'll never die. We'll be together forever." Maxine kissed his cheek.

"Forever is a very long time," Howard said. "It's impossible for my brain to take that in."

"But isn't it wonderful. We'll never have to say good-bye to each other, never have to be apart like we were this past year."

"I need to ask you about that, Maxine," Howard said, clearing his throat. "I was gone twelve months. I wouldn't blame you if you've met someone else."

"Howie, how can you even think such a thing? You know I was with you in California in thought and prayer every day. Let's sit over here in the corner and you can tell me all about it." She led the way to a far corner furnished with reading tables and chairs. "Now then, tell me everything."

"I think I already told you pretty well everything in my letters."

"Oh yes, I appreciated you writing to me so faithfully. I liked it when you described your day—it was like I was there with you, but you never really said whether the treatments were effective or not. Do you feel a change?"

"The sports and exercise were really good for me. I'm sure you can see the change—my belly is completely gone."

"Yes, you're looking very trim. How about your appreciation of women? Did the program help you with that?"

"Yes, we spent a lot of time talking about that." He told her about the dances with the tabernacle women, and the weekly porn sessions.

"I'm surprised a ministry bearing Brother Tingley's name would use pornography to treat you, but if it works, I suppose it's okay. Do you feel comfortable about marrying me now?"

"Maxine, I don't know what to say. I get so nervous every time I think of the wedding."

Maxine waved her hand as though shooing away an annoying wasp. "I remember my first husband, Frank, saying exactly the same thing. We women like a lot of fuss—the white dresses, the bridesmaids, planning the flowers and decorations, the seating and the food. I understand perfectly that men don't care about that, so I promise to keep the wedding simple. Will that make you feel better?"

"It's not just the wedding ceremony itself. It's the whole marriage thing. This is embarrassing, Maxine, but I just don't know if I could satisfy you." He paused, swallowed, took a deep breath. "You know, satisfy you in every way, if you get my meaning."

"Oh, you silly men! You think everything revolves around sex. Of course, it's important in a marriage, but Frank used to get hung up too, unable to perform properly. I was able to help him with that, and I'm sure I could do the same for you. What's the saying, *Love conquers all*? And I'm sure, with the help of God, love can conquer any problem we may have."

"Still Maxine, I don't know that I could—"

"Howie Honey, I'm not going to pressure you, and we don't have to decide anything today. I'm busy with CarolFest. Let's both pray about it, discuss it with our families, and see what God has in store for us."

That evening, while his mother was bathing, Howard sat down on the edge of the bed beside his father. "Dad, I need to talk to you."

"Sure, son. What is it? I've sensed that you've been worried about something since you came home from California. Is it me you're worried about?"

"No, Dad. Of course, I don't like to hear you say that you won't be around much longer, but it's Maxine I'm worried about."

"Why? Is she not well?"

"No, it's just that every time I think about marrying her I get all nervous inside. Is that how you felt before marrying Mom?"

"Nervous? I was ready to run the other direction as fast as I could."

"You mean being uptight is normal for straight men too?"

"Sure it is. Thinking of his wedding day scared your Uncle Bert right into the army, and you know Tabbers' view of killing people. 'Course, later on he and Janet eloped."

"I wish I knew it was just stress about the wedding day."

"That's exactly what it is, my son. Us men, we don't care about all them frilly things the women get excited about. The very fact that those things make you nervous is proof you've come back from California healed."

"What's this about California?" Howard's mother asked, padding out of the bathroom in her robe.

"Our boy tells me he's nervous about marrying Maxine."

"Nervous?"

"Yes, but I'm telling him every man's like a hog on butchering day. He'd like to tuck in his tail and run, but we all go through with it."

"Even I was nervous on our wedding day," his mother said. "You know everyone's going to be watching you walk up that aisle, and you're hoping everything will go perfectly. Afterwards you wonder what you were so worried about, isn't that right, Cal?"

"That's right. After it's all over you'll be glad you did it for Maxine's sake."

"I think it's more than just being nervous about things going well on the wedding day," Howard said.

"Now, now, son." His mother put an arm around his shoulders. "Both your father and I will be so happy to see you settled. We're happy for your brothers and sister, that they all have fine families, but we've been worried about you."

"That's right," his father said. "Your mother and I pray for you every day. All these years we've felt so sorry for you, that you didn't have anyone special in your life. Then Maxine came along. You seem to like many of the same things: hiking, going to concerts and art shows, attending services at tabernacle. We praise God for bringing Maxine into your life. I know I don't have long for this world. I would hate to close my eyes for the last time thinking I was leaving my youngest son alone, with no one to love him."

"Oh Dad, don't say that. You mustn't keep talking like you're about to die."

"But it's true son. Life is just like ranching. The wee calves are born in the spring, we feed and water them for a couple of years, then ship them off to market. I've been on this planet for ninety-one years, so it won't be long and I'll be shipped off to the heavenly country. I'll be able to go in peace, knowing that you are happily married."

"We'll all be happy for you, Howard: your brothers and sister, your nieces and nephews, Maxine, and Apostle and Mrs. Farida. And who knows, you're not too old to have some children of your own."

"But Mom, Dad, I don't think you understand why I'm nervous. You see, I'm afraid I won't be able to satisfy Maxine, be everything a husband should be."

"Oh my boy," his mother said, sitting down on the bed beside him. "On this planet no one is a perfect partner."

"You and Dad seem to get along fine."

"We've had our hard times, haven't we, Cal?"

"We have."

"You mustn't expect that Maxine will be the perfect wife. Things about her will annoy you. She won't always understand you."

"That's true, Howard. Your mother would have preferred to live in town. She doesn't understand what the country, what the home place means to me."

"Your father's right. I was a city girl, not used to country ways, but we made do, didn't we, Cal? That's what all successful marriages are: two people making do with the good in each other and overlooking the bad."

"I'm sure you'll feel differently in the morning," his dad said. "You've had a long day. You're weary from all the skating and everything. Let's talk no more about it tonight. Good night, son. Your mother and I love you very much."

The final concert was a Christmas Eve candlelight service. Howard bundled his father up in his overcoat, scarf and boots. Fresh snow squeaked beneath their feet as they joined the other families walking the short distance to the floodlit stone tabernacle. Inside, the flames from hundreds of candles were reflected on the backs of the polished wooden pews, the stained glass windows, and burnished organ pipes. The four hundred choir members were wearing white robes trimmed with red.

As he stood to sing the familiar carols, Howard looked around at the families with a touch of envy. Everyone was wearing their finest clothes, the fathers in dark suits, the mothers in long skirts, many with sprigs of holly pinned to their blouses. Their children sat between them, little girls with green or red bows in their hair, boys squirming on the hard pews and poking each other.

And there was Maxine in the front row of the choir. She gave him a little wave and he waved back. She had been so patient and decent when he had first revealed his affectional orientation. Many women would have shunned him, or passed his little secret on to everyone in the tabernacle. She had done nothing but support him, telling him about the change ministry in California, keeping in touch with him all the months he was away, always expressing her faith in him.

As Howard helped his father stand for the final carol, *Silent Night, Holy Night*, he looked around the tabernacle. He knew many of the people by name. He had gone to summer camp with some of them. He had been baptized right here in the Mother Tabernacle during a CarolFest when he was ten years old. Like everyone else, he believed in Brother Tingley's visions.

After the final prayer he asked his brothers to help his father back to the hotel. He hurried forward to the choir room where he waited for Maxine.

"Would you like to come for a walk with me along the riverbank?" he asked.

"That would be lovely." She took his arm as they walked down the hill to the river where small bonfires lighted the walkway, casting long shadows across the ice.

"That was a beautiful service," Howard said, "and during the singing of *Silent Night* I made my decision. God seemed to be speaking directly to me in all the carols tonight. Same with the readings about the sacredness of family life. Maxine, will you marry me?"

"Oh Howie Honey. Yes. Yes. Of course I will." She stood on tiptoe to kiss him on the cheek. "And don't be nervous about it, Howie Honey. Every groom is nervous and—"

"That's what my dad said."

"You need never be nervous around me. With God's blessing we can work out any problems that arise. Oh Howie, I love you so much."

Howard took Maxine's hand in his as they turned to walk back to their hotels. He couldn't wait to tell his mom and dad the good news.

Chapter 15

Every morning during Christmas vacation Marc checked for a message from Howard. There was nothing. Was their meeting in vain, a flash of familiarity that would never be repeated? Had their meeting meant nothing to Howard? Had his promise to keep in touch been a polite brush-off?

Marc had been back to school for a week when the coveted message arrived late on a Friday night.

Hey Marc. Was good to see you. Didn't get to Greenfield during holiday. Family went to Beeverville for CarolFest. Been busy supervising a project in Kenora. Back home now. Howard

Marc decided to play it cool, to wait until the middle of the week before replying, but by Saturday night his self-control imploded.

Hi Howard. Sounds like you've been busy. It must be difficult to have to be away from home so much, or do you enjoy the itinerant life? Perhaps you got used to it in Africa. Some day I'd like to hear all about your trip and see some photos—you probably took lots. You didn't tell me much about your work there when we had coffee. Anyways, just saying, Hi. Marc

Howard replied Sunday morning.

Hey Marc. Not crazy about being away from home. Helps me climb the corporate ladder. Must get ready for tabernacle—Maxine is picking me up. Let me know if you ever come to Winnipeg. Howard

Three weeks later Marc received notice that French teachers were required to attend two days of workshops in Winnipeg. He texted Howard, asking if they might get together for dinner one evening.

Hey Marc. Good to know you're coming this way. Xtra bed in living room. Stay with me. Maxine has symphony tickets for Friday night. Howard

At six-fifteen Thursday evening Marc buzzed Howard's apartment. *I won't stare into Howard's fiery blue eyes,* he promised himself as he rode the elevator to the twentieth floor. *I won't gaze at the perfect symmetry of his ears, nor think about what could have been. I won't grill him about his plans to marry Maxine. I'll just be cool and friendly and let Howard get used to having me around again.*

Howard came to the door, the sleeves of his white dress shirt rolled up, showing off the furry forearms that had always felt so good wrapped around Marc on those cold winter nights in the dorm.

"Welcome to my tiny abode in the sky," Howard said, reaching to shake his hand. "Let me take your coat, and then you can stash your gym bag beside the futon." He led the way into the living room.

"Do I see a professional decorator's touch?" Marc asked, looking at the papered walls, a light tan background sprinkled with faint images of protractors, compasses, dividers and other mathematical instruments.

"Just my own efforts." Howard pointed to a black leather armchair in the corner while he sat down on the futon.

"Looks great. You have a good eye for colour. I wish I was smarter in that area. I've got that big house of Auntie Belle's to redo. Maybe you'll come out to Greenfield sometime and give me a few ideas?"

"Sure thing. Would you like a drink?"

"What have you got?"

"Grape juice, mango-banana, water, Ginger Ale."

"Ginger Ale please."

When Howard returned with the drinks he noticed Marc looking at the dining table set with three places: black placemats, black napkins folded to look like swans. "Maxine'll be joining us for supper," he said.

"That the reason for the fancy cloth napkins and candles?"

"More for you, actually. Maxine's not so fancy. I got fresh salmon steaks, flown in from the coast. Hope that's okay with you."

"Sure is. I never tire of salmon. While living in New West I'd sometimes head down to the quay and get a whole fish off the boat."

The telephone jangled twice. Howard picked it up. "Come on up, Maxine."

"I think you'll like Maxine. I was lucky to meet her. She works at city hall, assistant to the mayor."

Maxine knocked on the door a minute later. "What a horde of people in the elevator. Hooligans with boxes of beer. If they cause a rumpus you'll have to alert the super, Howie. Oh, you must be Marc." She pulled off a black leather glove and reached to shake Marc's hand.

She was a thin woman, a head shorter than Howard, with a narrow horse-like face, but not at all unpleasant. Her carefully shaped black eyebrows contrasted startlingly with her no nonsense copper-toned hairstyle shorn close-cropped against her head. She wore over-sized glasses with tortoiseshell frames.

"Howie, take this chicken casserole off my hands while I remove these boots."

"Didn't I tell you I was getting salmon steaks?" He took the cloth bag with the glass baking dish and set it on the kitchen counter.

"Well Howie, I got to thinking that Marc's probably sick of salmon."

"I never tire of salmon," Marc said.

"Oh, you must be absolutely sick of it, living in Vancouver as you do."

"Marc's not in Vancouver anymore," Howard said.

"No? Where do you live?"

"I'm teaching in Greenfield."

"Of course. Howie did tell me." Marc took her coat and hung it in the closet while she straightened the jacket of her dark blue business suit and tightened the matching blue bow threaded through the collar of her white blouse. "I love visiting Greenfield, such a pleasant little city in the river valley, but I'd never live there. I'm a big city girl. I'd absolutely die without my symphony and art gallery. Howie, did you put the casserole in the oven? Three hundred degrees. Now, let's go into the lounge."

"The lounge?" Marc stood aside to let Maxine pass in the narrow hallway.

"Maxine's an anglophile," Howard called from the kitchen. "She calls the trunk of her car the boot, and the hood the bonnet."

"My folks were posted to the Newcastle tabernacle for six years when I was a teen," Maxine said, sitting down on the futon. "England's absolutely the most wonderful country. Old and decrepit, but it all works. I do hope we'll have our honeymoon over there. Howie Honey, have you thought anymore about that?"

Marc flinched at the *honey* endearment. It seemed to diminish Howard.

"Howie Honey, did you hear what I asked you? Have you had time to plan our honeymoon? I'd absolutely love to show you around England."

"I've been busy with that project in Kenora. Marc, it's a new bridge and the foundations—"

"Oh, you and that bridge. Will we never hear the end of it?"

"Where did you guys meet?" Marc asked.

"The tabernacle," Howard said, coming into the living room.

"I knew the moment I saw Howie that he was the man for me," Maxine said, patting the futon to show him where to sit. "I'd just moved back to Winnipeg from Montreal after Frank died—Frank was my husband, car crash, terrible thing—and when I walked into the tabernacle that morning it was like God beamed a message straight down to me. *Maxine, there is the man you will marry.* And we've never looked back, have we Howie Honey?" She reached for his hand and moved it to her knee. "Now Marc, do tell me, are houses really as expensive on the coast as they say?"

"I'm sure they are still expensive though I'm in Greenfield now."

"Of course. How foolish of me. Howie Honey, how much was that house we were looking at in St. Vital last week?"

"Two thirty, wasn't it?"

"I'm sure it was two fifty, but it was worth every penny, a heritage house, solid brick with four bedrooms and the kitchen and bath all updated. Howie Honey, we really should move on it soon or it'll be gone."

"Have you guys set a wedding date?"

"Not yet," Howard said.

"And I don't know why we haven't." Maxine crossed her legs. "Howie keeps saying he may have to head off to Bulgaria in the fall to work on a project, but I don't see why that needs to stop us getting married. I wouldn't mind going to Bulgaria. I hear wonderful things about those odd little countries. I think the people are good with their hands. Don't they make ceramic tiles or something?"

"That's Turkey, Maxine."

"Oh yes, you're always better with names of countries than me. Say, I bet that casserole is ready. I'll check it, and you fellows come to the table and we can eat."

Once they sat down Maxine reached for Marc's hand. "We like to hold hands while thanking God for our food. Will you join us?"

Marc let her take his left hand, then noticed Howard, on the other side of the table, was holding out his hand, wanting him to join them. Marc suppressed the urge to cry while Howard prayed. The last time he'd held Howard's hand had been that last night they'd shared a bed in the dorm. He wondered if Howard was remembering the same night.

"There. Now we can eat," Howard said, winking at Marc as he handed him the salad bowl.

"We're hoping you'll be able to come to tabernacle with us on Sunday," Maxine said. "Apostle Farida, that's my father, will be preaching, and if I do say so myself, he's so good, absolutely the best. He's totally, and I mean totally, unafraid to call sin by its right name."

"What about cross-country skiing?" Marc looked at Howard.

"We can go to tabernacle first, then head out to Bird's Hill Park after lunch."

Maxine nodded. "That sounds like an excellent plan, and in the evening there's a praise service, but we don't have to go for that if we're too tired from skiing." She smiled indulgently, as though like the pope, she had granted them some special leniency.

Marc hoped Maxine wasn't going to tag along the whole weekend. He wanted some time alone with Howard, and skiing seemed the ideal opportunity to do some man to man talking, to find out just how thrilled he was about marrying this woman who appeared ready to bring her civic organizational skills to bear on every aspect of his life.

It sounded like she was totally in control at city hall. "I shouldn't really be telling you this" she began each story, then went on to paint herself as the heroine who had saved the mayor, and the city, from certain disaster. "More casserole, Marc? Howie Honey?"

After dinner they returned to their original seating assignments in the lounge, where Maxine continued her anecdotes. Every time Marc asked Howard something, Maxine was reminded of some crisis at city hall and she galloped away with another tale. As the evening bored onward Marc began to question Howard's description of Maxine. A decent woman would shut her mouth from time to time. A decent woman would give her fiancé an opportunity to say a word or two. A decent woman might even ask her fiancé's friend a thing or two about his life. Marc briefly imagined the two of them in bed, Maxine giving Howard play-by-play instructions. The thought made him nauseous.

When Maxine finally left, Marc helped Howard wash and dry the dishes. "What should we do with this leftover chicken?" Marc asked. "It's been sitting on the counter all evening so it won't be safe to eat."

"We mustn't throw it out."

"Why not? Will Maxine commit suicide if you throw out the remains of her casserole?"

"What do you think of her?"

Marc knew that being honest was risky, but if a word or two would stop Howard from getting himself into something he'd most certainly regret, he'd better say it. "I wouldn't have thought you'd want someone quite so forceful," he said. "She seems so into herself. She didn't give you, or me, a chance to say much this evening."

"I think she was nervous tonight, about meeting you. When we're alone she doesn't talk quite as much."

"I can't imagine Maxine being uptight about meeting anyone."

Howard ignored his remark as he dried his hands. "I'll get you some pillows and a blanket. The sheets are already on the futon under that quilted throw."

"Thanks for letting me stay."

"It's good to see you again. I'll brush my teeth and use the bathroom and then it's all yours. Sleep well, my friend."

There was no hug or kiss or pat on the butt from Howard, but Marc supposed those once familiar endearments were too much to expect with Maxine's perfume still hanging in the air.

Chapter 16

Friday morning Howard got to the office early, completed the latest progress report for the Kenora bridge project, then went looking for Jim Bronnel. Jim had to sign off on it. Jim wasn't in his office so Howard walked down to the staff lounge. Isabel, Jim's secretary, was making coffee.

"You ready to hunker down for the weekend?" she asked, nodding towards the window overlooking the parking lot. "Looks like a blizzard's setting in."

"I have company visiting, an old college roommate," Howard said.

"Forecast is for this snow to continue all day."

"It won't be the first time we've had a spring blizzard. Is Jim coming in today?"

"Speaking of the devil, there he is."

"Whose calling me the devil?" Jim Bronnel asked, stomping snow off his boots and shaking out his parka.

"I need you to review the progress report on that bridge in Kenora before I send it off to the Ontario Ministry of Transportation," Howard said.

"Give it to me now," Jim said, reaching for the report, "and then come see me before ten. I'm heading out to North Kildonan to check on that new development. We've run into a problem with the routing of the sewer and water lines. You'd think by now we'd—" Jim cocked his head to one side. Someone wearing high heels was approaching along the corridor.

"Well, good morning!" Jim sucked in his belly before reaching to shake the young lady's hand. "You must be the temp for reception."

"That's right. Bonnie McFey." She pulled off a knitted hat and fluffed up her silvery blond hair. "I was told to report to the Administrative Secretary. They didn't give me a name."

"That's me," Isabel said, taking a step forward. "You can hang your coat in here and pop your lunch into the fridge. Then I'll take you out front and explain your duties."

As soon as the women had left the room Jim winked at Howard and gave a low whistle. "Some pair of legs on that one, eh?"

"She's a nice looking girl."

"A nice looking girl? Is that all you can say? Surely they taught you a better line than that in California. Looks like she just stepped off a movie set. We men'll have to keep our doors closed if we want to get any work done today." Jim chuckled and strode out of the room, taking the long route to his office so that he could walk past Reception.

Howard hurried back to his own office. He sometimes wondered how good a Tabber Jim Bronnel was, talking about women the way he did. Did he not believe Jesus' teaching that to lust after a woman is the same as committing adultery?

Howard reviewed some preliminary drawings for a new development in Portage la Prairie, went over some change with the tech, then walked down to Jim's office.

"Ah, you needn't have rushed," Jim said. "With all this snow it doesn't look like I'll be heading up to North Kildonan today. In fact, I'm going to close the office early so we can get home before we get snowed in. Sit down while I check this report and then I'd like to hear about your time in California. I'm sorry I haven't had time to ask about it before this, but the new year is always so busy, getting new projects underway. I sure missed you while you were gone, but I hope the program down there did you some good."

Howard picked at the cuticle on his left thumb as he watched Jim skimming the pages, pausing now and again to make a note in the margin. He wondered how much he should tell Jim. Each time he described the program at TITC, it sounded sillier: sweaty bike rides, Bible reading, searching his past for abuse that had never happened—how could such activities change the core of anyone's personality? And yet he did feel more confident about himself and proud of the weight he'd dropped from around his middle.

"Good report, as usual," Jim said, pocketing his pen. "I've marked a couple of points you could flesh out a bit. Now, about California, where was it you went?"

"Pomona, to the Tingley Inversion Therapy Center."

"Oh yes. And did they invert your centre?" Jim grinned.

"That's the idea."

"I'm curious to know how they did that."

"It would take hours to tell you everything."

"Well, just the highlights then. I'm not trying to be nosy, Howard. I'm curious because there was a report on CNN this morning about some ministry in California. One of their star pupils came out of the closet, said they weren't changing anyone's sexual orientation. What's your take on that? Have you been changed?"

"I found the program helpful, but change is a lifelong project."

"I don't know much about homosexuality, but I presume before going to California you wouldn't have found that new temp at reception hot. Is that right?"

"I know when a woman's physically attractive, always have known. It's just female attractiveness never awakened any burning desire in me."

"But this morning you felt desire for Bonnie at reception?"

"Well, not really. As you know, Jesus said lusting after a woman was the same as committing adultery, so I try to guard against that."

"But you could see she was hot, her shapely calves, her tits so perky, her long blond hair. You could see all that?"

"Yes, I could, but I'm sure you've heard that Maxine and I are going to be getting married."

"Yes. Yes, I did hear that. Congratulations. And you're excited about that?"

"I think Maxine and our mothers are more excited, but that's usually the way with weddings, isn't it?"

"Yes, of course. I remember wanting to run away and hide until mine was over. Well, make the changes to this report and then you can send it off to Ontario. Then you'd better get out of here. I'll go tell Bonnie to phone everyone to head home before this storm gets worse. I wonder if she needs a ride."

Chapter 17

Marc shivered as he walked through the skyway to the adjoining hotel's restaurant. The streets had almost a foot of snow on them, and the few cars and buses were slipping and sliding in slow motion.

When the workshop reconvened, the presenter took a vote to see who wanted to skip the afternoon break and leave early. When they were dismissed at three-thirty Marc was glad he didn't have to drive. It was difficult enough wading through the snow the few blocks to Howard's apartment building. He hoped the storm would have sent Maxine home early too, leaving Howard and him with some quality time alone.

When he reached the apartment he found the door open. Howard was standing in the entranceway, half-way out of his parka, talking on his cell.

"Maxine, the road's are really heavy. You'd better go straight home...I know your Accord has front-wheel drive, but before the evening's over...I wouldn't advise it...Maxine, we can do without dessert...well, suit yourself."

"Even *our* office closed early today," Howard said, turning to Marc as he laid the phone down. "We've never done that before. They're forecasting another twelve hours of this storm."

While Howard peeled potatoes and took the salmon steaks out of the fridge and put them in the oven, Marc set the table and cut up vegetables for a salad. They were sitting in the living room drinking hot chocolate when the phone jangled. Maxine was on her way up.

"I went to all the trouble during my lunch hour to pick up this black forest cake, and I certainly wasn't going to sit at home and eat it all by myself," she said, handing the box and a plastic container to Howard, while like a rambunctious black lab she shook the snow off herself. "And that other is a tub of chicken soup from the deli. It seems a good night for soup."

"But I have the salmon steaks all ready to go," Howard said.

"That's fine, Howie Honey. We'll have the soup followed by salmon and whatever else you've got."

After dinner Marc tried to curb Maxine's nonstop dialogue. "Could I take a look at the photographs you took in Africa?" he asked.

"There's absolutely nothing to see," Maxine said. "Just piles of pipes, and pumps, and things."

"Surely you took some shots of the villages where you were working. I'd like to see those, and even the pipes and pumps. I'm sure they'd be interesting to me."

"Maxine's right," Howard said. "They're pretty boring for people who aren't engineers."

"Let's play a game," Maxine said, taking Howard's hand, the same hand that Marc used to grope for in bed when Howard awakened in the middle of the night, nervous about some test or class project. Marc would weave his fingers through Howard's, and comforted, Howard would go back to sleep.

"Where's the Scrabble, Howie Honey? Remember, I gave it to you for Christmas a year ago, and we haven't played it since."

"I'd rather see the photographs," Marc said. "My brain's been on high all day in that French workshop. Couldn't we just look at your photographs, Howard?"

"They look much better projected on the wall," he said, "and I don't have a projector at home."

"We can play Scrabble at the dining room table," Maxine said. "You get the game Howie and I'll make us all another hot chocolate. That'll be a cosy way to spend the evening."

They played until almost ten when Howard turned on the television to get the news and weather report. The newscaster read a long list of cancellations. Then the police chief warned people not to travel unless it was absolutely necessary. Fire trucks and ambulances would have enough difficulty getting around without having to dodge abandoned vehicles.

"What an exciting storm," Maxine said. "I'm sure the city will be closed down until Monday. I may have to walk to work from here."

"What?" The exclamation leaped out of Marc's mouth.

Maxine glared at him. "You don't expect me to drive in this snow, do you? I live way out in East Kildonan. They probably won't plough my street until sometime late Sunday or even Monday, but that's okay. I brought an overnight bag with me just in case. It's down in the car."

"Maybe I should go to a hotel," Marc said, not relishing the idea of bunking in close quarters with Maxine. "I could walk back to the Holiday Inn. It's only a few blocks."

"No guest of mine will stay in a hotel," Howard said.

"So where are we all going to sleep?"

"You can bunk in with me."

"But don't you and Maxine want to—"

"What kind of girl do you think I am, Marc? I'll have you know that I'm very much looking forward to my wedding night. Then, and only then will I sleep with my husband for the *first* time."

"I didn't mean to—"

"You probably think us Tabbers old fashioned, and we are, but we don't apologize for it, do we Howie Honey?"

"No. Maxine and I aren't going to rush into anything."

"There'll be no need for anyone to bunk in with anyone else," Maxine said. "I remember once when I was a child in England. We had more company than beds, so you know what we did? We lifted the mattress off the box spring. That gave us two beds instead of one. The spring isn't all that comfortable, but it's okay for one night. We can pad it with quilts and blankets."

"I don't have any quilts and blankets, other than what's on the bed and futon," Howard said, "and besides, my bedroom isn't big enough for that. You can have the futon Maxine, that is if you don't mind sleeping on sheets that aren't fresh. I don't have any extra sets and the laundry room closes at ten. Marc and I'll sleep in my bedroom. He can have the bed and I'll dig out my old air mattress and sleeping bag. They're in the storage room, somewhere."

While Maxine was downstairs getting her overnight things Marc moved his gym bag from beside the futon into Howard's room. Howard couldn't find the pump for filling the air mattress, so they sat down on the floor and took turns blowing into it. "Not quite my idea of a blow job," Marc said.

Howard laughed, his face beet red, whether from the joke or from blowing into the mattress, Marc didn't know.

When Maxine returned there was a bit of awkwardness about using the bathroom until Maxine urged the men to go first. Marc brushed his teeth, washed his face, and then, just in case Howard was inspired to do more than sleep, he dropped his clothes on the floor and stepped into the tub for a quick shower. He didn't see how anything major could happen with Maxine lying watch in the next room, but best to be prepared.

While waiting for Howard to finish in the bathroom, he lay in bed remembering another blizzard when he was just a kid, a few years before his brother Claude leaped off that bridge into a frozen eternity. They were still living on the farm north of Greenfield. Father Dann, the same one who would condemn Claude to eternal hellfire, came to visit, as he did once a year. By the time the supper dishes had been cleared away a blizzard was creating a whiteout on the country roads. His parents had insisted that Father Dann stay the night, and by some luck, Marc was chosen as his sleeping partner.

His mother warned him to keep his eyes shut to give Father Dann some privacy. That night he kept the promise, perhaps because he was already asleep when Father Dann came to bed. The next morning when his father called, "Time to get up and milk the cows," Marc had sat up in bed, and as he swung his legs over the edge, he'd sneaked just the tiniest peek over his shoulder at Father Dann's naked backside beneath the flannelette sheets.

What he saw became engraved upon his grey cells as though they were coated with a particularly sensitive film emulsion—two beautifully rounded and firm cheeks dusted with curly dark hairs. Not having had much experience with naked men, his first thought was that Father Dann, having hair on his butt, was some sort of freak. He had wanted to ask his father about it while milking the cows, but it didn't seem the sort of thing to discuss with him. He certainly couldn't inquire of Claude who would have tattled that he hadn't kept his eyes closed as promised.

When Howard came out of the bathroom Marc heard him say good night to Maxine and thought he heard them kiss, though it didn't sound like an embrace by passionate lovers. Perhaps Tabbers didn't believe in French kissing before the wedding night, if even then, though Howard used to be extremely adept at it.

No one had warned Marc to close his eyes while Howard shucked his clothes. He watched his friend fold his shirt before dropping it into the laundry hamper, then hang his pants in the closet, creases carefully lined up. He took the same care with his socks and underwear and then turned, full frontal view.

"How come you've managed to keep a six pack stomach while mine has morphed into a one pack, despite my workouts at the gym?"

"It's a struggle," Howard said. "Did a lot of physical work in Africa."

"I guess I should do more," Marc said as Howard flipped the light switch, then crawled into his sleeping bag.

"You going to be comfortable down there?" Marc asked.

"Used this mattress and sleeping bag for years on the ranch. Summers we boys would set the tent up behind the house and sleep there."

"If you get uncomfortable, there's lots of room here. I promise not to—"

"I'll be fine, Marc. Sleep well."

Marc closed his eyes and gritted his teeth, resisting the powerful urge to throw himself off the bed and onto Howard, to bury his face in that thick mat of salt and pepper fur on his chest, to kiss him tenderly, to let the passion he felt boiling up inside him explode all over this man who by now could have been his partner for almost a quarter century. If Howard had accompanied him to Vancouver as planned, those sodden winter nights wouldn't have been so lonely. They could have cuddled under the sheets, jogged around Stanley Park on sunny summer evenings, spotted each other during workouts at the gym, and camped in the mountains during summer vacations.

Marc wasn't so naïve as to think there wouldn't have been rough times with Howard. Like any couple, they'd have had battles. Howard's careful folding of clothing that was going into the laundry hamper and other precise ways might have driven him crazy.

In turn, Howard would scold him for returning the Shreddies box to the cupboard when there was only a spoonful left. He would get fed up with Marc never putting things back in their place, for leaving half-read books lying all over the apartment, but they would have kissed and made up joyously in bed, feeling their bond growing tighter over the years.

"Will you have to work tomorrow?" Marc asked, once he'd swallowed the lump of regret in his throat.

"I often work Saturdays, but I've got this weekend off. In this climate we use January to do a lot of planning, drawing up blueprints, and getting approvals for projects that will take off in the spring and summer."

As they talked of work, Marc kept waiting, praying for Howard to sit up, to make the first move, to reach across the quarter century and heal the wound in their relationship. He wondered if Howard remembered those nights in the dorm, or had he erased them from his mind? When he needed to take care of his own needs, right in this bed, what did he fantasize about? Surely he didn't imagine being with Maxine. You'd have to be a milk and toast army private to be in love with her sergeant major ways. Perhaps he kept a stash of bodybuilding magazines at the bottom of his sock and underwear drawer like he'd done in the dorm.

Eventually Marc lost consciousness. He was awakened around three when Howard got up and padded into the bathroom. When he returned he closed the door firmly, then instead of crawling back into his sleeping bag, got into bed beside Marc. "Sorry to wake you," he whispered. "My back's killing me. Guess air mattresses aren't so good for someone my age."

"No problem," Marc said, sidling over, though not too far. "Lots of room here."

Howard turned onto his side, his back to Marc. In their dorm year that had always been an invitation for Marc to flip onto his side, put his arm over Howard's chest and snug him in close. Should he do it now, or would Howard freak, cry out, leap out of bed and alert Maxine?

When Marc next awakened the green numerals on the bedside clock read seven-thirty. He was alone in bed. His first thought was that Howard had snuck into the living room to snuggle with Maxine. Maybe they were huddled together on the futon, hypocrites like television preachers who advocated sexual purity while screwing prostitutes of varied genders in cheap motel rooms.

Then Marc heard the toilet flush, water running into the sink. He closed his eyes, pretending he was asleep, felt the sudden draft of cold air and the mattress tip as Howard slipped between the sheets once again. When Marc opened his eyes Howard was lying flat on his back, his eyes closed. Marc shifted a leg to show that he was awake. Maybe Howard would reach across, pat him on the belly or kiss him on the forehead like he used to do when he slept through the alarm in the dorm.

Howard's breathing became heavy and regular, then he turned onto his side, facing Marc. His eyelids fluttered, opened, then closed, a slight smile on his lips, his breathing evened out again. Marc flipped onto his side, facing Howard. He studied the faint web of lines radiating from the corner of his eye, his thick black as charcoal eye brows and long lashes, the scattering of grey in his paint brush moustache, the red blush on his lower lip. His hand was lying flat on the wine coloured sheet, half hidden where his cheek rested on it. Marc studied the pattern of pores, the fine black hairs speckling his knuckles—and suddenly the tears welled up in his eyes. He swallowed once, twice, trying to suppress the groan of what might have been.

Marc wiped the tears away with the back of his hand, then reached out and brought his hand down on top of Howard's. He watched as Howard opened his eyes, looked at the hand on top of his with puzzlement for a moment, then looked at Marc. He smiled shyly, then pulled his hand away. He brushed his hair off his forehead, then brought his hand down on top of Marc's. He threaded his fingers through Marc's, grinned, snuggled into the mattress, and closed his eyes.

Marc's impulse was to jump his bones right then and there, but best not to spook him. Holding hands was a first step, a good one, a comforting one. Without letting go of Howard's hand, he snuggled himself closer, closed his eyes and drifted off to sleep.

A knock on the bedroom door awakened him, and Howard too, judging by the way he jumped. He let go of Marc's hand and flipped onto his back.

"Are you guys going to lie in all day?" Maxine called.

"We're waiting for you to serve us breakfast in bed," Howard said.

"Yes, I thought that was the plan," Marc added. "How come I can't smell bacon and eggs?"

"Male chauvinists," Maxine snorted before going into the bathroom.

Mark raised himself on his elbow, bent over and kissed Howard on the forehead.

"Hey, no kissing."

"Okay, my friend, but if you decide Maxine isn't the one for you, I'm here. I'll always be here for you. I still love you, Howard. I wish—"

"Please Marc. Don't say anything more."

"You must feel something for me, for what we had."

"Those days in the dorm were a long time ago. I've changed since then, just as I'm sure you have, and I do love Maxine. She understands me, and I think she'll make me a decent wife." He gave

Marc's hand a squeeze, then heaved himself out of bed and put on his robe.

While eating the toast and scrambled eggs Howard had prepared, a sudden roar of diesel engines sent them running to the window. A blitzkrieg of yellow city trucks fitted with ploughs was stampeding down the street, their boxes heaped with sand and salt.

"Looks like you may be able to get home before too long, Maxine," Marc said.

"It'll probably be hours before they get to my street, but it doesn't really matter. I packed an evening gown with me just in case this happened, so I can go straight to symphony from here tonight."

"Do you think the concert will go ahead?"

"Yes, absolutely. The main streets will be cleared by noon," Maxine said. "This is Winnipeg. We're prepared for snow, unlike you jam tarts in Vancouver who faint at the first sniff of the white stuff."

"You might not be so cocky if you had Vancouver's hills."

"What will we do with the day?" Howard asked as he and Marc finished washing and drying the breakfast dishes. "Make angels in the snow? Build a snow fort? Have a snowball fight?"

"I really would like to see those African pictures. Can't you show them on your laptop? I saw one on your desk in the bedroom."

"You wouldn't find them very interesting. Like Maxine says, a lot of close ups of water pipes and fittings. I didn't go on safari or anything. Besides, some people don't like having their pictures taken. They think you're hog-tying their souls."

"I know what we can do, Howie Honey," Maxine said, coming into the kitchen after brushing her teeth. "We can have a ping pong tournament in your rec room."

Marc found that somewhat juvenile, but it was better than sitting in the living room watching Maxine hold Howard's hand.

After lunch Howard borrowed a couple of snow shovels from his neighbours and they all got a workout digging Maxine's Accord free of the snow. Marc enjoyed stretching his muscles, and the cold, fresh air cleared his brain. So what if Howard hadn't wanted to go farther than holding his hand? No wedding date had been set. There was still a chance he could win Howard back.

That evening's symphony concert wasn't of any interest to Marc, though he'd anticipated sitting beside Howard, holding his hand on the down low. Maxine made sure that didn't happen by manoeuvring herself between them. When they exited the concert hall just before eleven, traffic was moving like normal, as though the blizzard had been a figment of their imaginations. Marc expected Maxine would head home. Instead she whipped out her phone and called the superintendent in her building. "The plough's been down the street once but he hasn't done the back lane," she reported.

"You'd better stay the night again," Howard said, rather too eagerly, Marc thought. Maybe he was afraid that morning's lite hand-holding would advance to a more dangerous level if Maxine wasn't present to chaperone. On the plus side, maybe that was a good sign, a sign that Howard felt a whisper of yearning for those dorm days.

Sunday morning both Maxine and Howard urged him to come to tabernacle with them, but Marc pleaded a need to get home to prepare Monday's lessons. When they parted at the door, Marc spread his arms for a good-bye hug, but Howard just held out his hand.

Chapter 18

Howard had been glad to see Marc, but it had been stressful having him around. He had been uptight the whole time, frightened that Marc and Maxine would lock horns. It was clear that Marc didn't approve of Maxine, didn't approve of him getting married at all. Several times he had been tempted to share his experience at TITC with Marc, but Marc, who was always so sure of himself, would probably have died laughing when he learned about the program.

And maybe Marc would have been right. Maybe his own nervousness about getting married was more than normal groom jitters. Maybe he really wasn't ready for marriage, and yet, he'd resisted Marc's kiss, his obvious desire to do more than just sleep together. They'd held hands in bed, but didn't they do that at TITC too, at least at church when they'd sat in that healing circle or whatever it was. The fact that he and Marc had done nothing more must be proof that the program had done him some good.

That Sunday morning as Howard looked around the tabernacle he was relieved Marc hadn't come with them. The tabernacle's service would probably have appeared tawdry to a former Catholic, used to a church filled with artwork and beautiful music.

The choir was small, a handful of old folks who had difficulty matching their voices to the piano. The building had an ugly stain on the ceiling where the rain had seeped through. There was a thick layer of dust on top of the replica of the leaf from the heavenly tree of life that hung over the pulpit. While Maxine's father, Apostle Farida, preached that Sunday, droning on about the prodigal son, Howard watched a cobweb hanging down from the leaf. Each time the furnace kicked in, it swung back and forth like the serpent in the Garden of Eden. Was it about to tempt Apostle Farida, and what would the temptation be?

The faded leaf really did look silly, but every tabernacle in the world was obliged to hang a replica of the real one on display in Beeverville. Howard remembered, as a teenager, touring the workshop where the leaves were made. He had watched the ladies crafting the spools of wire, green silk and golden sparkles into leaves. If he remembered correctly, it took an hour to make one. Then the Head Apostle blessed it by sprinkling it with water brought over from the Jordan River. Finally, the leaf was carefully packaged, ready to be sent to hang over a pulpit in some distant corner of the world: New York City, Brisbane, Australia, or some tiny village in Africa.

Africa! Howard wished he'd never agreed to camouflage his time at TITC with the lie about Africa. He guessed he could have broadened the lie by showing Marc pictures he took one weekend when Rafe led the counselees on a visit to the LA zoo. He had pictures of tigers and elephants, lions and monkeys. There had been quite a few black folk at the zoo too. The photos might have fooled Marc, unless he questioned why all the animals were behind fences.

On the way to tabernacle Maxine had asked him what Marc thought of her. "He didn't say very much," Howard had said.

"Nothing at all?"

"Well, he thought you were a little intense."

"Intense?"

"Yes, about the casseroles, about not wanting him to see my African pictures."

"Well, I needed to be a bit intense about that. Do you think he's still after you?"

"He thinks I'm making a mistake by marrying you."

"Of course he would. It's clear that he's still in love with you. I noticed how after prayer at the table he dropped my hand like it was a dead fish, but hung onto yours for several moments."

After tabernacle folks crowded around them. Some had just heard the news about their engagement and wanted to congratulate them.

"I'm so happy for you. What a lucky girl you are, Maxine. Aren't you the lucky man Howard, snaring the apostle's daughter. I'm so thrilled for you both. You're such lovely Christian young people. I'm sure you'll have a long and happy life together."

A handful of the men swarmed them too. "Caught at last, eh Howard. Thought you'd escaped the marriage trap, but you're about to join the rest of us in leg irons. Congratulations son. Joining us big guys in the major leagues, eh?"

Howard held Maxine's hand. He smiled. He nodded. He prayed silently that the knot in his stomach would unravel. Why did he feel uptight when people congratulated them? Must be groom jitters. While at TITC, Sister Bergus had told him most men would rather elope than go through the details of a full-blown wedding ceremony and reception. She advised him to ignore this feeling. If he truly loved Maxine, he was to embrace all the wedding details. That would make Maxine happy.

Chapter 19

When Marc arrived home Sunday afternoon he vacuumed the house from top to bottom, ironed a few shirts, and picked up a pizza for supper, all the while abusing himself for not playing it cool with Howard. If he hadn't tried to kiss him, perhaps he would have gotten more than a handshake at the door when he said good-bye.

Before going to bed that night he checked his messages.

Hey Marc. Good to see you. Too bad the storm spoiled your visit. Maybe we can get together when the weather's better. We can do some hiking. Maxine enjoys the outdoors too. Howard

It wasn't the storm that spoiled my visit, Marc thought. It was Maxine, hanging about like Howard's secret service agent. He wondered how long Howard would tolerate her organizing ways after they were married. Eventually he'd resist, wouldn't he, and then what? Did Tabbers permit divorce, or would they have to tough it out forever?

To Marc's surprise, Howard's emails became daily events. He rarely mentioned Maxine, except to report a trip to the symphony, art gallery, or some function at city hall. She could be his sister for all the excitement he expressed about her.

Marc never mentioned his frequent trips to Riverside Park. He hated himself for cruising the riverside trails, but the RAV4 had a mind of its own. Every time a hot guy at the gym, or on the street, or in the grocery store, caught Marc's attention, the RAV4 ran to the park.

Occasionally, he had a semi-satisfying encounter, someone whose body fit perfectly with his own, someone who brushed and flossed their teeth, changed their underwear daily, and best of all, wanted to linger in bed for an hour or two after the main event. Sometimes they even fell asleep together, arms and legs entwined, but inevitably there was a stirring, a bleary stare at the bedside clock, an exclamation of "Good God, look at the time," and that night's Mr. Right Now ran into the bathroom to clean up, pulled on his clothes, and dashed away to make excuses to his loving family.

By mid-April Howard and Marc were texting each other at least twice a day, once in the morning to describe their plans for the day, again at night to recount what had happened. Even when he had to travel to supervise some project, Howard rarely missed contacting him.

Hey Marc: You might of heard about the hog plant coming to Greenfield. Bronnel won the contract for design. There's lots of other work too with new housing subdivisions. Bronnel will open an office in Greenfield. I'm coming on Thurs to look for suitable office space. Can I stay with you? I'd love to see your house. Howard

Hi Howard: You can stay as long as you want. I get home from work 5:30ish so come by anytime after that. Looking forward to seeing you. Love, Marc.

Marc had begun signing his emails *Love, Marc* and so far Howard hadn't taken offence, though he never reciprocated. Maybe this visit would lead to greater intimacy.

The morning of the visit, Marc wakened with an awful thought. Would Maxine be coming too? It would be very odd if she did, but having seen how bossy and possessive she was, he wouldn't be surprised if she showed up clutching that infernal overnight case. He thought of emailing Howard to ask for clarification, but decided not to risk it. Howard might take it as an invitation to bring Maxine.

The white Ford 150 pickup with Bronnel Engineering inscribed on the door pulled up just after six Thursday evening. Marc watched from behind the curtain in the living room as Howard got out. Apparently, the secret service hadn't come. As Marc watched him open the front gate and walk up to the house, he thought this is how it should be all the time. Every night he should see his Big Man coming home after a day at work.

"Get yourself in here," Marc said, opening the door and extending a hand for Howard to shake. After hanging up his jacket and the usual small talk, Marc led him upstairs. "This is your room any time you come to town. That chest of drawers is empty and the closet has a few hangers in case you want to unpack anything."

"I'm only staying a couple of nights."

"I know, but I want you to be comfortable. The bathroom's just across the hall—the white towels are yours and the matching bathrobe on the back of your bedroom door is for you. I didn't prepare any dinner, not knowing what time you'd be here, so whenever you're ready we'll go out to eat."

"Aren't you going to show me through the house first? I've been looking forward to seeing it. I want to compare it to what we've been looking at in Winnipeg."

Marc winced at the intrusion of *we*. "Since we're up here we might as well start at the top and work our way down. Watch the sloped ceilings when we get into the attic. I wouldn't want you to ruin my plaster by smashing a hole in it."

"Thanks, Marc. Your concern for my head may go straight to my head."

That sounded more like the Howard Marc knew from dorm days, the one who, though quiet and studious, could get a joke and heave it right back.

"This larger room would make a great train room," Howard said.

"Train room? You mean training, like exercise equipment, a treadmill and stuff?"

"No. Trains, model railways. This is the perfect space for an N scale layout. You should look into that."

"I had an electric train set when I was a kid."

"I've got a whole box of locomotives and running stock in my locker, just waiting for the day we buy a house, and that's one reason I wanted to come to Greenfield with the chief."

"You're going to buy a house here, in Greenfield?"

"No. Maxine would never live here, but this weekend is the Greenfield Model Train Show. I'd like to go tomorrow night, if you're okay with that."

"Sure." Marc lead the way downstairs, biting his lip to keep from telling Howard that the attic, the whole house, was his to share if he'd just forget Maxine.

When the tour was over they drove to the Golden Cow, Greenfield's only Chinese buffet. Sitting across the table from Howard, Marc studied his face. He looked haggard, the tiny muscles around his eyes and across his forehead tight. As Howard talked of the challenges he was having with some of his projects, Marc noticed that he rarely looked him in the eye, and then only for a second or two before glancing down at his plate or across the restaurant.

Marc talked about his teaching job, the queer Bill Fuches who taught sixth grade next to him. Then they talked about their families. Howard's uncle had died during the winter. "It's kind of nice to know he's in a better place now," Howard said.

"You sure about that?"

"Of course. He's safely in the heavenly country. Isn't that where your Auntie Belle is?"

"Since Claude died I've never been sure of anything. I'm positive Father Dann lied when he said Claude was roasting in hellfire.

Why would a loving God torture a sixteen year old forever and ever just because he lost his head over some girl? Doesn't make sense. I guess everything's pretty straight forward in your religion?"

"I know what I believe," Howard said.

"So you never doubt, never review your beliefs?"

"What do you mean?"

"Let me give you a silly example. Dad always drove General Motors products. He said Fords were no good. I grew up thinking Ford products were junk. Later I bought a little Mustang, and it was one of the best cars I ever had. What I'd learned previously was just Dad's prejudice.

"I think it's the same with religious beliefs. As a Catholic I was raised to believe it was a sin for priests to marry. I used to think the Anglican priest would burn in hell because he was married. Later on I learned the whole celibacy thing has nothing to do with the Bible."

"Our apostles can marry. Maxine's dad is an apostle."

"I know that. I'm just using celibacy as an example. Maybe some of the things we grew up believing to be true aren't based on anything solid. That's why we all need to take a hard look at our beliefs, turn them inside out, check whether they still stand up or not."

"That's done every year at the annual conference in Beeverville. The apostles present papers on various topics."

"But that's someone else checking things out. Shouldn't you do that personally? I mean if Maman hadn't checked things out in her Bible after Claude jumped off the Twentieth Street bridge, she'd still believe what Father Dann told her. The thought of him being tortured in hell would have driven her crazy. She probably would have followed him off that bridge."

"So you think Father Dann was lying?"

"Maman thinks so, and before I ever get involved in religion again, I'll sure check things out. I think everyone should."

"Marc, if you're telling me to check out the Tabber's view of gay marriage for myself, I've done so many times."

"And?"

"It's a puzzle. The Bible seems so plain when I hear Apostle Farida preach, but sometimes I get so lonely that I—well, better not go there." Howard looked at his watch. "We better get back to your place and into bed. I've got a long list of potential office sites to check out tomorrow."

When they got home Marc was too wound up to sleep. He went into the den, popped an episode of *Upstairs Downstairs* into the DVD player, and sat down to watch it while Howard hopped in the shower. When Howard came out wrapped in the white robe, he sat down in the other recliner. "I see you're watching Maxine's favourite show," he said, "She's still after me to have our honeymoon in England, which reminds me, I've got something for you." Howard padded across the hallway to his room and came back a moment later with an envelope. "My friend, you are the first to get one of these."

Marc had to suppress the urge to cry out in pain at the sight of the ivory-coloured envelope. He yanked out the invitation.

Alfred and Moira Farida
and
Calvert and Bella Hildebrandt
Invite you to the marriage of their children
Maxine Agatha Farida
and
Howard Richard Hildebrandt
2:00 p.m.
Saturday, September 15th, 2012
Winnipeg Tabernacle of Believers' Assembly
Reception to follow at the Farida home
238 Riverside Crescent

"Thanks, Howard. I guess I'm honoured to be the first to receive an invitation. Does this mean you're really going ahead with this marriage?"

"Yes, and we both want you to be there."

"Howard, I know I may be speaking out of turn, in fact I am, but do you really think—"

"Please, Marc. I'd prefer not to discuss it. I've got a new life ahead of me and—"

"But is this the life *you* want, or is it the life Maxine, her parents, your parents, and the tabernacle want?"

"Marc, I don't want to talk about it. You probably think I'm being stupid, but we'll just have to disagree about that. Can we just leave it alone? The reception's going to be in the Farida's backyard. The leaves should be changing colour by then so it should be nice."

"Nice."

"Should be."

"Come on, Howard. You know it won't be nice. It'll be a disaster."

"Marc, please don't react this way. I knew you wouldn't be pleased, but I've made my decision, and I don't want to discuss it."

"I think we'd better discuss it. You and I both know you're as gay as I am. If you won't be honest with me, don't you think you need to be honest with Maxine? Will it be fair to become her husband, a man who can never love her the way a man should?"

"No, Marc. No—" Howard leaped out of his chair and dashed into the bathroom, banging the door behind him. Marc heard the toilet lid snap up, then silence. After a few moments he went to the door and knocked.

"Howard, are you okay in there?"

"I'll be okay."

"You need anything?"

"Just leave me alone."

The next moment Marc heard a gulp followed by the unmistakable sound of Howard's stomach turning itself inside out. He knocked on the door again. "I'm coming in."

"Stay out, Marc. I'm warning you—"

Howard was sitting on the toilet, doubled over, the new bathrobe lying in a heap at his feet. He straightened up, looked at Marc, then away as a second powerful regurgitation of his all-you-can-eat Chinese dinner shot out of his mouth. The vomitus spewed like fire from a dragon's mouth, splaying a stinking swath across the bathrobe, the floor, the tub and the tiled surround.

Teaching elementary students who occasionally suffered from stomach upsets had prepared Marc for this sort of thing, but their regurgitations were tiny compared to Howard's. Marc grabbed a facecloth from beside the sink, ran it under the hot water.

"Big Man, what did you eat for dinner that's made you so sick?" Marc knelt down and reached to wipe Howard's chin and chest.

"No, Marc." Howard twisted away. "Leave me alone. Just get out of here and quit treating me like a brainless child."

"What do you mean?"

"You don't know? You really don't know what I mean? You're a pompous ass who claims to have all the answers to life. You figure you can give me advice anytime you like, but if you're so smart, how come you're living in this big house all by yourself? Tell me that!" Tears poured down Howard's cheeks. Marc reached to wipe them away with a clean towel.

Howard swatted his hand aside. "Get away. I can clean up by myself."

Marc stood up and took a step back. "I'm sorry, Howard. I suppose it is none of my business if the man I loved back in dorm days wants to marry a woman. But why are you so defensive if you feel it's a good thing? Why are you so uptight about it?"

"Since when do you know what's inside me? Just leave me alone. I should never have come here. I'll clean up and go to a hotel."

Marc knelt down again. He put his hand on Howard's shoulder. "I'm sorry to've upset you, but I love you Howard. I don't want you to make a mistake. I'm sorry if my concern comes across in the wrong way. Maybe I do sound like a pompous ass. I know I haven't made any great success of my own life, but that's all the more reason to help you avoid a mistake. Besides, it's not too late for you and me."

Marc started to blub, tears rolling down his cheeks. "We can have a good life together. One word from you and I'll give up my teaching job here. I'll move to Winnipeg." He paused, waiting for Howard to say something. He hung his head, refusing to respond or look at Marc.

"I've never stopped loving you, Howard. You know how hard it was for me to lie in the same bed with you when I stayed with you in

Winnipeg? I so wanted to touch you, hold you, make love to you. And I think you still love me too. I think, deep down inside, you regret not coming to the coast with me all those years ago." Marc put an arm around Howard's shoulder, kissed him on the cheek. "It's not too late."

Howard shook his head. "I can't. I can't live with a man."

Marc sighed and stood up. "I'm sorry to hear you say that, and I guess there's nothing I can say to change your mind."

Howard shook his head again and stood up. "Look what I've done to your lovely bathroom, the one you worked so hard to modernize. I'm so sorry."

"Lucky I ran the tub surround right up to the ceiling." Marc reached into the sink and handed Howard another face cloth. "Wipe yourself down while I clean out the tub. Then take another shower. Would you like a hot drink before you go to bed?"

"Are you kidding?"

"Peppermint tea is supposed to be soothing to the stomach."

"Please, no."

"I think you should drink something. It'll settle your stomach."

"Marc, stop it! There you go again. I said I don't want anything to drink but you won't listen. You always know best."

"Why does it upset you so much when I suggest something, but you let Maxine tell you what to eat, where to sit, like you're her run-and-fetch dog?"

"Please, Marc. Just leave me alone."

Marc shook his head, then took the soiled robe and towels down to the clothes washer. After setting the cycle he plugged in the kettle. When he got back upstairs with two mugs of peppermint tea, Howard was in bed.

"I'm sorry I spoiled your bathroom," Howard said, "and your evening."

"It's not *my* evening. It's *our* evening, and don't keep apologizing. You're human. You get uptight. You throw up. Besides, I made you do it trying to hammer some sense into that handsome head of yours. From now on I'll try not to—"

Howard's cell phone announced its presence by playing the first few bars of some musical thing. "Can you reach that for me? It's in my pants' pocket."

Marc went over to the chair where Howard had carefully draped his pants over the back. He reached into first one pocket, then the other, a task he found intensely intimate. He handed the phone to Howard.

"Hello. Oh hello Maxine...Yes, I got here fine...I know you worry about fog at this time of year but I got here before dark. Yes, I'm all settled for the night."

Marc went across the hall to the den to shut down the DVD player and TV. He kept one ear cocked toward Howard's conversation, expecting him to tell Maxine where he was, maybe pass on greetings from Maxine, but he hung up without mentioning him.

"How's Maxine?"

"She's fine." Howard put the phone on the bedside table, then sat up and reached for the mug of tea. "This does smell good. Maybe I'll just wet my mouth with it, see if it stays down."

"You going to be alright now?"

Howard nodded. "Sorry about my meltdown, Marc, but you are pushy at times. Still, you're a good man. You don't even get upset when I throw up all over your new bathroom."

"Isn't that what love is about—good times and bad times? You get some sleep. I'll see you in the morning. Love you."

Chapter 20

Howard pulled up the covers and closed his eyes. He wished Marc wouldn't say the word *love*. It took him back to their dorm days when they snuggled in bed every night. Marc was always kissing him and saying "I love you...Love you lots...Couldn't love you more, Big Man". Had he ever said the word back? Maybe, after sex, but he always felt that the prophet Brother Tingley was standing in the shadows. He was recording Howard's every thought, word, and deed, shaking his head sadly at what a disgrace he was to the tabernacle.

At TITC they had taught him that words of endearment were important to women. They'd spent several mornings sitting in a circle, repeating phrases as Sister Bergus flashed them on the overhead screen.

I love you.
Thank you for mending my shirt. You're such a sweetheart.
Honey bunch, I do so love you.

Let me give you a hug, Sweet Pea. I love how
you painted the bathroom.

At first the guys felt like new immigrants learning a strange language. However, after shouting out the phrases a dozen times, the blush faded from their faces. The words started to come naturally.

Then Sister Bergus asked them to tone it down, speak in natural voices, wrapping their vowels with affection. She turned on the PowerPoint. Slides of women appeared on the screen. Some were Asian, skinny as steel fence posts. Others were snugly black mommas, others Caucasian like you'd see any day at the supermarket. Sister Bergus instructed the group to say the phrases as though speaking to each woman in turn.

Finally she'd asked them to speak individually. "Imagine the model is your partner and you've just come home from work. Let her know that she is cherished, that you love her to distraction."

Howard had wished he could die, especially when Sister Bergus chose him to begin. He'd felt such a fool speaking to each in turn when Sister Bergus clicked the wand. The photograph of a platinum blond with a bony rack of shoulders wearing a long, red evening gown flashed on the screen with the words he was to say. *Samantha*—all the models had names—*Samantha, thank you for dinner. That is the best pork roast I've ever eaten. It just melted in my mouth. I'm so glad I have a lovely wife who can cook. Thanks, Love. You really are special to me.*

He had to repeat the lines until Sister Bergus was satisfied with his intonation. By that time his cheeks and neck matched the scarlet of Samantha's gown, and his black t-shirt was soaked through with sweat, back and front.

Boxer was sitting across the circle from him. When it came his turn, Howard was embarrassed to see that his eyes strayed to him each time he repeated his lines. *Darling, I love you so much. I'm thrilled that I married you. I couldn't have asked for a better partner. I really believe God brought you and me together.*

"Wife," Sister Bergus had corrected him. "I couldn't have asked for a better *wife*."

But Boxer had insisted on *partner*, never taking his eyes off Howard. Poor little Boxer. He had a partner back in Atlanta, but he'd fallen hopelessly in love with Howard. He'd always been offering to do things for him—wash his laundry while doing his own, make his bed, hold his hand when they knelt by their beds to pray before turning in for the night, dry his back when he came out of the shower, give him a rubdown after a particularly exhausting bike ride. It hadn't been that difficult to resist. Boxer wasn't his ideal: too tiny, too effeminate, but most of all, he didn't want Boxer to go back to Atlanta feeling guilty about cheating on his partner.

But that had been in California. That was in the past. Tonight he was in Greenfield, in Marc's house. Marc had just said, "Love you." The words made him feel warm and safe inside, but scared too.

Chapter 21

Friday after work Marc picked up a roast chicken from Safeway, and from the freezer section French fries, green peas and a Sara Lee cake so they could eat in. After washing up the dishes, they set out for the model railway show in the Greenfield arena.

Howard paid the admission for both of them. The arena was crowded with families. Marc wished they'd come before dinner when there might have been fewer people around.

Howard strode over to the first table and dove into a serious discussion with a bookseller about the year Canadian National adopted its green-black-gold passenger train colour scheme. Later they were watching the Greenfield Valley Model Railway club's layout when Marc glanced over to the other side and saw Bill Fuches, the sixth grade teacher. Marc waved. Bill barely nodded, blushed, then turned away and disappeared into the crowd.

After an hour Howard said he needed a drink so they headed for the concession. It was a relief to get off the hard cement floor and to put some space between themselves and the crowd. They had barely sat down with their drinks when Dr. Beale came into the snack bar with her twins and husband. Marc hadn't seen her since that awful night in her medical office when he'd had to milk his oozing dick for her. She headed straight for their table, smiled and stuck out her hand. Marc shook it, then introduced Howard to the family. While he made small talk with her and the twins, John Beale and Howard discussed railway stuff.

"I'd like to get one of those caps you're wearing," Howard said to John who was sporting a baseball cap emblazoned with The Milwaukee Road's orange wafer.

"The hobby shop from Fargo's selling them," John said. "Their booth is over there." He pointed to a far corner of the arena. "The caps are in a box under the table, but if you want one you'd better hurry. There were only a few left."

"I'm going to run and grab one while I can," Howard said. "I'll be right back."

Marc visited a few more minutes with the Beales. When they got up to leave Dr. Beale asked, "Is Howard your partner?"

"I wish," Marc said. "He's getting married in September—to a woman!"

"Too bad. You two look great together, and I can tell by the way you look at him that you love him." She patted his shoulder. "Good night, and I hope you find someone soon."

Marc finished his Coke, then flipped through a book about CN locomotives Howard had bought. After ten minutes he began to get worried. Had Howard had a disagreement with the guy selling the hats, gotten tense, thrown up all over someone's train set? Or had he collapsed and been carried off to the first aid station, or whisked away in an ambulance without his knowing? Panic tightened its grip on him as the minutes ticked by.

He finally set off in the direction Howard had disappeared. As he excused his way through the crush of people a man laughed beside him, spewing forth a stream of half-chewed hot dog that made him wretch. A child screamed. A woman scolded her children. The lights seemed to flicker, casting a sickening green miasma over the crowd. Marc shook his head. He was starting to see black dots wherever he looked—on the light blue jacket of the man in front of him, on a display of railway posters, on the giant logo for the Greenfield Grits hockey team hanging on the distant wall. A kid riding on his dad's shoulders blew a wooden steam train whistle in his ear and laughed.

Marc grabbed onto the edge of a table displaying used books, took one up and began leafing through it, seeing nothing, praying that equilibrium would return, that Howard would appear, and at that moment a hand came down on his shoulder. "Here you are."

"Howard, thank God you've come."

"I've been looking all over for you. Why did you leave the snack bar?"

"I didn't know where you were. I thought maybe you'd left."

"Without you? How could I? You drove us here. You've got the keys."

"I know, but I thought maybe you'd met someone and—"

"You're trembling, Marc." Howard put a hand on his shoulder. "Are you all right?"

"I'm okay now that you're here, but crowds make me nervous."

"What's to worry about?"

"Fire! What if there was a fire like when I was a wee kid?"

"What happened?"

"It was at our church's Christmas concert. It was always held in the church gym where tables were set up and decorated with pine boughs and candles. I was in the Kindergarten class. We'd just gone up front to say a recitation when someone brushed against a table. The paper tablecloth, pine branches and candle tumbled onto the floor and exploded into flames."

"That would be frightening. Did everyone get out?"

"Dad ran forward and lifted me off the stage and grabbed my brother Claude. Mom had our coats but we couldn't get out because everyone was stampeding towards the doorway. Our catechism teacher was standing right in front of it, jumping up and down in her black and white habit and screaming, 'Oh sacred Mother of God, have mercy on us.'

"Finally someone slapped her on the face and pushed her out the door. Otherwise we'd probably all have been overcome with smoke."

"The place burned down?"

"No. Dad and some of the other men filled their coats with snow and ran back inside. I remember being terrified he'd be burned alive, but I guess the fire wasn't all that big. They put it out. Since then I'm always nervous in a crowd."

"How do you manage at school, all those kids yelling and running about?"

"That's different. I'm in charge."

"Come along. The exit's over here. We'll head out before everyone makes for the parking lot at the same time."

It was just after nine when they got home. Howard sat down at the kitchen table while Marc poured milk into a saucepan and set it on the stove to heat. Then he sat down across from Howard.

"Your hands are still trembling," Howard said.

"Still coming down from my panic attack in the arena. I was sure you'd ditched me."

"Why would I do that?" Howard reached across the table and cupped his hands on top of Marc's.

"It happened to me once in Key West. Richie was this other teacher. We were boyfriends, sort of. We'd been dating for a few weeks and had gone to Key West for Christmas break. We stayed in a crummy little hacienda, at least that's what the owner called it, but it was more like a fleabag hut. New Year's Eve we walked into town to join the other revellers. We had a few drinks at the Bourbon Street Pub, then checked out another bar.

"Richie took off to the restroom while I finished my drink. When he didn't return after fifteen minutes I went looking for him. He wasn't in the restroom, or outside on the patio, or out front on the street. I wandered around the bar for about an hour, getting more and more scared.

"I imagined all sorts of things. Maybe he'd been attacked in the restroom, his wallet stolen, his body bundled into a car and dumped off a dock. Finally I made my way back to the hacienda. On the table lay a note scribbled on the back of Richie's airline boarding pass. *Met someone Hot-Hot-HOT! See you at the airport in two days.*"

"That's awful. I don't suppose you dated him again."

"You got that right, and that's been the story of my life."

"What do you mean?"

"Last night when you said my love life hasn't been such a success, you were right. It's been a complete failure. How about your love life? Did you try dating guys and give up on men? Is that why you're engaged to Maxine?"

"I haven't been with a guy since you."

"You're putting me on."

Howard shook his head.

"That's incredible, but tell me one thing. Were you gay back then, or were you just faking it when you and I snuggled in bed?"

"I wasn't faking it. I did love you." Marc winced at the *did*.

"So what brought about the change? You said it was guilt that kept us from being together, and I guess I can understand that, considering what you hear at that church you attend, but what makes you think you'll be satisfied with a woman?"

Howard shifted on his chair again, laced his fingers together, unlaced them and crossed his arms. Marc got up to make the hot chocolate. "I'm not trying to make you uncomfortable, Howard. I need to know that you're going to be happy with Maxine."

"I might as well tell you."

"Tell me what?" Marc handed him his mug and sat down again.

"I never went to Africa. Well, I did go."

"I don't understand. You went to Africa, but you didn't go? And what's Africa got to do with you marrying Maxine?"

"I did go to Africa, but not on a mission trip. I went to an engineering conference in Cape Town, for one week. I didn't want to show you my pictures because there really aren't any except the usual touristy things in Cape Town."

"So where were you last year?"

"I was in California. The tabernacle has a ministry there."

"A ministry?"

"A ministry that changes gay people to straight."

"You mean one of those places where they attach electrodes to your dick and show you pictures of naked men, then zap you within an inch of your life?"

"Nothing like that. It's called the *Tingley Inversion Therapy Center* or T-I-T-C. We guys called it Titzy. I read about the Center in the Tabernacle Times. I thought it was worth a try, that maybe I'd be able to find happiness with a woman, have a family even. I'm not too old for that. Lots of guys are having kids when they're my age, even older."

"So you spent a year at this TITC place." Howard nodded and leaned back in his chair. "How'd you get the time off work?"

"Jim Bronnel, the firm's owner, he's a Tabber. He gave me a sabbatical."

"So he knows you're gay?" Howard nodded. "How much money did this TITC place extract from you for the cure?"

"Three thousand a month."

"That's thirty-six big ones for the year. You engineers must do very well for yourselves."

"My parents, and the tabernacle helped."

"So let me get this straight. Your employer gave you time off, the tabernacle and your parents paid part of the fee, and now you're going to marry the priest's daughter."

"Apostle. Tabbers don't have priests. Maxine's father is Apostle Farida."

"Whatever. I'm just tallying up all the people who seem to be involved in this cure of yours."

"People are very kind."

"Hmm, guess that's one way of looking at it, but I'm wondering where that leaves you in this plan to marry Maxine. You must be feeling quite a bit of pressure to marry, to prove that you're straight."

"It's what I want to do."

"What did they do to you at TITC to make you straight?"

"A lot of different things. Prayer, Bible study."

"But you've been doing those things all your life. I remember you sitting up in bed every morning in the dorm reading your Bible, and you always prayed before your meals, so there must have been more than that. What else did they do to *repair* you?"

"They taught us how to fix cars, change tires, spark plugs, flush the rad, replace light bulbs, that sort of thing."

"But you did all those things on the farm when you were growing up. I remember you taking me out to the shed on your ranch where you were helping your dad tear down a tractor."

"I know."

Marc didn't want to cause another barf session, but he couldn't keep his mouth shut about such nonsense. "If changing spark plugs on the farm didn't make you straight, how could it have that effect in California? Is there something special about California spark plugs?"

"There were other things. We played baseball and soccer and went hiking in the mountains. Learned little things too, some of them kind of stupid."

"Like?"

"We learned how to change in the locker room, how to drop our sweaty clothes on the floor or stuff them into our gym bags wet and creased like straight guys do."

"Well my dear man, I've got news for you. You failed that course because when I was staying with you in Winnipeg I saw you fold your clothes before you put them into your laundry hamper. Maybe you flunked the whole program."

"We learned how to act around girls, went to dances with—"

"Hold on there. I thought you Tabbers didn't dance."

"We don't, so they weren't really dances, more like marches. They played music like *Onward Christian Soldiers* and we marched around the gym holding hands with the girls."

"And because of that you now have an eye for the ladies? Walking down the street you find it hard to keep your eyes off their tits, or whatever it is straight men get off on? You get hard just thinking about what's couched between their legs? Can you look at me and tell me you can't wait to get Maxine into bed?"

Howard's head came up and he actually looked Marc in the eye. "No, I can't say that, but so what? At least I'll have a companion. We'll probably be as happy as any couple. One thing they taught me down there is that no one can completely satisfy another person. No marriage is perfect, but at least I won't have to come home to an empty apartment every night. Haven't you ever been lonely?"

"I've been lonely ever since that night in the dorm when you ditched me, but at least I know that a woman can never come close to satisfying me physically or emotionally."

"I know Maxine won't be everything to me. No wife can be, and I know she's a bit pushy."

"A bit?"

"But she's decent."

"I wish you'd quit using that word to describe her. It's like you're describing a budget motel or restaurant, decent and clean."

"At least with Maxine I won't have guilt gnawing at my insides all the time, like when you and me were together."

Marc nodded. What could he say to that? It would take more than words to chip away at the core of guilt the Tabbers had instilled inside Howard. "I guess it's time we hit the sack," Marc said, getting up and going over to the sink. "Hope you're not sore at me for quizzing you like this." He put an arm around Howard's shoulder as he came to rinse out his mug.

"Marc, I understand where you're coming from. I know you mean well, but I have to do what I know is right."

"Yes you do. I just wish it could be different. Please know that I love you and I'm always here if you want to talk—before your marriage—or after."

"Thanks, Marc. I hope we'll always be friends."

Chapter 22

Howard lay on his back. He flipped onto his left side. He tried his right side. He thought about what Marc had said about those who had a stake in his marriage to Maxine. *Lord, don't let me do the wrong thing,* he prayed. *I've done everything you've told me to do. I've read my Bible. I've prayed. I've taken counsel from Apostle Farida. I've gone through the program at TITC. You've got to make my marriage work. If I'm not supposed to marry Maxine, then tell me. Speak to me like you did to Abraham, to Moses, to Brother Tingley.*

There was a knock on his door. "Howard?"

It was Marc. "What is it?"

"You're not sleeping yet?"

"No."

"Can I come in?" Without waiting for a reply Marc walked in, lifted the covers, and slid into bed beside Howard.

"Hold on, Marc. What are you doing?"

"Can I hold you for a few minutes, just in case it's the last time we're together like this?"

"I don't think Maxine would—"

"Never mind Maxine. I promise not to molest you. I want to snuggle one last time. Can you handle that?" Marc flipped onto his side and laid his head on Howard's chest. Howard lay still for a few moments, thinking Marc would leave when he didn't respond. But he didn't. Finally Howard lifted his arm and brought it down around Marc's shoulders.

"Thank you. I've missed this," Marc said. "It feels so good to have you hold me, to hear your heart beating, to feel my skin against yours. Let's pretend for a few minutes that we've always been together, that we're buddies, partners, husband and husband."

Howard chuckled. "Husband and husband? That is weird Marc, totally weird, but I suppose that's what they pronounce at the end of a gay wedding. I've never been to one. Have you?"

"I've been to several. Sometimes the minister pronounces them husbands for life, other times partners for life, lovers for life."

They lay without speaking for several minutes, snuggling deeper into each other's skin. Howard spoke first. "I spilled my big secret about going to TITC. Now tell me what your life's really been like."

"What it's really been like? I could say I lived the high life in Vancouver, boyfriends stashed in every closet, but if you believe that I've got a few rusty old ships to sell you."

"You never found anyone permanent?"

"At first I didn't want to get involved with anyone. I thought you'd change your mind. I wrote to you care of your parents and when you didn't answer I sent a letter to you at Bronnel. Did you get my letters?"

"Yes. In fact, I still have them. Over the years I'd get them out and reread them."

"Why didn't you write to me then?"

"I wanted to."

"But you didn't."

"I was afraid I'd mess up our lives again."

"How so?"

"The guilt thing. I figured we might get back together. Then I'd start feeling guilty again and want to break it off. I didn't want to hurt you twice."

"I rushed home from work every day to check the mailbox for a letter, and then the phone for a message, but there was nothing. You know what I used to do Friday nights?"

Howard shook his head.

"This is going to sound so stupid, so pitiful, but I used to drive out to the big Canadian Tire store and sit in the parking lot, watching the guys going in and out."

"You hung out at Canadian Tire?"

"Yeah. I know it sounds dumb, but that's where I thought macho guys like you hung out, so I used to park there until closing time."

"You picked guys up there?"

"Oh yeah. I'd sidle up to some greasy hunk fingering high performance spark plugs and suggest he come to my place to find out what real high performance was all about."

"Really? You used that line?"

"Course not. I'd park near the entrance and think about you. Sometimes I'd go in to buy a package of gum, a drink, wander around the hardware section, check out the latest tools, dream of having a place of my own with a garage so I could restore an old beater. Then I'd head back to my car. Sometimes I'd see a guy who reminded me of you and that was so fuckin' painful. Why'd you flinch just now?"

"Your language."

"Oh sorry. You Tabbers don't use four letter words. You know, I always liked that about you, that you didn't talk filth. I admired you for that. Still do. Oh damn it, there's your phone again. Where is it?"

"In my pants pocket."

Marc hopped out of bed and searched it out. "Here. Maxine I suppose. What's she doing calling you at this hour?"

"Probably been working late."

Marc made a sour face, then went across the hall to the bathroom, slamming the door behind him.

"Did I hear a door closing?" Maxine asked.

"Kind of a noisy place, this motel. Thin walls. How was your day?"

Howard stifled a yawn as she talked about her day. When Marc came back from the bathroom he sat on the edge of the bed. He brushed his fingers lightly through the hair on Howard's chest and belly. Howard yanked the sheets up and swatted his hand.

"Is Jim Bronnel with you?" Maxine asked. "Have I called you at a bad time?"

"No, I'm alone, but I'd better get to sleep. I've had a long day. I looked at a lot of offices. Several look promising…Okay, you have a good night too…Yes, I'll see you Saturday for lunch…our usual place…Good night."

Marc took the phone and dropped it back into Howard's pocket, then slid back into bed. "Does Maxine know you're staying with me?"

"No."

"Why not?"

"She'd be upset. I told her I was staying in a motel."

"What's happened to Howard, the good Tabber boy, who would never tell a lie? First the story about Africa, and now you're hiding the fact that you're staying with me. Is this escape from the truth something new?"

"I hate lying, but sometimes it's easier than trying to explain things to people who won't understand."

"Maxine wouldn't understand you coming to stay with me?"

"Probably not. She tends to see plots, probably because of her job at city hall where the politicians are always plotting strategy against each other."

"I hope you won't lie to me anymore."

"This is no lie, Marc. After we graduated I really wanted to stay in touch with you. I even drove past your apartment building one time."

"When? Where?"

"In New Westminster."

"You were right outside my building but you didn't phone?"

"I came to an engineering conference on the coast. I looked you up in the telephone directory to see if you still had the same number you'd given me in those letters you sent."

"And you drove past my place?"

"I rented a car and searched out your building, a concrete high-rise on Agnes Street."

"That's right. So, you drove right past my front door, but didn't come in?"

"I know it sounds as dumb as sitting in the parking lot at Canadian Tire, but I figured you'd be angry with me, wouldn't want to see me, or you'd have a husband as you put it a few minutes ago."

"I would have been thrilled to see you, even for a few minutes."

"Did you never have a husband, as you put it?"

"I could entertain you for hours describing all the guys I tried to connect with. The one time I got really close to a good and *decent* man, to use your word, he died when a gravel truck wiped him out."

"I'm sorry."

"Well, that's in the past. I'm here. You're here. Let's just snuggle and get some sleep. Will you hold me, like you used to do in the dorm?"

Marc turned onto his side, facing away from Howard. "Please Howard, just one more time. Hold me like you used to do in the dorm?"

"Okay, but only if you promise no funny stuff."

"I promise, no funny stuff. I just want to sleep with you one last time."

Howard flipped onto his side, put his arm around Marc's chest, and pulled him close, but even as he did so he felt the guilt snaking its ugly tentacles around his heart. What would Maxine think if she could see him now, or her father, or Brother Tingley?

Chapter 23

Monday evening Marc arrived home late from school and the gym. Actually, he was late because he'd spent two hours patrolling the trails in Riverside Park. The hours had been wasted because he hadn't connected with anyone.

He picked up some KFC on the way home, and after gnawing it down in front of the tube he crawled into bed, depressed and lonely. Snuggling with Howard had felt so good, so right. He'd kept his word—no funny business—yet he'd noticed that Howard had avoided looking him in the eyes during breakfast. Obviously guilt still had him by the balls.

Tuesday morning a message was waiting for him.

Hey Marc. Thanks for your hospitality. Sorry I threw up over your new bathroom. What a terrible baptism for it! I'm glad we had our talk. I'm going to stop lying. I told Maxine everything, how I stayed with you. She's glad I came clean. She says hello. Keep in touch. Howard.

Marc wasn't sure he liked the idea of Howard telling Maxine everything, but telling the truth would be most commendable, especially if he'd quit lying to himself about his affectional orientation.

In mid-June the Department of Education offered another workshop in Winnipeg for French teachers. Howard invited him to come Saturday afternoon, attend an outdoor concert at The Forks in the evening, and go hiking on Sunday, before the Monday workshop.

When Marc arrived at Howard's just before dinner on Saturday evening, Maxine was removing her casserole from the oven. This one was a gluey macaroni and cheese thing garnished with flaccid branches of broccoli and bright pink slivers of ham.

"Marc, I'm so glad everything is now out in the open between us three," Maxine said after the prayer had been concluded. "As Howard has shared with you, I supported him going to California for sexual inversion therapy, and I praise God for the miracle that occurred there."

"Has he told you how they tried to turn him straight?"

"Howard has shared absolutely everything with me."

"But Maxine, you're an educated woman. You have major responsibilities at city hall. Don't you find it curious that things as simple as learning how to change spark plugs or dropping your gym clothes in a pile on the floor are able to change the bent of your affections?"

"I think we're all more complex than the medical profession has yet discovered," she said, "but that doesn't mean that some little thing like concentrating on manly ways might not have an overall effect. I'm sure you've heard of people using herbal tinctures to cure cancer and heart disease."

"But Maxine, say you started to wear leather and learned to change spark plugs on a Harley Davidson, would that turn you into a lesbian, into a dyke on a bike as they're sometimes called?"

"Oh Marc, what a preposterous idea! Imagine me on one of those greasy things, but I'm sure I could adopt that lifestyle if I wanted to, and there you have the most important factor. You see, Howard wanted to change, didn't you, Howie Honey?"

"I really don't want to discuss it," Howard said. "I'm just pleased that I now have someone to attend concerts with, go on hikes, that sort of thing." He reached out and patted Maxine's hand, the first time Marc had seen him do that.

"I don't believe anything can change affectional orientation," Marc said. "I've heard the Mormons tried using electricity to shock it out of the system, but it didn't work. It may have turned guys off the physical act of sex, but it didn't change their attraction to other men."

"But Howard told me how you crawled into bed with him a few weeks ago when he was staying at your place—and absolutely nothing happened."

"Howard, you told her that?"

"I want everything to be out in the open between Maxine and me. No more secrets."

"And don't you be upset that he told me." Maxine wagged a finger at Marc. "Howie and I are building our relationship on complete honesty. I understand you snuggled together all night and didn't have sexual intercourse."

"Howard, you really did tell her everything!"

"He did." Maxine patted his hand. "And if Howard was able to resist touching you inappropriately, what more proof do you need that he's changed? Praise God and the TITC ministry." She patted his hand again, then ripped a slice of bread in half to mop the cooling scab of cheese off her plate.

"I just want to live a normal, peaceful life," Howard said, laying his fork down on his empty plate and looking at his watch. "And now we'd better stop the talk and get away to The Forks. The orchestra will be playing one of the Brandenburgs and I don't want to miss that. It should be a magical evening."

Marc remembered exploring The Forks where the Assiniboine River meets the muddy Red when Howard and he were in university. Then it had been a derelict Canadian National Railway yard, lined with abandoned warehouses and weed-choked storage tracks stocked with surplus passenger cars. Now the warehouses had been transformed into a public market, and the riverbank had been landscaped with grassy terraces leading down to the point where the two rivers met.

A small string orchestra was seated on a stage cantilevered over the river, with the audience seated on the terraces. Water taxis zipped up and down the rivers, unloading concert-goers. Maxine spread a blanket on the ground and sat down. Howard sat beside her. Marc sat on his other side.

All classical music sounded about the same to Marc—a string of notes spilling out of the instruments in a predictable fast – slow – fast pattern. He preferred country, John Berry singing *If I Had Any Pride Left At All*, accompanied by his inimitable brand of squinting and squeezing out of tears. Howard was really into the classical genre, leaning forward, nodding and tapping his fingers in time to the music.

A couple of guys with a cocker spaniel settled themselves one terrace down. They spread out their Snoopy blanket, then sat down, their shoulders touching, their hands meeting as they stroked their doggie.

Maxine clucked her tongue, leaned forward to look past Howard at Marc. "See that? Bold as brass. What a horrid public spectacle. Now, you can't tell me that's what you want."

"That's exactly what I want," Marc said. "I think it's beautiful to see two guys so in love with each other."

"Well then, Marc, all I can say is that Howard and I will pray for you, won't we, Howie Honey."

"Hush. They're starting the Brandenburg," Howard said.

The musicians were leaning into their instruments and sawing away like their lives depended upon it. Both he and Howard were leaning back on their hands. Howard's hand was just inches from his. If Marc stretched out his little finger he could caress the back of Howard's hand. Did he dare?

Keeping his eyes on the orchestra Marc lifted his finger, reached over and stroked the edge of Howard's hand, a touch as light as the wings of a moth fluttering by in the evening air. There was no reaction. Marc stroked again, applying a little more pressure. Still no reaction. Okay, be stubborn in your determination to be straight, Marc thought, sitting forward with his hands in his lap.

As the sun set behind the cliff of high rise apartment buildings to the west, a cool breeze wafted off the water, mixing its clammy breath with the smell of buttered popcorn and hot dogs. The gay couple on the terrace below wrapped their arms around each other in a warm, but perfectly respectable embrace.

As night fell in earnest, the conductor raised his baton for the last number. The players leaned into the music, and from across the river a rocket shot into the night sky, raining a shower of pink and green stars over The Forks. Others followed in quick succession but Marc couldn't concentrate on the music, or the fireworks. A moth was fluttering at the edge of his hand, and then it interlaced its fingers with his. He smiled, and in the dark snugged his shoulder against Howard's. Finally the night had taken on a magical quality for him too.

The concert over, they strolled up Broadway to Howard's apartment, Maxine on Howard's left side, Marc on his right, the two men occasionally brushing hands as they walked. Back at the apartment Maxine collected her casserole dish and kissed Howard on the cheek. Marc noticed that he didn't kiss back, just sort of snuggled his cheek against hers like he might do when bidding his grandmother good-bye. He had been a good kisser when they'd made love to each other in the dorm, not like some of the guys Marc had met on the coast who were afraid to open their mouths in case romance flew in.

"Now, you men behave yourselves," Maxine said as she shook Marc's hand. "I trust you completely, Howie Honey. I know God will direct your ways, and your ways too, Marc."

"And how is God going to direct our ways tonight?" Marc asked when the door closed behind Maxine.

"How do you mean?"

"Do you want to snuggle?"

"No. We'd better not. I'd have to tell Maxine."

"That sounds like if you didn't have to tell Maxine you'd not be averse to a bit of skin to skin."

"I know we snuggled at your place, Marc, and I enjoyed that. I even enjoyed holding your hand tonight, but even as we were doing it I felt guilty. I knew it was wrong, so I've got to say no to snuggling. I'll get your pillows from the bedroom. The futon has clean sheets on it.

You have a good night now. Take a shower if you like. The green towels are yours."

Chapter 24

Howard didn't sleep well that Saturday night. He was worried about Sunday morning, about what Marc would think of the tabernacle service. They were cleaning up the kitchen after breakfast when Marc asked, "Which trail are we hiking this morning?"

"Uh, I thought maybe you'd like to come to tabernacle with me."

"I thought we were going hiking."

"Well, not right away. Maxine's coming to pick us up. She'll drive us to tabernacle."

"I haven't been to a Sunday mass since that day when the priest consigned my brother Claude to hellfire, but so long as there won't be any talk like that, I guess I can go. Do I have to dress up for this tabernacle of yours?"

"Most people do."

"I didn't bring a tie."

"I'll lend you one."

As they dressed Howard saw Marc was having trouble. "You forget how to tie a Windsor knot?"

"Yes. I always have to look it up online."

"Here, give it to me." Howard reached for the tie, turned Marc to face the bathroom mirror, and put his arms around him. "Watch me."

"I am watching you, and feeling your heat. You feel pretty good to me. Oh Howard, why—"

"Now Marc." Howard quickly finished knotting the tie, then stepped back. He patted Marc on the shoulders. "Let's not do anything we'll regret."

"You think you'd regret marrying me?" The phone jangled twice.

"Saved by the bell. That'll be Maxine downstairs. We'd better get going. She doesn't like to be kept waiting."

Marc didn't say anything, but Howard could see, by the way he kept fiddling with the tie, that he was nervous about going to tabernacle. It didn't help that when they walked in people were standing in clutches, whispering to each other, as though Tabbers were part of some secret society.

Howard was relieved when Maxine took over, introduced Marc to her mother who was at the welcome table, then took him into the office to meet her father. "Ah, the famous Marc LaChance," he said. "You're Howard's friend, and Maxine's. We've all been praying for you."

"I suppose that's good," Marc said.

"Conversing with God is always good," Apostle Farida said. "We're so happy that you've come to worship with us this morning."

Maxine lead them into the sanctuary, where she pointed out the large green leaf suspended over the pulpit. "It's a representation of the one Brother Tingley brought back from the tree of life in heaven," she whispered.

"And the stained glass windows are copies of those in the mother tabernacle in Beeverville," Howard said, hoping Marc wouldn't examine the dusty leaf too closely.

Once they were seated, an elderly man hobbled across the aisle to shake their hands. He waved the paper with the order of service in their faces. "Have you seen this?" he asked, pointing to the announcements section.

"Oh praise God! There's going to be a de-baptism this afternoon," Maxine said. "And isn't it about time! Brownie and Bertie Phyllson have been bringing disgrace upon the tabernacle long enough."

"Did she say de-baptism?" Marc asked Howard.

"Yes. It's when someone shuns all correction," explained Howard. "Brownie and Bertie have been involved in drugs for quite some time now, not just using them, but selling them to schoolchildren."

"We'll absolutely have to go to the de-baptism this afternoon," Maxine said when the man had hobbled back to his pew.

"But we promised Marc a hike," Howard said. He didn't like the idea of a de-baptism. That was all Marc needed to witness to decide Tabbers were complete nut bars.

"We can do both," Maxine said. "The de-baptism is being held in Bird's Hill Park. We can go to it, then hike some of the nearby trails."

"I don't know."

"Look Howie Honey," Maxine said, laying a hand on his arm. "It'll be good for Marc to see what would happen to you if you hadn't gone to that change ministry in California."

Chapter 25

After another of Maxine's vile casseroles for lunch, they drove up Highway 59 to Bird's Hill Park. As they turned in at the gate, Marc remembered the good times when Howard and he had hiked and cross-country skied there. This time they parked at the main beach.

"You don't have to come if you don't want to," Howard said as they got out of the car.

"Now, Howie Honey, don't you be tempting Marc to stay behind. He needs to witness this."

"But maybe he doesn't want to see a de-baptism."

"It sounds very strange," Marc said, "but I am curious."

"There! See!" Maxine glared at Howard. "Come along. We need to hurry if we're to see the whole thing." She took Howard's hand and led him to the edge of the parking lot.

Marc found the scene surreal: scores of people in their Sunday best, the ladies in flowered dresses, the men in black suits, white shirts and ties, all marching up the hillside. Their silent purposefulness was a dramatic contrast to the shouts and laughter of the children splashing in the water down at the beach.

"Don't you need water for a baptism?" Marc asked.

"Yes," Howard said. "Baptism is a washing away of sins. A de-baptism is confirming that people have decided to go on with their sinful ways."

"So what's going to happen?"

By this time, Maxine, in her spike heels, had fallen behind. Even so, Howard lowered his voice. "I wish you didn't have to see this. I think it's cruel. There's nothing in the Bible about de-baptizing people."

"Where are these two druggies, Brownie and Bertie?" Marc asked, scanning the line of Tabbers.

"I don't think they'll come," Howard said. "People don't usually show up to be de-baptized."

"How does it work then?"

"Just wait. You'll see."

As they topped the hill an apostle handed them each two small cloth bags. "Bean bags? Are we going to play some sort of game before the ceremony?" Marc asked, juggling his bags.

"These are for the de-baptism. They're filled with gravel, sand, dirt."

"For what purpose?"

"We're going to stone Brownie and Bertie."

"What?"

"They're as good as dead already, dead in their trespasses and sins," Maxine said, catching up to them.

"I'm certainly not going to stone anyone," Marc said. "I may be a pagan, as you seem to think, but I do remember the stories from Sunday school. Jesus told a bunch of pompous church people that only those who had never sinned should throw stones. You guys aren't going to throw any, are you?"

"You shouldn't have those," Maxine said, pointing to Marc's bags. "Only baptized Tabbers can take part in a stoning."

"You can have mine then," Marc said. "I wouldn't have used them anyways."

"It's only the men who throw stones. I'll give them back to the apostle."

"Is that right, Howard, only the men are allowed to throw stones?"

"Tabbers are kind of old fashioned." Howard was looking rather green and sweating, as though he might lose his lunch, which considering its glutinous quality, wasn't such a bad idea.

Apostle Farida directed the men to stand in a circle. "How can they stone someone if they're not here?" Marc asked, feeling like a second grader asking so many questions.

Howard pointed to a stout lady in a blue dress, her slip showing beneath the hem. "That's Althea Phyllson, the boys' mother. She'll have some of their clothing in that Wal-Mart bag she's clutching."

"Clothing?"

"Yes," said Maxine. "If people don't show up for their de-baptism a relative brings an article of their clothing. See, she's handing something to my father. Two measly shirts. Most people would bring a whole outfit, spread it out on the ground like the person was lying there, but the Phyllsons always were lax in their spiritual practice, even before that dead-beat husband of hers was killed jay walking across Portage and Main."

"This is barbaric," Marc said. "The kids are half-way to being orphans and now the whole congregation is going to stone them?"

"Their mother asked my father to hold the ceremony," Maxine said.

"Why would a mother do such a thing?"

"She hopes they'll wake up, realize the seriousness of their actions, get scared and come back to the tabernacle."

"Howard, you're not taking part, are you?" Marc took a step back from his friend, leery of receiving a shower of half-digested lunch.

"I'd rather not—"

"Good. Then come with me. We'll go back to the car and wait for you there, Maxine." Marc reached a hand toward Howard's shoulder.

"Oh no you don't. Every baptized male *has* to take part," Maxine said. "It has to be acted out by the whole congregation. You absolutely must stay and watch, Marc. You'll see what Howie's parents would have gone through if he'd stuck with you."

"You mean they'd have stoned you for loving me?" Marc put an arm around Howard's shoulder.

Howard nodded, took a step back. "It's done for shock value. Like Maxine says, the shock of being stoned may bring them back to the tabernacle."

"More likely they'll never set foot in church again," Marc said.

Apostle Farida moved to the centre of the circle. "Althea Phyllson, do you swear before God that these garments, stained in sin, belong to your sons Brownie and Bertie?" He held aloft two shirts, one white with blue pinstripes, frayed at the cuffs and stained with grease, the other a lemon yellow with pale red stains that could be tomato sauce or blood. Mrs. Phyllson nodded, moved her lips soundlessly, and dabbed at her eyes with a paper tissue.

"I, Apostle Most Holy Franklin Somerset Farida, do hereby declare before God and before the assemblymen hereby convened, that I have fulfilled my duty in advising Bertie and Brownie Phyllson, members of the Winnipeg Tabernacle of Believers Assembly, of their sins most grievous. Despite the shame of having their sins made public, they have refused to make confession to the most holy assembly, and therefore I have the solemn duty of conducting this sad rite.

"Brownie Phyllson, I now cast thy immortal soul into the hellfire that burneth without end. May the finality of this sentence bring thee to thy senses. May thou plead with God for mercy. Peradventure thou repentest not, thy soul shall writhe in agony throughout eternity amidst the flames prepared for the devil and his angels." He threw down the shirt with the blue pinstripes and stamped upon it.

When he had finished pronouncing the same curse on Bertie, and flung his shirt down, he removed from his pocket the two dirt bags, took a step backward, raised the bags over his head, and shouted, "He that hath a clean heart, let him cast the first stone."

Apparently he had a clean heart for he hurled one bag at each shirt, shouting, "To hell with sinners!" Then he stepped aside and shouted, "Let the women sing! Let the assemblymen speak!"

Marc watched in horror as each man left the circle, cursed the two boys, and covered their shirts with heaps of dirt bags. All the while, the women droned something about being lost in sin. When it came Howard's turn he hesitated, but Maxine pushed him forward. "Howie Honey, if you don't take part, people will think you don't have a clean heart." He nodded and walked to the centre of the circle. Marc was heartened to see that he dropped, more than hurled, his bags onto the heaps, and his condemnation was more a whimper than a shout.

"What will they do with the shirts?" Marc asked as they returned to the car.

"My father will take them home and burn them," Maxine said.

"I think that's a totally wicked ceremony," Marc said. "If they're drug dealers, then they are doing something evil, but I don't see how throwing rocks at them, even in effigy, will help them to reform. What you're telling them is that if they don't love God he'll burn them forever and ever. That's a totally evil and dishonest representation of a God who is love. It's just as bad as when Father Dann sent my brother Claude to hell for jumping off the bridge. Imagine what their mother must be feeling. Surely there must be a better way to help them change their ways."

Marc looked around. Howard was lagging behind them. "Howard, are you okay?"

"Of course he's not okay," Maxine said, falling back to take him by the hand. "He's just seen what would have happened to him if he'd given in to his unnatural desires. I thank God that he found healing in California."

Howard smiled weakly but kept his eyes on the ground. "Come on, Howie Honey. Let's change and head out for that hike. Which trail would you like to do?"

They retrieved their hiking shoes and clothes from the car and went into the washroom down by the lake to change, then hiked the Cedar Bog Trail. It had been Marc and Howard's favourite during university days. They had often driven up to the park to run through

177

the cedar bog after class, then showered together, and fallen onto the bed to massage each other in loving ways before falling asleep in each other's arms.

Back at Howard's apartment after the hike, Maxine insisted on staying to help wash the dishes. Then she sat down beside Howard on the couch, took his hand in hers, and described in boring detail the challenges facing her and the mayor at city hall in the coming week. When she suggested heating up the leftover casserole for dinner, Marc insisted on treating them to a restaurant meal.

When she finally left, she shook Marc's hand, and said, "You men be good for one more night, and the next time I see you Marc, will be at our wedding."

The moment she was out the door Howard said, "I'm sorry she stayed so long. I can see you're tired."

"She'll be staying a lot longer once you're married. Are you going to be able to live with all that?"

"All what?"

"With her constant chatter, her pushy ways, with her devotion to the tabernacle? I noticed you didn't exactly hurl those dirt bags at the boys this afternoon."

"It's a nasty rite, but under the circumstances I guess it was the right thing to do. Selling drugs to schoolchildren is a really nasty crime."

"I thought Christians were supposed to be like Jesus. He never stoned anyone, and if anyone had an excuse to throw rocks at all those big shots who were persecuting him, it was Jesus."

"I know it seems harsh, but who knows. Maybe the Phyllsons will come back."

Marc dropped the subject, then said, "I notice you never kiss Maxine, and you never take her hand. It's always she who does the touching. It's like you're not really into her at all."

"I'm not into all that kissy stuff."

"I remember differently."

"Marc, quit trying to split Maxine and me. We're getting married in another few weeks, end of story. I loved you once and we did things that no two men should ever do together. I'm not going back there. You'll have to give up any fantasy you have about us getting married, or whatever you're thinking. I don't know what you see in me anyways. I'm very ordinary, about as dull as last year's newspaper."

"I don't find you dull. We always did interesting things when we were rooming together. Remember the hikes, and skiing, and road trips, going to concerts and things. As for ordinary, yes, you are ordinary and that's what I like about you. You've been holding down the same job for twenty plus years. You earn enough to pay the rent and keep clothes on your back. You walk and talk like an ordinary guy. You know how to drive. You'd be surprised how many gay guys don't even have their driver's license. You're a good solid guy, and after all the disappointments I had on the coast, you're exactly what I want. And if that isn't enough, I find you hot to look at."

"Marc!"

"You are. I remember the first time you walked into the dorm room. If I was the delicate type I'd have fainted at the sight of you, a tall hunky guy with curly black hair and that thick paintbrush moustache. You know what you made me think of?"

"I'm afraid to ask."

"Those statues of Greek gods. As a kid I used to spend hours looking at them in the encyclopaedia at school, like Michelangelo's sculpture of David."

"David was not a Greek god."

"You know what I mean. Nice chest. Nice ass. Thick thighs. You were everything I wanted to be, and I fell totally in love with you."

"But that was over twenty years ago. Look at me now."

"Yes, just look at you. Hot salt and pepper hair. Bet you still use the same belt size as when we were rooming together. Any man in his right mind would be stupid not to find you hot."

"Listen Marc, I'm marrying Maxine. Now let's quit talking and get to bed—"

"I thought you'd never ask."

"You know what I mean. I'll get your pillows."

Chapter 26

Howard was relieved to have his apartment to himself when he got home from work on Monday evening. He had picked up a pizza and was looking forward to an evening alone. While eating he propped open a biography of Isambard Kingdom Brunel. He could remember reading an entry about the famous engineer in a schoolbook, and that had inspired him to follow in his footsteps.

Interesting as the biography was, Howard couldn't concentrate. His thoughts kept veering to Marc. His friend was as stubborn as their old dog Shep on the ranch when he'd grab a rat. He wouldn't stop shaking it until he'd broken its neck, and Marc wouldn't drop the issue of his marriage to Maxine until he broke his resolve to marry her. That wasn't going to happen. Marc was right that the program at TITC had not changed his basic nature. He still found men attractive, but TITC had taught him how to avoid looking at them as sex objects, how to avoid thinking impure thoughts.

"Let Jesus take your load," had been TITC's advice. "Jesus overcame every temptation, and he's eagerly waiting to clear your mind of impure thoughts if you'll just surrender your will to him."

Howard had been sceptical at first, but found that it worked. "Jesus, take these thoughts and deal with them. I'm too weak to resist," he now prayed, when tempted to run his eyes over some fellow, and miraculously, within seconds, he'd begin to think of other things. With Marc around, he'd had to pray those words constantly. Marc was getting a bit of a tummy and his copper hair was threaded with grey, just like his own, but he was still a smart looking guy and Howard did remember those nights in the dorm: snuggling, hugging, kissing, doing other things that felt good, but were so wicked. With Jesus' help he'd been able to resist Marc's invitations.

After dinner he settled on the couch to read some more about Brunel when the phone jangled twice. "Hi Howie. Can I come up? We need to go over some things about the wedding."

Howard buzzed Maxine in and marked the place in his book.

"I was heading home from seeing about my wedding dress," Maxine explained as she came in the door. "I looked up and saw your light was on. Figured I might as well come in and go over a few things with you."

They sat down in the lounge. She pulled a notebook out of her purse. "I've got a list and we need to go over it."

"I'm rather tired, after being up late with Marc, and—"

"He kept his hands off you, did he?"

"Nothing funny happened."

"I'm glad to hear it. You know, Howie Honey, he's your friend, so I don't like to say anything, but it's clear to me that he doesn't want us to get married. He's like all homosexuals, determined to ruin marriage, bring disaster to families. In our case, he wants to corrupt you, pull you back into that evil lifestyle."

"Marc means well."

"I disagree."

"Please, Maxine. I'm tired."

"Okay, we'll just go over a few things. First, we need to talk about what you're going to wear. Since I was married before, I can't wear white in the tabernacle. I've chosen a silvery material for my dress but you're a virgin. You can wear white."

"You're forgetting about Marc and me."

"Whatever you did with Marc at university doesn't count. Have you thought about what you want to wear?"

"I've been so busy at work that I haven't had time to think about it."

"You need to order your suit soon."

"I thought I might wear that tan coloured one I sometimes wear to tabernacle."

"You don't want a new suit for your wedding day?"

"Nothing wrong with what I've got."

"Well, suit yourself—ah, that's a pun—suit yourself about the suit, get it? But never mind. Now, about the reception. We absolutely must choose the caterer."

It was almost midnight when Maxine left. Howard was exhausted, but too uptight to sleep. Thinking about the wedding made him nervous. He was sure he wouldn't be able to eat so much as a slice of bread for a week before the big day, and nothing at all at the reception. He hated wedding receptions, the guest tapping their glasses with their spoons, urging the bride and groom to kiss. It was disgusting.

Sometimes he wished he'd stayed in the closet, never confided his struggles to Maxine, to Apostle Farida, to his parents. He wished he'd never gone to TITC. Life would have been so much simpler. He might be lonely, but his life would be his own. Now there were times when he wanted to run away, find a cabin in the woods, have nothing to do with Maxine, nothing to do with marriage, nothing to do with the tabernacle. He'd live the simple life with no men to tempt him to sin, no women to propose marriage, no family cheering him on.

Chapter 27

Marc got to school early so that he'd have time to sort out what the substitute had done while he was in Winnipeg. The lazy bum had left a stack of quiz papers to be corrected, so he attacked those first. It was a quarter to nine when he finished, and looking over the lessons for that day, he saw that he was going to teach colours to his fourth graders. He rushed down to the office, grabbed the key to the storage room, and hurried to the end of the hallway.

The storage room was a narrow dogleg tucked around the furnace room, so it was always hot as a sauna. He left the door open to let some air in while he went to the far corner to get some coloured construction paper. While counting out the sheets he heard approaching footsteps. He glanced around the corner. It was Bill Fuches.

"Hi Bill. Did you have a good weekend?" He'd been trying to be civil to Bill ever since learning that he lived with his invalid mother, apparently an old battle axe of a woman.

"I'm hot," Bill said.

"Yeah, this room's always warm, even when the furnace isn't running. Guess it's the water heaters for the gym's showers."

Bill shuffled toward him, hands in the pockets of his shapeless corduroy jeans. "That's not what I meant, Marc."

Marc was in the middle of a count so didn't respond.

"Did you hear what I said, Marc?" Bill was standing close enough that Marc could smell his foul tobacco breath.

"Yes Bill. I heard you say it's warm in here."

Without any warning Bill yanked his hands from his pockets, grabbed Marc around the neck, pulled him forward and planted his wet, tobacco stained lips over Marc's.

Marc dropped the stack of construction paper, yanked Bill's hands off his neck and lunged backwards, only to bang into the shelves behind him. "What the hell! Get your filthy hands off me!" He covered his mouth with his hand, ducked, and scurried down the narrow corridor between the shelves.

"Don't be upset, Marc. I'm hot for you. That's what I meant. Now how about a kiss? A nice big kiss for Billy?"

"Bill, you're sick." Marc spat onto his palm and wiped his lips again, then kept his eye on Bill as he stooped to gather up the sheets of coloured paper.

"Yeah, I'm love sick, Marc. You and me—"

"There is no you and me." Marc shoved Bill against the wall. "Don't you ever touch me again or I'll have your hide and your teaching license flapping from the flagpole."

"Don't know what you're getting so upset about, Marc. I'm just trying to be friendly, thought maybe we could be friends, like you and that big guy I saw you with at the model train show last fall." Bill followed him as he hurried out of the room.

"Bill, I mean it. Leave me alone."

"You married to that big guy?"

"What are you talking about?"

"I followed you guys. I saw how you were sitting in the snack bar. I saw how you looked at that guy, like you wanted to drill more than your eyes into him, if you get my drift." Bill showed off his tobacco stained teeth in a frightening leer.

"I definitely am not interested in your drift."

"Mr. Grant might be interested in my drift," he said, then turned, tipped his chin up like Marc had offended him, and marched down the hallway to his room, the leather patch on the right sleeve of his mousy, tweed jacket flapping.

Marc locked the storage room, and hurried to return the key to the office before the bell rang. Then he took up his position at the doorway into his classroom. "Are you nervous Monsieur LaChance?" asked one of the girls.

"Why are you asking me that?"

"Your hands are shaking, just like my grandma's."

Marc laughed it off, but put his hands behind his back while he greeted the rest of his students. Somehow he managed to get through the first lesson. Once he'd assigned some seat work, he hurried to the men's room where he filled his hands with soap and rubbed at his face and lips, trying to get rid of the smelly tobacco odour.

Tim Grant caught him coming out of the washroom as he was leaving. "Everything alright, Marc?"

"Yes. Just had to give my nose a good blow."

"Good. Good."

All morning Marc debated whether he should report Bill's attack. He finally decided to say nothing, though not because he was afraid of being outed. The staff, including Tim Grant, knew he was gay. The subject of affectional orientation had arisen earlier that spring when Orillia Wiggins, who taught fifth grade, announced her son was getting married. Everyone offered congratulations and then wanted to know who the lucky girl was.

"Well, it's not a girl," Orillia had said. "It's a fellow he met at university in Saskatoon where he's studying to be a vet. A very nice fellow. At one time I would have been disappointed, thinking I'd never have any grandchildren, but of course things are different these days, and they say they want children."

In the discussion that followed, Marc had come out. Most of them already assumed he was gay. "No man who's unmarried by the time he's forty can be straight," Orillia had said. The topic had been dropped as quickly as it had arisen. Bill, who rarely socialized with the staff, had probably been sulking in his classroom over some perceived slight. He'd missed the whole conversation.

At noon Marc hurried down the street to the drug store, purchased a bottle of Listerine, and rinsed his mouth several times. However, the reminder of Bill's slimy kiss wouldn't be washed away. As the afternoon wore on Marc felt an increasing sense of violation over Bill's smelly smooch, but somehow he made it to the end of the day.

He went straight to the gym, hoping the flood of endorphins would help erase the morning's horror, but if anything, they increased the sharp edge of revulsion he felt. How did people get over a rape, he wondered, if one vile kiss could cause him so much angst? No wonder people needed months, even years of therapy, to recover.

Lying in bed later that night, remembering Howard's affectionate kisses during their dorm days, it occurred to Marc that his own recent expressions of love and uninvited snuggling might have been perceived by Howard, not as affection, but as a violation of his personal space, an assault on his emotions, if not his body.

"What the hell have I been doing?" Marc blurted into the darkness. "Thinking only of myself, that's what I've been doing, and all the time I thought I was showing Howard that I still love him. Oh God, if I still love the guy I need to respect his space."

Chapter 28

Howard read Marc's email for the third time.

Hi Howard. First off, thanks for the accommodation last weekend when I was in town for the French workshop. It was good to spend some time with you. I want to apologize for giving you a hard time about marrying Maxine, and for snuggling with you when you were last at my place. Maybe you didn't want to snuggle. I shouldn't have been so pushy. I'm truly sorry if I made you uncomfortable. I won't do it again.

Next Saturday one of the churches is sponsoring a workshop on homosexuality and the Bible. I know you won't change your mind about marrying Maxine, but why don't you drive out to hear what this speaker has to say? I intend to go, and would like to have your company. You're welcome to stay the night with me afterwards—or not, whatever you're comfortable with. Here's the info.

Workshop on Homosexuality and the Bible, Saturday, June 21, 10 a.m. to 4 p.m., Greenfield First United Church, Admission $10, study materials and lunch provided.

Howard didn't know how to reply. The only words about homosexuality he'd ever heard inside the tabernacle were words of condemnation. Apostle Farida frequently brought the subject into his sermons. He told the congregation how wicked gay people were. They were responsible for mass shootings in North America and tsunamis in Asia. Their filthy couplings caused air crashes and train derailments. Their right to marry was destroying family life in North America.

Howard could see that some of these statements were outrageous. Family life had been breaking down long before the Canadian government approved gay marriage, but he was curious about more liberal churches. How could they justify marrying two people of the same gender?

He had never dared enter a church of another denomination. He knew that would be a sin, for only Tabbers, thanks to Brother Tingley and his visits to the heavenly country, had *the truth* about the great issues of life. He'd never questioned that certainty, but since the de-baptism he'd begun to wonder. Marc had been right when he pointed out that Jesus never de-baptized anyone. He never lashed out physically at his enemies. Could the Tabbers be making a mistake when they de-baptized someone? Could they be making a mistake in trying to change gay people? Brother Tingley's writings didn't say one word about the gay issue, which seemed odd if it was such a great sin.

Years ago he'd asked Apostle Farida about that. "Well, my son," he'd said, "Brother Tingley died in 1910, long before this wickedness was known."

"But surely men have been, you know, meeting each other for centuries," Howard had said.

"Well yes, we know about the Greeks and Romans doing filthy things with each other, but then it died out, so I suppose God felt it wasn't important during Brother Tingley's time."

Howard went off to work without replying to Marc's invitation to the workshop. He'd think it over, pray about it. Maybe Maxine would go with him.

"No. Absolutely not! Never in a million years will I expose myself to such wickedness," Maxine said that night when he spoke to her over the telephone. "You know how wishy-washy the United

Church is. For goodness sake, Howie Honey, they even have gay and lesbian ministers. How could you even think of stepping inside one of their churches?"

"But maybe they're right and we're wrong." Howard said. "Besides, Marc came to tabernacle with us, and to the de-baptism. I think it's only polite that we accept."

"No, Howie. You've already spent too much time with that pagan."

"He's not a pagan."

"He doesn't go to church. Therefore, he's a pagan. You should tell him you're not coming and cut off all association with him. Now, have you been going over that list of wedding details we have to decide upon?"

Hi Marc. Thanks for the invitation to the workshop and to spend the night at your place, but I'm afraid I won't be able to get away from work on Saturday. We're in the final design stages of that new hog processing plant in Greenfield. The owners are flying into Winnipeg to have a final look at the plans on Monday. Sorry. Love, Howard.

In all his messages to Marc, he'd never signed off with the word *Love*. He didn't know why he'd done it now. It just came out of his fingers like they had a mind of their own. He paused, wondering if he'd be giving Marc the wrong message if he left it in. His finger hovered over the Delete key for a moment, but then clicked *Send*.

It was nine-thirty Saturday morning when he arrived in Greenfield. He had to ring the bell several times before Marc finally came to the door. He was wearing his robe and rubbing his eyes. "Did I get someone out of bed?" Howard asked.

"Howard, you big old dog. What are you doing here so early?"

"It's not early. It's after nine-thirty. I'm here for the workshop. Are you not going?"

"I wasn't going by myself. I thought you had to work today."

"That's what I told Maxine."

"Howard, you're not lying again, are you?"

"No. Well, not really. I drove past the site for the hog plant, took a few pictures."

"Well, come on in. I'll put the coffee on—or no, you don't drink brew. You'll find some juice in the fridge. Help yourself while I dash upstairs and get myself ready."

Howard was nervous as they walked into the church hall. Would God strike him down with a bolt of lightning for being unfaithful to the Tabernacle? He was surprised to see the walls hung with banners quoting Bible texts, and even more surprised when the female pastor—an unthinkable appointment in the tabernacle—opened the session with a prayer that sounded like those he heard every Sunday.

The guest speaker was a Barbara Mosley, a black lady with a massive tease of hair. She was wearing a long, blue dress and a string of bright orange beads around her neck, which wasn't a costume Tabber women would wear. She had a doctorate in theology and spent the morning explaining the Old Testament passages used to condemn homosex, as she termed it.

"What do you think?" Marc asked as they walked over to the buffet at noon.

"I don't know. I really don't know," Howard said. "She makes it all sound so simple, so common sense. But can she be right?"

"About what, for instance?"

"Well, about Sodom. You heard her. She said today's Sodomites are not gay people, but big city bankers who live in mansions and have yachts. They take billions of dollars from the government while they kick poor working stiffs out of their homes when they can't make their mortgage payments. Can that be true?"

"I think she's spot on about that."

"Why hasn't Apostle Farida figured that out then?"

"Do you think he's ever seriously studied the gay issue?"

"Maybe not, at least not the way she has, but do you think this speaker's a lesbian?"

"She says she's married to a man and they have kids, one of them gay."

"But can she be trusted?"

An elderly man joined them at their table. The skin on the back of his trembling hands was almost transparent, the colour of an oven-roasted turkey's skin, purple veins visible beneath.

"I just learned my son is gay a few months ago," he said after introducing himself.

"And how did you take the news?" Marc asked.

"I would have whipped him good if he wasn't bigger and stronger than me. He waited all these years, until I've got one and a half feet in the grave, to tell me this important piece of news. Can you believe it? I keep asking myself what I did to make him afraid to come clean with his old man. You're a nice looking couple. I hope you boys have told your parents about yourselves."

"Oh, we're not a couple," Howard said.

"You should be. A fine looking one you'd make."

"We've known each other since university," Marc said. "I told my parents when I was still in high school. Dad's dead now. Both he and Maman were upset when I first came out, but they became very supportive. Maman still is."

"I'm glad to hear that. I don't know why children build walls around themselves. It's as though they think their parents are aliens from some distant planet where people never have emotional or sexual needs. How about you, young chap?" He looked at Howard.

"I'm getting married in September."

"Congratulations. You've found yourself a fella?"

"A woman."

"So you're like me, straight?"

"I—I don't want—I can't live the guilt of being gay."

The old man dropped his sandwich. "Young man, I have only one word for you. Dumb ass."

Howard felt his stomach muscles tighten. He put down his sandwich. He scraped his chair back from the table. He hadn't come to be insulted by some stranger who wasn't even gay.

"Dumb ass is two words," Marc said to the old man, at the same time laying his hand on Howard's knee.

"You expect an old codger like me to be able to count?"

"Why did your son tell you now?" Marc asked, hoping to give Howard time to settle his stomach.

"Cancer," the old fellow said. "I've got three painful months, maybe six if I'm unlucky. Last time Ron was visiting—he lives in Toronto, some big shot in broadcasting down there—I told him I didn't have any more time to play games. I told him I didn't want him to bury me thinking I wouldn't love the real man he is. I always knew he was different from most other boys, into the art world, and ballet, and high brow music, all that stuff, and no wife, never even a girlfriend. Parents always know, though some don't like to admit it."

"I'm not hiding from my parents," Howard said, pulling his chair back up to the table. He picked up his sandwich again. "In my religion, it's not easy to be gay. Mom and Dad are glad I'm getting married—to a woman."

"Dumb ass. There, I've said it again, and don't take offence because I don't mean to insult you, my boy." The old man put his bruised hand on top of Howard's. "I think you're making a mistake. The Bible says a leopard can't change its skin, and your parents, if they're thinking people, know in their hearts that you're making a mistake."

"You don't know my religion. It tosses people like me into hellfire."

"Maybe your religion is wrong. Do you know how many different versions of Christianity there are in the world? Hundreds, maybe thousands. And why is that? It's because even the experts can't agree on what the Bible says. Maybe what you hear today will change your mind about what your church teaches," the old fellow said. "Now, I've got to find the men's room, and in a hurry!"

Barbara spent the afternoon reviewing St. Paul's statements in the New Testament that straights used to condemn homosex. Then she surprised Howard by referencing several passages throughout the Bible, which validated, even celebrated, same sex love. Howard could just imagine what Maxine and Apostle Farida would say about that kind of biblical scholarship. It couldn't possibly be true.

Barbara closed by reading the passage where Jesus responds to a question about marriage put to him by the religious leaders. In that culture, if a man died without children, his brother was expected to marry his widow to make sure she had children. The big shots proposed that seven brothers married the same widow in turn. They asked which of the brothers would be her husband in heaven. Jesus told them that marriage relationships wouldn't be carried over into the next life. People would be like angels, not marrying.

"So what's the big deal about the gender of the person you love if ultimately we're talking about an experiment that even God considers temporary?" Barbara asked, before opening the floor for questions.

Someone asked her to repeat her comments on St. Paul's warning about worshiping idols in the first chapter of Romans. She'd barely begun her reply, something about Paul's comments referring to the Emperor Caligula and his lustful activities, when a voice familiar to Howard and Marc interrupted.

"Lies! Lies! Absolute lies and rubbish! How can you stand inside a building dedicated to the worship of God and tell all these lies? How can you encourage these sin sick souls to defy God and his law? Don't you realize that *you* will be responsible for sending them to hellfire?"

Howard felt the colour drain from his face. He looked at Marc, then turned to see Maxine and her father standing in the doorway at the back of the hall.

"Yes Howard," Maxine said, taking a step into the room and pointing a finger at him. "I figured you were lying to me about having to work today. Dad and I've been sitting out here in the lobby for the last hour listening to this rubbish. Everything this woman says is a pack of lies. Are you, Howard, and the rest of you poor fools going to let this—this foreign, lying lesbian lead you into the devil's trap?"

"I believe the Bible pronounces a curse on those who judge, and call others fools," Barbara said calmly.

"Silence, Evil One," Apostle Farida said. "I come in the name of the Lord." He held up his Bible. "I challenge you to a debate on this topic."

"I would gladly have debated you earlier," Barbara said, "but as you can see, it is just now four o'clock, the time I promised these good folks I would be finished. However, let's take a vote. How many of you are willing to stay for, say, half an hour, to hear what this gentleman has to say?"

"A year is as a day in the Lord's sight," said Apostle Farida, taking several steps forward.

Howard prayed that no one would raise their hands, but the majority were in favour. Apostle Farida, a look of triumph on his face, strode forward to stand beside Barbara. Maxine came to where Howard and Marc were sitting, pulled up a chair and pushed her way in between them.

"I'm disappointed in you, Howard," she said. "I thought we were being honest with each other."

"I did visit the site of the new hog plant," he said. "I took pictures."

"Yes. I'm sure you did, but—"

"I shall give you ten minutes to introduce yourself and make your case," Barbara said. "Then I will once again open the floor for questions which we will both answer."

"I am Apostle Farida, a man appointed by God to preach the good news of salvation, the good news of deliverance from sin, from the sin of Sodomy." He quickly listed off most of the Bible verses Barbara had discussed throughout the day. He then paused, lowered his head as though praying, then looked at Howard. "But, I need say no more, for within your midst is a man who was once enslaved by sodomistic thoughts and actions, but by the power of God he has been delivered from evil. Howard, my soon-to-be son, will you please come forward and give your testimony?"

Howard shook his head.

"Very well, my good man, my future son-in-law, I will give your testimony for you." He spoke of the day Howard came to visit him in his office, of his confession of homosexual temptations. He went on to tell the audience about the Tingley Inversion Therapy Center and of the healing Howard had found there.

Barbara joined him at the podium, told him his ten minutes were up, and invited questions.

To Howard's chagrin, everyone wanted to hear more about TITC. How long did the cure take? What treatment methods were used. Could Howard now say he was heterosexual?

"Please, my son, come forward," urged Apostle Farida. "You are better able to answer these questions than me."

"I'll go up with you," Maxine said, taking his hand.

"No, let me go with him," Marc said, standing up and putting a hand on Howard's shoulder. Reluctantly Howard allowed himself to be led to the podium.

"I was at TITC for a full year," he said. He described the intense physical training, the Bible reading and prayer, the counselling sessions, the field trips and dances.

Finally someone said, "I know this is a very personal question, but since we're here to talk about homosex, do you no longer fantasize about sex with men?"

"TITC taught me how to control sexual thoughts," Howard said, blushing.

"I'm not trying to make you feel uncomfortable," said the questioner, "but I'm truly curious. When a sexual thought pops into your mind, is it about men or women?"

"At TITC I learned to think of sex in relation to my future wife, Maxine."

"We really are out of time now," Barbara said. "I promised the church we'd be out of here by four so they can set up for tomorrow's Sunday school, and we're already a half hour late. Some of you may wish to speak privately with Howard, but please move outside to do that."

Howard prayed that no one would stay around, and this time his prayer was answered. Everyone hurried out of the hall and disappeared into their cars.

"I hold you responsible for this, Marc LaChance," Maxine said. "Howie would never have come here, would never have had to endure this embarrassing grilling, if you hadn't encouraged him to come."

"Please, Maxine, let's not fight," Howard said. "I told Marc I wasn't coming. He didn't put any pressure on me."

"Then why did you come?"

"I wanted to hear the other side of the argument. I spent a whole year of my life at TITC. It only seemed fair to—"

"And isn't that what the devil has been tempting people with since the beginning of time? God says, don't eat the fruit, don't indulge in homosex, as that evil woman called it, but the Evil One wants us to find out for ourselves. And he uses pagans like you to tempt others." Maxine pointed a finger at Marc.

"Please, Maxine. I told you, Marc had nothing to do with this."

"He sent you the invitation, didn't he? If that isn't temptation, I don't know what is. Come on. Get into the car with Dad and me."

"Howard's truck is at my place," Marc said. "Why don't you all come over, have a cup of coffee and—"

"Oh sure, it's coffee now, is it? You want us to drink demon caffeine. Well, no thanks. We'll come by your place so Howard can get his truck, but we won't be coming in, will we, Dad?"

"The good prophet advises us not to set our feet beneath the table of sinners." Apostle Farida got behind the wheel.

"I'm sorry, Marc," Howard said, "but I'd better go with them. Thanks for telling me about the workshop. I enjoyed spending the day with you." He waved to Marc and got into the car. His hands were trembling so much he had trouble buckling his seatbelt.

Chapter 29

"*Mon pauvre garçon*, you should know better than to get involved with people from those strange religions," Marc's mother said, trying to comfort him. "They attract unbalanced people."

It was Sunday afternoon. They were strolling around the circle in Riverside Park. It was mid-August and the flower beds were at their finest. His mother found joy in each bloom's shape and colour while Marc couldn't find joy in anything. It had been three weeks since Maxine had dragged Howard away from the workshop and he hadn't contacted Marc since.

"You're probably right about Howard being unbalanced, Maman. His mind has been twisted by that cult-like religion of his, and that change ministry he went to in California just damaged him all the more. Why can't I get him out of my system? Am I damaged too?"

"No. No, my boy. You were terribly hurt when Howard played that nasty trick on you in university. But listen to your old maman. You have to leave him free to live his own life. Surely there are other men. Maybe there's someone right under your nose that you haven't noticed."

"I haven't met anyone, Maman, and I'm going to be forty-nine in a couple weeks and you know what that means. Next year I'll be fifty, and there's nothing nifty about that."

Monday morning, Marc attacked the garage roof. The shingles were dried and curled. If he didn't replace them the fall rains would seep through to the sheeting and rot would set in. He was shovelling the last of the old shingles off the roof when his mother hurried around the corner of the house. "Maman, you're coming to help me?"

"*Mais non.* I am too old for that. You want to see your Maman with a broken hip or worse?"

"No way. What brings you here? I thought you and cousin Arlene were picking berries today."

"We did, early this morning, while it was still cool. I went to Safeway to get some freezer bags. I saw Amy Hildebrandt."

"Howard's sister-in-law, the nurse? How is she?"

"She's fine, but Howard's not so good."

"What do you mean?"

"He's in the hospital in Winnipeg. He tried to kill himself. *Mon Dieu*, it's like our Claude all over again."

"Maman! *Non! C'est impossible!*"

"It's true. He swallowed pills."

"And?"

"He's alive, thank God."

Marc tossed the shovel to the ground and started down the ladder. "I'm going to see him. Which hospital?"

"Winnipeg's Health Science Centre, the psych ward."

"Oh Maman, I was afraid of this. Maxine and her family and that damn tabernacle are going to be the death of Howard."

"What about the roof?"

"Howard is more important than any roof."

When Marc walked into the psych ward late that afternoon he found Howard alone. He was sleeping so Marc pulled up a chair and sat down beside him. He was shocked at how much his friend had aged since Maxine and Apostle Farida had dragged him from the workshop.

The lines fanning out from the corners of his eyes were deeper. There were dark circles beneath them. The grey strands seemed to be taking over his hair and moustache. Every once in awhile he twitched, then twisted his head from side to side and groaned.

What a waste, Marc thought as he gazed at his friend. The agony Howard was putting himself through was all so pointless. Surely God operated on the KISS principle, keep it simple, stupid— love other folk and don't cause them any grief. Why did churches have to make life so complicated? The poor guy would never find peace so long as he clung to a teaching that labelled his natural yearning to love and be loved as defective.

If only I could spirit you away from these people who want to straightjacket you into their own narrow mindset, Marc thought as he took a tissue and wiped the sweat from Howard's handsome head, a head that should have been lying on a pillow in bed beside Marc rather than in a hospital room. Marc reached for another tissue to wipe a trickle of drool from the corner of Howard's mouth.

"Uh. Get away. Leave me alone. Leave me alone!" Without opening his eyes Howard swiped at Marc's hand.

"It's okay, Big Man. It's okay. It's me, Marc." Howard opened his eyes, took a moment to focus, smiled briefly, then looked frightened.

"Marc! What are you doing here? Is Maxine—"

"Relax, Big Man. It's only me." Marc reached for Howard's hand but he slid it beneath the white sheet.

"How did you know I was here?"

"Maman met Amy in Safeway this morning. I came as soon as she told me. Oh Howard, thank God you didn't do yourself in."

"Does Maxine know you're here?"

"Of course not."

"What time is it?"

"Quarter to four."

"Then you've got to leave. Get out before Maxine comes. She always comes right after work."

"Forget Maxine, Howard. She's the reason you're in here. Maxine and her parents and that wicked tabernacle. They're the reason you're here."

"Maxine mustn't find you here. She blames you. She says I wouldn't have, wouldn't have taken the pills if you hadn't—"

"But I haven't been in contact with you in weeks. How can she blame me for making you swallow a medicine cabinet full of pills?"

"It wasn't a cabinet full of pills. Just a few extra Prozac."

"Prozac? How long have you been taking Prozac?"

"I started while I was in California and I just kept on. They really help, Marc. You know how wild things have been at work with supervising plans for the hog plant and our new office in Greenfield."

"I thought you were never going to tell another lie, Howard."

"What do you mean?"

"Your depression has nothing to do with work."

"You try to juggle a half dozen projects at once with the boss breathing down your neck, knowing there'll be a penalty to pay if design isn't completed on time."

"But you love your work. Your depression is all about your marriage to Maxine. Admit it. Stop lying to yourself. Shake yourself loose from her and her damn family."

"Please Marc, don't start. If you came all this way just to give me a hard time, I'd rather not see you."

"But it's the truth, isn't it?"

"Why can't everyone just leave me alone?" His voice broke and tears spurted from his eyes. "And why do you, who claim to be my friend, always have to be so overbearing?"

"What do you mean?"

"Exactly what I'm saying. You were like that in college. Always pushing me to do things I didn't want to do. You never cared about my opinion. If I didn't want to do things you'd just bulldoze me until you got your way."

"When did I ever push you to do something you didn't want to do?"

"Remember that time you forced me to go cross-country skiing with you in that blizzard?"

"No, I don't."

"Well you did. You pushed until I agreed to go and I got a terrible cold that turned into pneumonia."

"I'd forgotten about that."

"And how about the time you wanted to see that movie with Tom Hanks. I forget the name, but you knew I didn't go to movies. No good Tabber goes to movies but you pushed and pushed until I went with you, just to shut you up."

"Why didn't you tell me you thought movies were sinful?"

"I did tell you. Maybe not in those words, but I told you movies were against my religion, but you wouldn't leave me alone. You made me feel so inadequate and stupid, like you were the only one who knew how to do things, and when I disagreed with you, you accused me of being too thick headed to know my own good. Now you're doing it again. You're like a runaway bulldozer."

"You're saying I'm a pompous prick."

"Remember the time you wanted to go to the pub to hear that band? I forget their name, Country Warblers or something. You knew I didn't drink and didn't like the kind of music they were playing, but you pushed until I went along with you. It was one of the worst nights of my life. The music, if you can call it that, was so loud we couldn't even talk."

"And I suppose I forced you to sleep with me, and make love to me?"

"I admit that I was happy enough to snuggle with you, but I probably wouldn't have had sex with you if you hadn't taken the initiative."

"Had sex with me? Is that how you thought of it?"

"What else was it?"

"I thought we were making love. I know it's an awkward term, sounds like we're building a go cart or some piece of furniture out in the garage, but I thought we were caring for each other, loving each other in the most intimate way two men can. Is that not what it was for you?"

"We were doing something sinful."

"So if gay marriage had been legal in Canada then, like it is now, you wouldn't have considered marrying me?"

"No. I couldn't have. Like I said then and still say, the guilt would have split us up. Besides, you're not a Christian."

"Not a Christian?"

"The Bible says we're not to be unequally yoked together, which means a Christian isn't supposed to marry a non-Christian. It would never have worked."

"That's rather exclusive, isn't it?"

"It's not meant to be. It's just that when two people are Christians they're more likely to get along than if one of them isn't."

"So if I'd been a Christian, would you have married me?"

"It's pointless to discuss this now. What's that sound?" Howard lifted his head off the pillow. His eyes darted to the doorway. Marc heard it too, the click of high heels approaching. "Oh crud, Marc. Get out. Get out before—"

Maxine strode into the room. "Well, if it isn't the devil himself," she said, glaring at Marc as she laid three yellow roses on the bedside table.

Howard looked at his watch. "You're early Maxine."

"Yes, I got off work early today, and it looks like God had a hand in that. Just how long have you been here?" She looked at Marc like he was a roach that had crept out from under the bed.

"I heard my Big Man was in trouble and came to help."

"You're the reason he's here," Maxine said. "If you hadn't fooled around with him, leaving him with a load of guilt, he wouldn't be here. You and your filthy kind are destroying marriage in this country, and now you're trying to destroy ours before it even begins. I'll thank you to leave now. Howie needs his rest."

"Do you want me to leave, Howard?"

"Maybe it would be best if you went."

"Would you like me to come back this evening? Or sometime tomorrow when the room isn't so crowded?"

"You're leaving right now, and you are never coming back. And remember, you're not coming to our wedding either," Maxine said.

"Howard?"

"Please go." Howard closed his eyes and gripped the edge of the sheet with both hands.

"Howard, do you want me to come back?"

"You will not come back," Maxine said. "I will give orders to the nurses at the desk not to let you in—family only. Hear that? Family only, and you are *not* family and *never* will be."

"Howard?"

Howard waved him away.

"Alright, but be strong, Big Man. Remember, I'm always here for you. If you need anything, just call me. And I'm glad we had a real talk today. I'll think about what you said about me being a runaway bulldozer." Howard smiled weakly. Marc patted his hand. "I love you, my friend."

Heading back to Greenfield, Marc shoved John Berry into the CD player, selected *I'm standing on the edge of good-bye* and pushed repeat. In a fog of tears, regret and self-recrimination he drove home.

Am I really a pompous prick? he wondered. Is that why he'd never been able to connect with anyone on the coast? Did he squeeze people out of his life by whacking them over the head with his own opinions? Is that why he was still alone in bed every night?

Chapter 30

Marc was feeling some discomfort as he finished clearing off the garage roof the next day. It was his own fault. When he got home from visiting Howard in the psyche ward, he was feeling depressed, to put it mildly, so the RAV4 took him straight to Riverside Park. Luck was with him. It took only a couple of circuits to find someone, bring him home, and get his shot of endorphins from the resulting orgasm. He'd been a fool though, not asking the guy to remove his wedding ring. It's sharp edge had chafed a sensitive part of his anatomy. He'd anointed it with Polysporin ointment but still it smarted as it rubbed against his underwear.

At least the roof project gave him something to think about besides Howard's plight. As he tacked down the roofing paper he had an image of Howard lying in that sterile hospital bed like a forlorn little orphan, and hovering over him, Maxine with her Woody Woodpecker haircut and blood red nails, the nurse from hell.

The next afternoon Marc was wrestling bundles of asphalt shingles onto the roof when a young man walked towards him down the back lane. He was a wiry little fellow wearing a paint-stained t-shirt and camouflage shorts. "Hey, let me give you a hand with those," he said, picking up a bundle of shingles as though they were made from Styrofoam. He bounded up the ladder and handed it off to Marc.

"Careful you don't injure your back."

"I roofed my garden shed earlier this spring," he said. "My brother-in-law helped hand things up, so I know an extra set of muscles comes in useful on a job like this."

"I haven't got a brother-in-law in town or anyone else who can help right now. I just moved here from the coast a year ago and haven't made many connections yet. You one of my neighbours?"

"Yes and no. Me and the wife just bought a townhouse in the south end, but I'm caretaker at the church on the corner here. You've maybe seen me biking past. I cycle to work when the weather's decent. I was putting out the garbage when I saw you wrestling with these bundles."

"I appreciate your help."

"Pete Stemgirder." He stuck out a calloused hand for Marc to shake.

"I'm Marc LaChance. I teach French in that new school in the south end."

"We've got two little ones, the oldest in nursery school. Maybe you'll teach them one day. If you're interested in meeting new people I'd love to see you at church on Sunday morning."

The sudden shift in conversation raised alarm bells for Marc. Did this guy figure heaving three bundles of shingles onto the roof gave him the right to shove his religion in his face?

"I'm not much of a church person."

"Hey, no pressure Bud. Just thought I'd invite you. We like to think we're a church where you don't have to check your brain at the door."

In spite of his unease Marc laughed. "That is a novel idea! What exactly do you mean?"

"A lot of churches get uptight if you don't agree with everything they teach. We like people to question things. After all, it's only by questioning and discussing that we learn something new, right?"

"Guess so, but church isn't for me."

"That's okay, but if you change your mind you'd be welcome to give us a try. We have quite a few people your age, both singles and marrieds. For the most part they're folk who've almost given up on Christianity, been abused by churches. You'll find us pretty laid back."

"That's good to know, but I'll pass."

"No sweat, my friend. This is the last bundle, and now I'd better get back to the church. I left the door unlocked. If you change your mind you know where to find me. Nine o'clock Sunday morning."

"That's kind of early."

"Not for our crowd. They're pretty active folk, like to hike and bike and all that good stuff on the weekends, so they come early and leave early. By ten-thirty everyone's pretty well gone. You have a good day and if you need a hand with something don't be afraid to ask."

"Thanks." Marc shook his head as Pete walked up the lane. Nice enough guy, but Marc had as much interest in going to church as he had in wearing women's panties and rolling his hair onto curlers every night. Still, what an intriguing idea: a church that didn't ask you to check your brain at the door.

Sunday morning he was lying in bed feeling sorry for himself because there still hadn't been any word from Howard. He'd messaged him a couple of times, asking if he was back to work. There had been no response. For all he knew, Howard had taken another overdose.

He was still lying in bed thinking these debilitating thoughts when he heard the church bells ringing. Pete's invitation flashed into his mind. He'd said there were both single and married folk attending. Since Howard was out of his life for good, he should get out and meet people. Maybe there'd be one or two gay guys at a church that encouraged questions, perhaps someone who wanted more than a quick snuggle. He glanced at the bedside clock. A quarter to nine, hardly enough time to shower and shave and brush his teeth, never mind grab a cup of coffee. Yet, maybe it would be better to be late.

That way he could slip into a back row and leave if he didn't like what he saw and heard.

As he walked up the steps twenty minutes later, he had the uncanny feeling that he was being watched. It was the feeling he'd had the first time he'd walked into a gay club. He imagined that cameras were snapping, phones were being picked up, the authorities were being informed about his movements. His face would be printed on posters. They, whoever *they* were, would be waiting to arrest him when he came out.

At the top step he hesitated. Maybe this was a stupid idea, but then the door swung open and Pete was sticking out his calloused hand for the second time that week. "Good to see you, Marc," he said. He was wearing the same camouflage shorts he'd had on the day he helped with the roof, but wore a clean t-shirt. "There's coffee in the corner. Grab yourself a cup and then sit wherever you like. We're just starting."

The comforting odour of fresh brew couldn't quite mask the scent of burning candle wax, musty old hymn books and Bibles. Marc filled a cup, added cream, and was wondering how rude it would be to walk out with the brew when a young man with a guitar stood up and began to sing *Blessed Assurance*, a song on John Berry's latest CD. Marc sat in the back row, telling himself he'd listen to the song, then leave the moment anything strange started happening.

Something strange did happen. Instead of a hellfire sermon, a fellow about his own age, casually dressed, shared his master's thesis with the congregation. A graduate student from the University of Winnipeg's School of Theology, he theorized that God was not a terrorist. Those Old Testament writers who attributed vicious killings to God were simply reflecting their own culture: a culture that blamed the gods for both good and evil events.

He concluded by saying that everything about God in the Bible should be tested by looking at Jesus in the New Testament. "There's no record of Jesus pointing a spear or firing an arrow at any of his enemies, even when they nailed him to a cross and flung it into the ground, so it's clear to me, and hopefully to you, that God is the victim of a bum rap. Those who wrote the Bible stories just didn't get what God is like. Let's make sure we don't make the same mistake."

Then he invited questions, something that had never happened in all the years Marc had attended mass. Some people agreed with the speaker. Others disagreed, but all the comments were respectful. Too bad Howard can't hear this, Marc thought. It might help him let go of his fear of burning forever in hellfire, but how did you get inside someone else's head? Only Howard could decide what, or what not, to believe.

After another song by guitar man, and a short prayer, the service was over. During coffee hour Pete introduced him to his wife and to several remarkably normal folk. By the time he left Marc was thinking he might return the following week.

And that's what he did. This time the sermon, if you could call it that, was by a physician who reported on the latest research into oxytocin, a hormone that floods the brain during sexual arousal and orgasm—he actually used the word *orgasm* in church, and no one jumped up to denounce him. Apparently oxytocin was a bonding hormone, one that promoted feelings of contentment and trust in one's mate, the mellow feeling partners feel while snuggling after sexual intercourse.

"God may actually have known what he was doing when he gave Adam only one mate," the physician said. "Studies suggest that promiscuity biologically confuses the psyche. Our grey cells don't know whom to bond with when there's a different face in the bed every night."

He concluded his talk by inviting anyone who was trapped in the web of sexual addiction, to attend the chapter of Sex Addicts Anonymous he had started at Greenfield United church.

As Marc walked home that morning he thought about his cruising in Riverside Park. He'd never considered himself a sex addict. He didn't go to the park every night, well, not absolutely every night. He knew the moment he found someone who wanted a long-term relationship he'd quit cold turkey. Still, it might not hurt to check out this Sex Addicts Anonymous thing. Even if he didn't benefit in any other way he might meet someone there.

Chapter 31

Monday after work Marc had phoned the number printed in the church program and talked with the doctor about attending SAA. "Is it okay if I'm gay?" he'd asked, after Frank had asked him a bunch of questions, like he was vetting him for a job.

"Gay, straight, transgender—we don't care. We're all there to help each other live healthier lives."

Now it was Thursday evening. The church was a busy place. Minivans dropped off Scouts and Cubs. Cowboys swung down from their mud-spattered pickups. Guys in shirts and ties, sleeves rolled up, pulled into the parking lot, greeted each other and walked into the church.

A white board in the entranceway listed a host of groups: Sex Addicts Anonymous, Alcoholics Anonymous, Al-anon and choir practice. He glanced into the main hall where the Scouts were gathered. He remembered the workshop on the Bible and Homosexuality. Oh Howard, he thought, if I had you I wouldn't be here now.

He walked down the hallway until he found the room designated for SAA. Half a dozen men, including the doctor who had spoken at church, were seated in a circle.

"I'm Marc. We spoke on the phone."

The doctor pointed to an empty chair. "Welcome. I'm glad you found us. We're just about to begin by introducing ourselves. I'm Frank and I'm a sex addict."

"Hi Frank." All the guys greeted him in unison.

"I'm Derek, sex addict."

"Hi Derek," everyone said.

"I'm Reinhold, recovering sex addict."

"Hi Reinhold."

"I'm Ken, sex addict."

"Hi Ken."

They were all looking at Marc. "Hi. I'm Marc. I don't know whether I'm a sex addict, but guess this is the place to find out, eh?"

"Hi Marc."

The doctor read the rules for the evening: a reminder about confidentiality, no cross talk, whatever that was. Derek read something called the group's traditions, and another reviewed the twelve steps. Frank then invited the guys to share what was on their minds. At first there was silence. Everyone seemed to be studying their hands or the titles in the bookcase along the far wall. Finally a shirt and tie guy unclasped his hands and told of the struggle he was having at work where a new receptionist had been hired.

"I can't stop myself from walking through the reception area. I keep glancing over the counter. You see, she wears these really low cut dresses, and boy, has she got boobs. But I know I shouldn't be doing that because then I act out in other ways." He twisted the ring on his fourth finger. "Today I masturbated twice, once in the men's room, the second time in my office. I've never done that before. It's getting really scary."

Marc looked at Frank expecting him to offer some advice. But no one said anything. Next a guy fitted out in faded jeans, checked shirt and a cowboy hat on his lap spoke. He picked up his hat and twirled it while confessing that he had driven fifty miles to reach a highway rest stop. He'd come up empty that week, but other times he'd found couples in motor homes who enjoyed threesomes.

The other cow poke was so hot Marc dared not look him in the face, or glance at his thick, calloused fingers he was picking at, for fear he'd reach across and grab him in a bear hug. However, once he opened his mouth, the allure rapidly drained away. He talked about coupling with the animals on his ranch.

By the time everyone had given their update, Marc felt totally turned off sexual activity of any kind. How could such normal looking people be so perverted and driven in their desires, he wondered. After a moment of silence, Frank asked Marc if he'd like to share.

Marc took a deep breath. "I don't think I'm really a sex addict," he said. "I mean, aren't we all supposed to be addicted to sex? Isn't that how we're designed? My main problem is finding a partner. I've been trying to date someone, but the individual seems determined to run away from me. I guess what I need to do is get that person out of my mind and move on in life. I find that really difficult."

He deliberately kept things vague. It seemed he was the only gay guy in the room, so he thought it wisest to be careful until he knew the others better. He didn't want to get wrestled to the ground and hog tied by one of the cowboys.

As he drove home he marvelled at what he'd heard. He'd always assumed, quite naively apparently, that the straight life would be simple. Straight guys could be up front about their needs, find a woman, marry her, and get their rocks off every night. Searching for love wouldn't be a covert activity for them, like it was for him.

Thursday evening SAA became a regular date on Marc's calendar. At the third meeting he shared the exact nature of his craving for a partner. Since cross talk was not permitted, no one commented on the pity party he was having over losing Howard, but on the way out the door the cowboy who was wrestling with the compulsion to visit highway rest stops clapped him on the shoulder. "Glad to hear you're climbin' on the hay wagon with the rest of us guys. Hang in there, Bud. I'll ask the Higher Power to send you a man. See yah next week." He reached to shake Marc's hand, then grabbed him in a bear hug instead. "Be strong, Bud."

Marc ran to the RAV4. He stuck the key in the ignition, then burst into tears, tears of relief at having come clean with the guys. None of them had judged him. They'd nodded encouragingly, as though they really understood. And now the cowboy had hugged him, called him Bud, like he cared.

"Oh Howard, why couldn't we have connected? Why are you so determined to marry Maxine when you must know it will never work?"

Chapter 32

September was always a tough month for Marc. He had a new crop of students to figure out and train to his classroom routines. That took a lot of talking, which after the summer's recess, left him with a burning throat and total exhaustion by each day's end.

That September he had the added burden of despair over Howard. He'd been counting down the days to the fifteenth, the day Howard would make the second biggest mistake of his life by marrying Maxine, the first mistake having been his rejection of Marc. On the eve of the wedding Marc sat down to message him.

Hi Howard. Tomorrow you'll be getting married. I have to respect Maxine's wishes (maybe your wishes too) and not come to the wedding, but I sincerely want all the best for you. You know how much I love you and so even though I'm disappointed that it's not me you're marrying, I hope you'll find some degree of peace with Maxine. I notice the sign Bronnel Engineering has gone up on your firm's office here in Greenfield, and furniture is being moved in. Perhaps you'll be out this way now and again to supervise projects. I hope you'll drop in to see me, or at least call so we can have coffee or dinner together. Love, Marc.

Marc read it over, then tapped Delete. He had to let Howard go, forget about him, well, maybe not forget, but quit running after him.

He spent Saturday in the garage, beginning restoration work on a '57 Chevy he'd bought off a neighbour. He was redoing the brakes and when that job was done he'd begin the messy job of scraping years of congealed prairie dust and oil off the engine block. He had hoped to distract himself from what was going on in Winnipeg, but he kept looking at his watch.

Twelve o'clock: Howard was probably getting into his monkey suit if that's what he'd decided to wear. Marc supposed his stomach would be turning somersaults. Maybe he'd skipped breakfast so that his nervousness wouldn't result in a nasty scene at the altar.

One-thirty: he'd be driving to the tabernacle, or one of his brothers would be doing the driving.

One-forty-five: he'd be closeted in Apostle Farida's office with his brothers. Would he be panicking, wishing he could call the whole thing off?

Two o'clock: he'd be standing at the front of the tabernacle watching Maxine walk up the aisle.

At that point Marc's mother came around the corner of the garage. "Oh, look at you," she said, "all covered in grease. I brought you some string beans for your cereal. Shall I just put them in the fridge for you?"

"Those aren't string beans." Marc pointed to the basket of raspberries she was holding. The last few weeks she'd been mixing up her words. He wondered if she'd had a small stroke. Perhaps he'd soon be sitting beside her hospital bed, watching Amy Hildebrandt care for her, just like she'd done for Auntie Belle.

His mother put the berries in the house, and then they sat on the back patio visiting for a few minutes. When she left it was almost three o'clock. Howard would be hitched to Maxine. Marc felt a wave of depression well up in him, forcing tears from his eyes. In the past he would have jumped into the RAV4 and let it take him to the park to look for solace, but no more. The supportive guys at SAA had cured him of that method of dealing with loneliness.

At Monday's afternoon's recess Ian Hiddley asked if someone would volunteer to help him with cross-country running practice after school. Bill Fuches, who was making one of his rare appearances in the staff room, snorted and stomped out. Since the incident in the storage room, Bill had been ignoring Marc, walking right past him without making eye contact. Marc didn't know, nor did he care, whether that was because Bill felt ashamed for coming onto him, or whether he thought he was punishing Marc for rejecting him.

Marc volunteered to help Ian. The volunteer work helped fill the time he used to spend cruising Riverside Park. Besides, hanging out with Ian always left him pumped. After that day's practice he stayed to help Ian set up equipment for the next day's gym classes. When they were done, Ian suggested they go out for dinner.

"My better half and the kids are going to a birthday party which fathers have not been invited to attend," Ian said. They drove over to The Green Diner, a vegetarian restaurant. Ian was into healthy living: no meat, alcohol or tobacco. They both ordered veggie burgers with all the fixings. Marc had his with fries. Ian had a salad.

Afterwards they shared a healthy slice of triple layer chocolate cake, the flavouring made from the carob bean. Apparently it was healthier than demon chocolate. They were scraping the last of the frosting off the plate when Ian popped the question. "Tell me Marc, have you met anyone special since moving back to Greenfield?"

"Special?"

"Yes, special as in, *I'm so in love I gotta get married?*"

"Haven't had any luck in that department. There don't seem many possibilities in Greenfield."

"I've heard that a back corner in The Grain Bin is where gay guys meet in this town."

"That smelly old bar? Nothing but old guys looking to get laid while their wives are knitting or whatever wives do while their husbands are out drinking beer."

"Oh, sorry to hear that. I guess there isn't anywhere else to meet guys like yourself?"

"I've accompanied my cousin Arlene to the art gallery and symphony concerts, figuring I'd be sure to find suitable men there, but so far nothing."

"Don't worry. He'll show up." Ian reached across the table and patted Marc's hand. "I think you're a pretty special guy and if I wasn't straight and already married I'd snap you up right away."

They split the bill, and outside the restaurant Ian hugged Marc. "I appreciate your help, Marc. Now go find that man."

Marc wished he hadn't said that. The depression that hit him lowered his resolve to stay out of the park. When he came to the corner, he let the RAV4 turn in that direction. Why bother saving himself for some mythical husband? He was as likely to show up as the apple trees were likely to bloom and produce a crop in the middle of a Greenfield winter.

He drove twice around the circle and then parked to watch the sun slip below the trees across the river. A murder of crows was gathering in the cottonwoods, holding a last conference before they started heading south for the winter. In a few minutes the night prowlers would be out, and if he was lucky there'd be someone new, someone able to inject a drop or two of excitement into his personal life, a life that must look chronically dismal if a young blood like Ian Hiddley noticed his loneliness.

After about ten minutes a new Caddie, all sharp angles for knifing through the wind, circled the drive, slowing each time it passed. The young driver couldn't be more than twenty years old, out for a spin in his daddy's toy. Looking down from the RAV4, Marc could see he was wearing shorts and a tank top emblazoned with the logo for the Greenfield Goons basketball team.

On his fifth circuit he stopped beside the RAV4 and lowered the passenger window. Marc lowered his.

"How you doin, Dad?" the kid asked.

"Fine."

"You lookin' for some company? I really like older guys." He reached inside the leg of his shorts and exposed himself. "How would Daddy like to get a hold of this one?"

"Uh, no thanks. I gotta go." Marc raised his window and sped around the circle and out the park gates. So that's what it had come to. He was in the Daddy category. How depressing was that?

He was relieved that it was dark by the time he turned onto Greystone Avenue and parked the RAV4. Even though none of the neighbours would know where he'd been, he didn't want to have to look anyone in the eye. If the kid hadn't called him Dad, he'd probably have brought him home, and blown his weeks on the wagon.

He was stepping out of the shower when the doorbell rang. Please God, don't let it be cousin Arlene, he prayed. He didn't have the mental energy to listen to her latest religious enthusiasm. By the time he'd pulled on his robe and started down the stairs the ringing had stopped. He flicked on the kitchen light, about to boil water for herbal tea, when the bell rang again. He pulled aside the drapes in the living room bay window to see who it was.

Howard? Was that Howard standing on his front step with a backpack slung over his shoulder? The bell chimed again. Marc ran to the door.

"Howard? What are you doing here?"

"Can I come in?"

"Of course you can." He noticed Howard glance over his shoulder as though he thought someone was following him. He closed the door firmly behind himself. He had dark circles beneath his eyes like he hadn't slept for days, a stubbled face, and his breath stunk like he hadn't flossed or brushed since the world began. "What's with the backpack?

"I'm—I'm—Oh Marc, help me." Howard's face crumpled, tears poured down his cheeks and he threw his arms around Marc.

"Whatever's wrong, Big Man?" Marc guided him down the hallway and over to the sofa in the parlour where they sat down. "You haven't swallowed pills again, have you? Should I call 9-1-1?"

"No."

"Then what is it? Tell me what's happened." Marc put his arms around him, gently rocked him.

"Here's a tissue. Blow your nose. Now, when you're ready, tell me what's wrong, or do you want something to drink first, something to eat? I've got a chicken breast—"

"No. Nothing to eat."

"Why not? Has something bad happened?"

"Yes. It's—it's Maxine."

"Maxine's sick?"

Howard shook his head. He wiped the tears from his face, straightened up, and took a deep breath. "I got married."

"So you went ahead with it after your time in the hospital?"

"Yes, but I'm a failure, Marc. I tried. I really tried, and I thought it would work, but I couldn't do it."

"Do what?"

"It! I couldn't do it—do it with Maxine. Oh Marc, you were right."

"You couldn't have sex with Maxine?"

Howard nodded, blew his nose again. "Marc, I'm still gay. I knew I was gay and I was scared. I've been scared stiff all these months. They told me at TITC that I'd be scared but God would come through for me. He'd help me. But he didn't help me, Marc. He didn't lift a finger for me. I prayed so hard but he did nothing, and so I let Maxine down something awful."

"What exactly happened?"

"For a wedding present her folks gave us the honeymoon suite at the Hotel Fort Garry. It was a beautiful room, its own Jacuzzi tub, a king size bed with a frame and curtains. Oh Marc, I stood at the window and wanted to jump."

"You couldn't get it up?"

"Oh Marc, I got it up alright. Just wait until you hear. She was so good. She let me have a shower first. Then she had hers and came out of the bathroom in this filmy dressing gown, or negligee, or whatever it's called. If the lights had been out, if I hadn't seen her naked, I think I could have done it, but I just couldn't. And poor Maxine, she was so decent about it—at least to begin with.

"When nothing was happening she thought she'd help. She climbed on top of me." Howard started crying again. Marc snugged him in close.

"What then, Big Man?"

"She flipped her negligee over her head and onto the floor and dropped down so that her tits were hanging in my face. At TITC we looked at lots of pictures of naked women, but nobody told me they'd have long black hairs growing out of their nipples. No one at TITC told me they'd be like that. They never looked like that in *Playboy* and *Penthouse*, the magazines they forced us to study in California. Why didn't they warn me? If I'd been warned I would have expected it. Maybe I wouldn't have been so grossed out."

"I doubt anything could inoculate you, or me, against a sight like that. So you couldn't get it up to have sex with her?"

"Oh no, I got it up alright. It's just that what came up wasn't what she was expecting. It was a replay of that horrible night in your bathroom. I upchucked my wedding supper: perogies, cabbage rolls and wedding cake—they had some Ukrainian friends cater the meal. You know what my stomach's like. I power vomited all over me, all over the bed and the floor, and worst of all, all over Maxine: her new nightie, her face, her hair."

"Oh Howard."

"It was the very worst night of my life. I'm a loser, Marc. I'm a complete failure."

"Of course you are. I'd be a loser too if someone asked me to make love to a woman. I'm not programmed for that. Neither are you. You were trying to do something your brain isn't hard wired to do. What did Maxine do?"

"How would you react if the man you'd just married threw up all over you?"

"I seem to recall when something like that happened here not so long ago."

"Don't remind me."

"I know it sounds completely crazy Howard, and maybe even a bit perverted, but that night you upchucked all over my bathroom I realized just how much I loved you. I didn't mind cleaning you up at all. In fact, you being sick just made me love you all the more." Marc put his arm around Howard, pulled him close, and kissed him on the cheek.

"Poor Maxine. She ran into the bathroom, took a shower, packed her bag and left."

"Didn't she say anything?"

"Not a word."

"That's not like Maxine. Where is she now?"

"She's in Winnipeg, in her apartment, I guess."

"You mean you haven't called her or gone to see her since your wedding night?"

"I can't ever go back to her. In fact, Jim Bronnel's been after me to leave Winnipeg. He wants me to head up the office here in Greenfield."

"And what have you told him?"

"I couldn't say yes when I was marrying Maxine. She'd never have moved here, but now—"

"But you are married. Won't you have to settle things with her, have the marriage annulled or something?"

"I can't talk to her right now."

"Why not? Some Tabber rule?"

"I'm too embarrassed. How can I face her after what I did?"

"You can't leave her in limbo. What's her number? I'll dial it for you."

Howard pushed Marc's arm away and stood up. "There you go, bulldozing me again."

"Well, you need bulldozing this time. It's not fair to leave her wondering where you are, or whether you'll ever come back to her. Give me her number and I'll punch it in for you."

"I can't talk to her. I won't talk to her."

"Someone has to speak to her. If you don't, then you're left in limbo too. You need to finish this thing. What's her number?"

"Get off your bulldozer, Marc."

"You can't leave that poor lady wondering what's happened to you."

"I thought you didn't like Maxine."

"That has nothing to do with it. She obviously loved you or she wouldn't have agreed to marry you. Now what's her number?"

Howard spat out her number. When the call was picked up at the other end, Marc handed the phone to him.

"Maxine? I'm sorry I haven't called sooner. I apologize for that. I know...We need to talk...Yes, I know you must be upset and I don't blame you for being angry...I'm angry too...No, not with you, Maxine. With myself, for thinking I could change...No, I don't want to try to make it work...Maxine, time won't make any difference.

"Maxine, we both have to face reality. It's clear to me, and should be clear to you too, that God doesn't go around changing gays into straights...How can you say that? I have given him a fair chance to change me: all those months at TITC, hours and hours of prayer and Bible study, counselling every day. What more could I have done?

"Maxine, I'm forty-nine years old. I gave it my best shot. I'm tired of fighting it...I can't help it if that makes you sad...I'm not going to waste any more time...No, counselling won't do any good.

"There's only one thing to do. We'll have to get an annulment. Then we can both get on with our lives...I know it will be embarrassing for both of us, but there's no other way.

"I'm in Greenfield...Yes, I'm at Marc's...I know you don't approve, but I need to start over. I'm going to accept Jim Bronnel's offer to be manager at the office here. I'll phone you when I come back to Winnipeg to get the rest of my stuff. We'll go to a lawyer together, see what has to be done."

Marc hugged Howard when he pocketed the phone. "Good man. You needed to do that."

"I guess I needed a bit of your bulldozing. Poor Maxine doesn't want to give up. She thinks I should come back to Winnipeg and we'll try to work things out."

"You're not going to do that, are you?"

"No way. I'm tired, Marc. I'm worn out trying to live up to other people's expectations: my parents, Maxine and her parents, the tabernacle. I can't go on doing that for the rest of my life."

"I'm glad to hear you say that."

"And I'm just plain exhausted. I haven't slept since that horrible wedding night."

"Then it's up to bed for both of us. I've had a long day too." Marc stood up, reached for Howard's hand and pulled him to his feet. "You remember where your room is. I'll put out some clean towels. What's in that backpack? Did you bring a toothbrush, your razor?"

"Those things and one change of clothing."

"Good enough." Marc gave Howard another hug, then went into his own room and closed the door. Good God, he thought, maybe, like they said in SAA, there really was a Higher Power in heaven. If Howard had put off the wedding at Marc's urging, he'd always have wondered if he should have gone through with it. This way, he'd learned his own lesson.

Marc crawled into bed, pleased to hear the sound of the water in the pipes, the dull patter of the shower against the tiles, the quiet followed by nose blowing, teeth being brushed, the click of the light switch, bare feet padding across the hallway floor, the door closing.

It was just after one in the morning when a tap on the door awakened him. "Marc?"

"What is it Howard?"

"You haven't come into my room for a snuggle."

"I didn't know how you'd feel about that."

"That never stopped you before. Can I come in?"

"Sure." Marc held up the covers. "Crawl in if you're sure it's what you want. I didn't want to force myself on you like I did before. I heard what you said about me being a bulldozer, and I've been trying to clean up my life. Besides what you said about me being too pushy, I had a nasty experience with one of the teachers at work, and I've been learning a lot of things at church."

"Marc LaChance is going to church?"

"Yeah, can you believe that? It's not very churchy. I don't know if you'd like it, but if you stay until Sunday we can go together.

"I'd like to stay, that is if you don't mind," Howard said.

"Well then stay. I've never given up the dream of making a life with you."

"Maybe we can make that happen. Once I find a place to live here in Greenfield we can get together like this every weekend, maybe even during the week sometimes." Howard kissed Marc on the cheek.

"What do you mean *find a place to live?*"

"I thought I'd get myself an apartment."

"You will not. You'll move in with me."

"Are you ordering me around again?"

"Sorry," Marc said. "I must remember not to be a bulldozer about it. What do you say? Will you live with me?"

"What exactly are you asking me?"

Marc flipped off the covers and slipped onto his knees beside the bed. He took Howard's hand in his. "Howard, will you marry me?"

"Oh Marc."

"Now Howard, don't answer me until you've answered this question. Say we did get married, would you be overcome with guilt after a week, a month or whatever period of time? That's what you've always said before."

"Remember that workshop we went to in June?"

"How could I forget it?"

"Remember how Barbara commented on that story of Jesus telling the big shots that in heaven we won't be married? We'll be like the angels?"

"Yes, but what's so special about that?"

"All my life I've heard apostles in the tabernacle preaching that there's only one thing we take to the heavenly country: our character. We don't take money or cars or houses. Nothing, except our character."

"I still don't see how that assures me you won't bail after a couple months of this." Marc squeezed Howard's hand.

"Because that tells me God doesn't care what sex my partner is. All he wants is for me to be a loving person, to try to be like him, to live like Jesus."

"Are you done with the Tabbers?"

"I've decided there's something far more important than being a Tabber, and that's being a Christian. I don't need to be a Tabber to love God and love others as much as myself."

"You're starting to sound like a preacher man."

"Sorry. I guess it's time we got some sleep."

"You don't want me to do anything with this?" Marc grabbed Howard's crotch.

"I thought you'd never notice."

"I noticed."

CPSIA information can be obtained
at www.ICGtesting.com
Printed in the USA
LVHW050023271118
598264LV00013B/112/P

9 781634 920476